Buried

in the

Records

Dave Pratt

PublishAmerica
Baltimore

Stella;
Thanks for
the fun at
WOOTB.
Dave Pratt
2007

First printing

At the specific preference of the author, PublishAmerica allowed this work to remain exactly as the author intended, verbatim, without editorial input.

ISBN: 1-4137-9693-1
PUBLISHED BY PUBLISHAMERICA, LLLP
www.publishamerica.com
Baltimore

Printed in the United States of America

For Jacqueline

"Practically perfect in every way!"

Acknowledgements

Of all the people in my life who have made this book possible, first and foremost among them is Zelma Orr, accomplished writer and mentor, without whom this book would not have been possible. She saw me through my first novel, then cajoled and encouraged me through this, my second effort, teaching me the worth of brevity, clarity and strong characterization.

To my publicist, Karen Sell, I offer my greatest appreciation, although her work is only beginning. My special thanks go to Police Chief Todd Stancil, for past discussions about practical police procedures, to Master Gardner Ann Marie Oda, and to Nancy Redden, RN, BSN, Kim Martin, RN, and Marge Ward, RN for their sage advice and council on hospital procedure.

Finally, my thanks to the editorial and production staff of PublishAmerica for taking a chance a relatively new writer. Their professionalism and quality approach to producing this book have made the task painless and ultimately rewarding.

Buried

in the

Records

Chapter 1

The hospital board room was thickly carpeted, quiet and dimly lit. Large plate glass windows flanked an expansive oak conference table and high backed leather chairs in the center of the room. Beyond the glass, tall evergreen trees waved their limbs in lazy cadence with a freshening evening breeze. Just visible through the tops of the trees, the sky rapidly darkened as it grew crowded with gray and black, rain-laden clouds. The air felt humid and oppressive, even to the two men and one woman who huddled at one end of the table in the air conditioned room.

"This is a disaster. I tell you, this man they're sending to audit us is top notch. He's an experienced ex-Army officer, and word has it that he's thorough and not to be fooled. He might just find us out." The speaker was a handsome man, in a classical way: tall with aquiline features, hair swept back from his forehead in a stylishly casual cut, and the long, soft fingers of a surgeon. "We've made it through audits before, but this one has got me worried. We've been taking a lot of patients, lately. It's not a good time."

The woman, who was markedly smaller than her two cohorts, shook her head and spoke in calming tones. "I've talked to the Director about this and our guidance is to hold to our guns and ride this audit out. We've weathered worse than this before and come out just fine. Besides, when you come right down to it, it's just a routine audit. He won't find a thing. We have our own people in patient records. I've checked with them, and everything's in order."

"But what if he does find something?" The second man's voice was high-pitched, whiny and there was hardly any hair left on his balding pate. A small paunch hung over his belt and parted his long white doctor's coat as he shifted his weight nervously in his chair. "What will we do then? I don't want to go to jail for murder."

The woman reached out with both hands and patted the two men's forearms, like a comforting grandmother or aunt. "No one's going to jail for anything. What's to find? We've been very careful about the patients we've selected. They all would have most likely died on their own, even if we hadn't helped them along. And in the remote chance that he did find something to implicate us, it would be very hard to prove under those circumstances."

"But what if he..." the paunchy doctor persisted.

The woman smiled grimly as she looked her two peers directly in their eyes, in turn. "We've already killed more than once. I suspect we could take care of one little auditor if we had to."

The surgeon slapped his hand on the tabletop with a crack like a rifle shot. "I'll have no part of deliberate murder!"

The woman's smile disappeared and her words came out sharp, demanding. "You keep your indignities to your self, Doctor. Your words are as much a fraud as you are. And as for murder, it's a little late to worry about that. How many patients have you dispatched already, with your own hands? And what of your bulging bank account? Are you prepared to explain all of that to the District Attorney?"

"I just meant..."

"I don't care what you meant or didn't mean. We stick together or we hang together. Now, you two just go about your job and try to relax. I'll handle this auditor personally, and I'll make sure there's no trouble for any of us."

Chapter 2

The two-day drive up the coast in his sleek Toyota Supra sports car hadn't been much of a burden. With excellent weather and a car that was a joy to drive, Bill Deming cruised along the winding reaches of the Cascade Highway as it wound up the green, tree-studded hills of the Pacific Northwest. Home, that's where he was headed; back to the land where he'd spent his formative years. And he was looking forward to it.

He exited east onto Highway 101, drove another forty-five minutes through increasingly dense traffic, and found the exit ramp for his hotel and turned off. He sighed as the hotel came into view. It wasn't exactly the home he'd known during high school, but it would do.

"End of the trail, Alex." He glanced at the chunky yellow lab sleeping on the passenger seat beside him. Alex blinked dark brown eyes and gave his owner a groggy look. "Yeah, it's been a long trip, but we're here."

He pulled into the hotel parking lot, found a spot, turned off the ignition and stretched his arms wide. It had been a long trip, but the scenery and the time on the road had been a tonic, just what he needed after the past few, demanding jobs he had completed for his employer. He had needed the break.

He reached across and opened the passenger side door. "Out you go, buddy, but don't go far."

He trusted Alex to do his business and not stray too far. The dog was well trained predictable and a sort of metaphor for his life: predictable, controlled, and *no* surprises.

Bill hummed an old Moody Blues tune as he left the car and headed for the hotel office. Another few minutes and he'd checked in and found his way to his room. It was on the first floor, not far from where he'd parked the car. He whistled for Alex, and by the time he slid the card into the key lock, the dog was beside him.

Once inside, Alex paced a quick survey of the small bedroom, bath and kitchenette, and then zeroed in on the couch. He was curled up on one end and asleep before Bill had dragged in the final suitcase. It was the dog's little ritual, and after a dozen road trips with Bill, the routine was more or less set in stone. Alex would be out for hours before he'd be ready to eat or go outside, and that gave Bill some time.

With Alex sound asleep in the room, Bill was back in the Supra and headed north on Interstate 5. Today was Sunday. Tomorrow would be the first day of his consulting assignment at Olympia's largest medical center, Wilkes Memorial. He liked to arrive at a new job a day early, so he could get settled and get the lay of the land before he had to dig in and get to work.

But even before he checked out the hospital where he would be doing his audit, Bill intended to visit his old stomping grounds in the little town of Lakewood, Washington. A suburb of Tacoma, Lakewood was where Bill had lived with his parents during his high school years. To some it might seem silly, but he had a need to see the old school after twenty-six years away. He had good memories of his high school days, but had only been back once since he graduated. He had promised himself this visit. Maybe he'd look up old friends; maybe one old girlfriend in particular.

"Wonder if she still hates me?" he said aloud. Would time have healed the breach in their friendship?

Bill left the freeway twenty minutes later, headed west toward Lakewood. He wound his way through scattered subdivisions, along the occasional lake, a golf course, and past shopping areas that hadn't been there the last time he visited. It pleased him to see that the wooded, slightly rural atmosphere he'd known as a teen remained. Taking his time, he cruised his old neighborhood, but failed to locate the house where he'd lived with his parents. Where there had once been lanes, gravel side streets and modest family homes, broad avenues, cul-de-sacs and large executive homes dominated the landscape.

Giving up the hunt for his old home, he aimed the car toward his old high school and was relieved when he found it a few minutes later. He turned into the narrow drive in front of the sprawling, single-story brick building and stopped the car before entering the parking lot. It was Sunday, and the school was empty of students. In their place, joggers filtered through the area in profusion of Spandex, baggy shorts, rainbow stripes, and day-glow colors. A large group emerged from his blind spot and ran in front of his car just as he put it into gear. "Idiots," he muttered. He could have hit one of them. When they were clear, he deliberately checked all of his mirrors, and then pulled forward and into a parking space.

There, right before him, was the place where he'd gone to school, made and lost friends, and found his first love. Amazing. It looked exactly the same.

Lost in his memories, Bill swung open the car door to step outside for a close look. Before he could get it all the way open, something slammed into it, and knocked him back into the driver's seat. There was the sound of gravel crunching, and a curse on the other side. He eased the door open wider, slowly, and stared at the small figure lying prone on the sidewalk.

"Are you hurt? I'm sorry, I didn't look …"

The woman was petite, with hair scattered across her shoulders in a tussled mess of brown and red highlights. Blood seeped through her torn sweatshirt from a raw patch of flesh on her elbow. The woman grimaced and took hold of the hand he extended.

"You didn't see me? I wouldn't have guessed. Or maybe you make a habit of lurking in schoolyards to assault joggers who run by your car."

The woman shook back her hair to reveal her face, a familiar face. High cheekbones, long bangs, startlingly clear blue eyes framed by thick lashes, pert nose and those same full lips that had driven him to distraction so many years before.

"Carole?"

The woman's eyes narrowed, and she squinted at him. "Bill? Bill Deming? This is just too weird."

"Weird isn't the half of it. Half an hour ago I was thinking of..."

His words were cut off when she threw her arms around him in a hug that threatened his spine. She pushed him away, held him at arm's length, and then punched him hard in the shoulder. "You come back after all this time to assault me with a car?" She punched him again. It was quite a punch for so small a package.

"What was that for?"

"The first one was for hitting me with the car. The second was for dumping me twenty years ago."

"You were the one who went off and got married." He gave her a lopsided grin. "Forgive me?"

"Forgiven, yes. Forgotten, no."

"I suppose that's a start."

"Of course it is." She dabbed at her bleeding elbow with the handkerchief retrieved from the glove compartment, and pointedly let her eyes drift over him, from head to toe. "The years have been good to you, Mr. Deming. Except for the gray smudge in your hair, you look all right for a man your age."

"Hey, our birthdays are only a few weeks apart." He sucked in his stomach and puffed out his chest. "Besides, a military career keeps a boy in shape, no matter how old he is. You look great yourself."

She studied him. "You? In uniform?" She grinned, the same grin that used to drive him insane when they were an item back in simpler days, when sports and girls filled his life to over-full. A familiar tension knotted in the pit of his stomach. He cleared his throat.

"I've been retired for a couple of years. I'm a consultant now, based in California. I'm here on a job." He hooked a thumb over his shoulder, indicating the jumbled silhouette of dark buildings against the fading evening light. "I came by to see if old Lakes High School was still standing. You still married to Kurt?"

Carole's expression changed. He recalled that her moods shifted constantly, unpredictably, and you never knew what would set her off from one minute to the next. Perhaps that lack of predictability was why things hadn't worked out for them all those years ago. She had married

Kurt Watson a year after she and Bill graduated and went their separate ways. He'd wanted college and for her to wait for him. She'd wanted a family right out of school. When Bill left, Kurt was right there to fill the void, the big hero captain of several of the school's successful teams.

Bill had returned the next year for the wedding. The ceremony had been one of those perfect Ken and Barbie events that cut him to the quick. Funny that he'd think about that now. That had happened decades ago.

"Kurt and I split up years ago. He was a jerk and still is, from all I hear. Took me a while to realize it." She looped her uninjured arm through his. "Looks like I let the good one get away. How about you? You got a missus and four little Bills running around the house in sunny California?"

"Never married," he said. "A military career, lots of moving around. I just never found the right girl."

"I'm just as glad. I've gotta run. Got a piece of paper? I'll give you my address, and if you have a chance, look me up."

Bill handed her a pad and pen from the map pocket in the driver-side door, and she scribbled her phone number on it. "I'd like it if you called me. Maybe we could get together and go to dinner. It would be like old times. Where's this job you're working on?"

"Wilkes Memorial Hospital, in Olympia. You know where it is?"

There was a distinct twinkle in her eyes when she replied. "Yes, I certainly do."

She turned and started to jog off, but then paused mid-stride and called over her shoulder, "Give me a call when you have a moment."

"Maybe I will," he called back.

She waved over her shoulder and disappeared around a corner.

"Maybe I'll do just that." He gave the old school a final, searching glance, and then climbed back into the car and headed back for the hotel.

Chapter 3

The surgeon's gloved hands were crimson to the wrists. Steel lamps the size of commercial spotlights wrapped the room in a harsh glow that illuminated the surgical table and the patient on it, who was split open from sternum to groin.

Nurses and technicians gathered around the patient in a crowd of anonymous, shapeless surgical scrubs and facemasks. En masse, they whispered orders, acknowledgements and hustled to do what was needed. At the patient's head stood the anesthesiologist, surrounded by a battery of gauges, cylinders and tubes that wandered off and into the patient. The room smelled of sterility, that bitter tang of cleaning agents and filtered air. The soft, mellow strains of guitarist Carlos Santana echoed in the background.

"Nurse, get the sweat out of my eyes," the surgeon said. His voice was soft, toneless, belying the heated intensity of his gaze as he ran his fingers along the patient's small intestine and up, past the stomach.

The head nurse, brows furrowed to a single dark line above piercing black eyes, glared from behind her face shield at a young RN, who snatched up a sponge and dabbed at the surgeon's forehead.

"Think he'll make it, Dr. Simmons?" In her twenty years as head nurse of this OR, Marge Rouche had seldom seen an auto accident victim like this one survive. And she'd seen more than a few cases since the Olympia to Seattle corridor had exploded with high tech firms and the resulting influx of people. They came to live in the mountains, valleys and plains of western Washington and congested the single interstate that ran through the area's most populated cities. It was a six-lane freeway in places, jammed beyond capacity on a twice-daily basis as the west side of the state commuted to their jobs. In the last two years, the number of horrific crashes on Interstate 5 had increased by a factor of eight.

Wilkes Memorial Hospital was located a few convenient miles off I-5 in Washington State's picturesque capitol city and it was one of only two Level two Trauma facilities in the southwestern quarter of the state. From the Columbia River to the northern reaches of Tacoma, Wilkes Memorial took care of the state's most complex cases, including the near-constant flow of auto crash victims. If it happened anywhere south of Tacoma, it went to W.M. On a really good week, that meant two or three cases like this one – on a bad week, more.

The surgeon nodded, motioned with his eyes to the resident across the table. The young surgeon-in-training reached in with suction and cleared blood from an area of bowel. "Surprising, but I think this one will make it. Most of the blood is from small vessels. The organs are amazingly intact. It's hard to imagine, but I don't see why our Mr. Terrance shouldn't come through the ordeal in good shape."

Marge smiled beneath her mask. "That's amazing news."

Simmons paused, frowned. "Cautery. The small vessel on the right, next to my thumb."

The resident swapped suction for cautery and slipped the hot tip of the device forward. A wisp of fowl-smelling smoke drifted up from the body cavity and the trickle of blood abated. Simmons wrinkled his nose, which made his surgical mask bob up and down on his face. Marge stifled a chuckle.

"As long as I do this job, I will never get used to the smell of burned flesh," Dr. Simmons said.

Several of the staff working at tableside mumbled agreement.

Dr. Simmons pulled his hands out of the patient's belly and sighed, his smile showing in his eyes as he glanced at the young resident across the table. He rolled his shoulders to ease the tension of five hours at the table and stepped back.

"That appears to be the last of the bleeders. Think you can close this one, Doctor?"

The resident nodded. "No problem, sir."

A moment later, the OR's paging system whistled through the room's overhead speakers. The sound was followed by a tinny, hollow voice that said, "Dr. Simmons, contact Dr. Harrison, stat."

The lead surgeon turned toward the head nurse. "Marge, how about you keeping an eye on our young protégé while I see what the beloved Chief of Surgery wants."

"Sure thing, Doctor."

Simmons backed away from the table and stepped over to the intercom on a nearby wall. He put his mouth close to the speaker as a nurse pushed the "speak" button. "This is Simmons. What 'cha need, Luke?"

A set of forceps clattered to the floor. Marge spun around and squared off with the OR technician standing nearest the instrument tray at the foot of the OR table.

"Nancy! How can you be so clumsy?"

"I'm sorry, Marge. I don't know what happened. One minute it was on the sterile tray. I glanced away for just a second and the thing fell to the floor. I have no idea what..."

"You're in charge of the instruments. Don't try to deflect the blame. Just pay attention and be careful. Get over to the cabinet and get a new sterile set."

"Yes, ma'am," the technician mumbled, and stepped away from the surgical table.

The clatter of the forceps hitting the floor and the animated exchange between nurses distracted everyone, particularly the resident, as he carefully stitched up the peritoneum, the body cavity's internal lining. His hands paused in their work and he raised his eyes and nodded at the head nurse and troubled technician. "Folks, this is only my second closing on a case this big. If we want to get out of here sometime today, you're gonna have to keep it down."

Marge locked eyes with the resident, capturing his attention for a long, tense second. Everyone in the room held their breath. No one admonished Marge or her staff and got away with it, except maybe

Dr. Simmons, but he was one of the team.

With everyone's attention on the nurse and resident, the fleeting movement of the anesthesiologist's hand was missed as he adjusted the flow of the narcotic running into the patient's veins, increasing it threefold. With a soft sigh, the patient slid irreversibly deeper and deeper into the depths of anesthesia, over the edge and into the sleep that never wakes. Another adjustment of a small knob, and the flow was returned to its previous level.

It took mere seconds.

A patient monitor that sat on a cart a few feet from the patient finally disrupted the tension of the room as the regular, staccato rhythm of the vital signs monitor faltered, skipped a beat, then another, then speeded into a rapid-fire machine-gun blast of chirps so close together that they almost sounded like a single, long tone.

Marge and Dr. Simmons heard it in the same instant and pushed their way up to the table where the patient jerked once, then again, and then lay still.

"He's arresting. Call the code," the anesthesiologist yelled through the silence in the room.

"Move, people! We've got work to do," the head nurse added, her voice calm, businesslike but with a sense of urgency that no one missed.

Simmons reached a gloved hand into the body cavity where the resident had yet to close, and began massaging the patient's heart. His forehead broke out into a thick sweat, but his words remained calm as he spoke to the resident. "Scoot around and assist anesthesia. I'll handle this end. Marge, get the crash team in here and then monitor vitals. Everyone else, move away from the table."

The head nurse jumped over to the intercom, slapped the speak button with the heel of her hand and yelled, "Code Blue in OR fourteen." Then she turned to a nurse standing nearby and said in a tone that allowed no question, "Get the defib unit fired up for the doctor, now."

The tech she'd spoken to already had the defibrillator cart rolling up to the surgical table, and Marge nodded in satisfaction. This was her team. They knew their jobs. She'd trained them, herself.

One of the nurses standing next to the surgeon with the contact paste for the defib paddles groaned and whispered, too loudly, "Not again. That man was okay."

Marge heard the words and spun to face the woman. "You heard the doctor. Away from the table! I'll take that paste."

Most of the OR team backed away from the patient as the *code team* raced into the room. Simmons smiled grimly as the Chief of Surgery, Dr. Luke Harrison, stepped up to the table beside him. "Didn't I just talk to you on the phone? Nice of you to be close by – I can use the extra set of hands."

Controlled pandemonium overcame the OR as the two surgeons and team of OR technicians fought to revive the patient.

"This shouldn't have happened," Simmons said as he worked defib paddles into place over the patient's heart. "This man was good. He should have survived. Clear!"

The staff all took a step back, away from the patient as a wave of electricity struck the body. It arched, and then settled back onto the table.

Dr. Harrison's eyes looked weary and sad through the protective face shield as he replied, "They can surprise you. We've both seen too many cases like this, where the patient is doing fine and then throws a clot or arrests for no particular reason."

"Yeah, but this one should have made it."

Simmons yelled "Clear" again and repeated the defib process again, without effect.

They each worked a different area, knowing their duties well after many practice sessions and too many actual cases. Methodically, they checked gauges, inserted a catheter, adjusted the anesthesia gas mix, and finally punched a shot of adrenaline to the patient's heart; a last ditch attempt to stimulate life.

It didn't work, and five minutes later both surgeons stepped away from the table. Their shoulders sagged from the prolonged effort. Harrison turned his head toward Simmons as he stripped off his face shield and surgical cap. "You call it. It was your case."

Simmons shook his head, stripped off his own face gear and ran his fingers through long, sweat-soaked black hair. He looked around until he spotted Marge giving instructions to a team of nurses, and waved her over. "Keep the ventilator in place and check his organ donor status. Bring in the harvest team if he checks out."

Simmons rubbed the heels of his hands hard against his eyes as Marge nodded her understanding. He turned his attention back to

Dr. Harrison. "This shouldn't have happened. It was a complicated case, but he was doing fine. I would have bet my last two paychecks this guy would have made it. The organs were all intact. Not so much as a bruise on the liver or spleen, and that's unusual for a car accident like the one he'd been in. I'd said as much to Marge just before he arrested."

Harrison sent a searching glance toward the head nurse, who turned away abruptly to consult with her staff. The nurses stood in a tight knot, whispering angrily among themselves. "I tell you, I saw a case just like this last week, and another a month before. It isn't right," one of them said.

Marge shushed her crew with a stern glare.

Harrison returned his gaze back to meet Simmons' perplexed expression. "Any idea what might have gone wrong?"

When Simmons failed to respond immediately, Harrison looked over at the large clock that dominated the wall above the OR's main entrance, his eyes flicking from there and back to the head nurse, then over to Simmons once more. "So, do we call the patient? I've got to be in Room 7 for another case in a couple of minutes and I'll have to scrub up again."

Dr. Simmons paused, and the room fell silent. "Yeah, I guess. Marge, start the recorder. Record the patient as deceased at ten o'clock, June twenty-fourth. Sign it Doctor Simmons, surgeon of record. Stop the recorder. I'm headed for the showers."

Harrison laid an arm across his colleague's shoulders as the two men pushed through the OR's swinging doors. "It was a tough case. You know you can't save every one."

Behind them, they heard the receding voice of the head nurse call out, "This man's an organ donor. Get the extraction team in here, STAT!"

Chapter 4

Bill arrived at the hospital early the next morning with the feeling that this was going to develop into an interesting assignment. Running into Carole yesterday, literally, he took as a very good sign. Because of the hour, it took only a few minutes to find a parking spot near the hospital's front entrance. He set the Supra's alarms on automatic and headed for the building's main entrance.

He'd studied the hospital's operations for a week prior to coming north, but had no idea of the layout of the building. He was pleasantly surprised at its setting, with ancient pines and fir trees hanging over the parking lot like an evergreen umbrella. A simple brass plaque to the right of the front door was inscribed with the name: Wilkes Memorial.

Wilkes Memorial was named for one of Olympia's founding fathers. Like a cleverly constructed woodsy retreat, its six-story nursing tower blended into the evergreens like it was part of the original forest. The morning sun filtered through the trees and reflected off broad, polarized windows that fronted each patient's room and offered a view of Mount Rainier to the east. A sprawling administrative wing swung north of the main building, its muted forest green and brown exterior lying like a shadow between tall rows of Douglas Firs that bordered an expansive parking.

Bill whistled as he admired the buildings and their clean lines. This campus had been carefully planned. He knew what it took to build and maintain a healthcare facility and this one would require quite a budget. Most of the other hospitals in the area were associated with a multi-hospital network, supported by vast national support structure and financing that could be used to build and maintain an expensive physical plant. Not Wilkes. Among them all, Wilkes Memorial stood alone. The sole independent institution in the capital city, Wilkes Memorial was the last of its kind, and by all reports was doing quite well.

Bill pushed his way through the revolving front door. Inside, he found a broad, open foyer dotted with clusters of hospital staff admiring a display what appeared to be Native American art hung on the walls and in a large display case in the lobby's center. He stopped to admire one of the paintings that seemed to reach out and grab his attention. The style was abstract, striking, with vivid colors and shapes reminiscent of Van Gogh. The brass plaque on the case indicated that an artist from the nearby Nisqually Reservation painted the piece ten years ago. The artist's depiction of everyday native life were rendered in bold relief and held Bill spellbound for several seconds, until he felt a gentle tap on his shoulder.

"Excuse me. Are you Mr. Deming?"

The words were repeated twice before Bill was able to draw his attention away from the painting.

"I'm sorry," Bill said. "But this piece is wonderful."

"Yes it is, and thank you very much. It was painted by my maternal grandmother."

Bill turned to meet the dark, laughing eyes of a very attractive woman. She had a tanned, oval face, and large wide-set eyes that were framed by thick black hair that hung past her shoulders in an ebony cascade. In her mid to early thirties, she stood only a few inches below his own five-eleven and gave off a radiance that brought a smile, unbidden, to his lips.

"Your grandmother?"

The woman nodded. "My family comes from the reservation. I lived there when I was growing up."

"Your grandmother was an amazing artist."

"You are Mr. Deming, then?"

Bill took a business card from the breast pocket of his sport coat and handed it to her. "I'm sorry. Yes, I'm Bill Deming." The words stumbled from his mouth and he suddenly felt extremely self-conscious. He was acting like a school kid, smitten by the first beautiful girl he saw. "I'm here to see Mr. Sterling, the Administrator."

She briefly examined the card he'd given her, and then met his eyes and smiled once more. She held out a hand and Bill shook it, noting the confident, firm grip, and the way a tiny electric shock seemed to travel up his arm from where they touched.

"I'm Jan McDonald-Sanchez." She waved a slim, long-fingered hand toward the painting Bill had been admiring. "She was a great woman in her time. She was an elder of the Nisqually Tribe. If you'll follow me, I'll take you to your first appointment."

"You work in administration?"

"I'm actually an intensive care nurse. I'm in the hospital's management internship program. I get to rotate through all the major divisions of the hospital. Right now, I'm working in the administrative wing with the hospital's leadership team. Mr. Sterling asked me to meet you. He's very excited about your project and wants to do whatever it takes to ensure that it goes well."

Jan led him out of the foyer and down a long corridor. He glanced around as they walked, getting his bearings. Signs along both walls indicated that they were headed for the administrative and ancillary support sections of the hospital. People in white coats, pastel uniforms and suits bustled in and out of doors that lined the long hall. One man pushed a cart full of medical records toward them. They had to pause and step out of his path as the rickety, wobbly-wheeled cart seemed to take on a life of its own.

"Better order a new cart, Rick," Jan said as the man moved past. "That one's about done for."

"Yeah, yeah. I hear you." The lab technician mumbled as he struggled the cart past. "See if you can get me the money, will you?"

She turned her attention back to Bill and he could feel the warmth of her gaze as a nearly tangible thing. "Speaking of which, the results of your audit could mean a lot of money for Wilkes," she said.

"At least enough for that new cart." He smiled, but kept his eyes forward as they neared the end of the hallway.

"So, exactly what does an audit entail?" Jan continued.

"A prospective patron wants a review of the hospital's business plan and books before he makes a large contribution. I'm here to do that review."

They came to the end of the hallway, where two large, carved wooden doors barred their way. Above the doors, the sign read, "Administration." Jan paused, her hand on the doorknob.

"That sounds pretty involved."

Bill glanced at her, not sure if her statement hadn't held just a hint of humor or cynicism in it, and noticed several strands of her long black hair that had drifted forward to tangle with her eyelashes. He found himself wanting to reach out and brush them back into place, and wondered how her hair would feel against his fingertips.

Instead, he shifted his briefcase from right to left hand and returned his gaze to the doors. He didn't have time for schoolboy fantasies.

"The audits are actually pretty boring for most people, when you get right down to it. I dig through the hospital's financials and medical records, compare performance against industry standards, and interview a few key stakeholders. It can be pretty tedious. Then I write up a very long report so the donor can feel comfortable committing his funds to support the new cardiac care wing that your hospital wants to build."

Jan lifted an arm to indicate their way through the heavy wooden doors. "I doubt I would be any good at that sort of work. Shall we go in?"

When he reached for the door to push it open, she touched his arm and stopped him. "Your work may be dull to you, but I think it could be very important to our patients. Wilkes is one of only two Level 2 trauma units in this section of the state. The additional cardiac capability would help us out a lot."

Bill nodded and followed her into the hospital's headquarters.

The administrative heart of the hospital's operations was a thickly carpeted open bay with busy workstations lining the perimeter. Near the center were three larger work spaces occupied by a young woman, a man in his early twenties, and an elderly lady that Bill would guess to be at least seventy years old. Each of the three larger modular work units was positioned in front of one of three doors that led to the offices of the hospital's Deputy Administrator, Chief Financial Officer and Chief Executive Officer.

The elderly woman worked at the station nearest the CEO's office and stood as they approached her desk. Short and matronly in a gaily-flowered dress and blue-gray hair, the woman's heavily creased face spoke of a person who had already lived a long time. The eyes, however, danced with a light that suggested much younger years. Bill smiled as he met those eyes. She was an exact picture of the grandmother he'd never met.

"Mr. Deming, I presume," she said. "I'm Ruth, Mr. Sterling's secretary. Darrel is looking forward to meeting you."

Jan laid a hand on the arm of his jacket and winked. "Keep an eye on Ruth. She's one of those rich widows you hear about. She's ruthless; eats men like you for breakfast."

"Oh, you," Ruth said. "I'm nothing of the sort. I'm just a kindly little old lady trying to do her job."

"She's the one who runs this place, have no doubt," Jan said. "I guess this is where I bow out. It's been nice meeting you, Mr. Deming."

The feel of her hand on his arm was electric and once more, Bill struggled with his composure. "The name's Bill, and it was nice meeting you, too. I hope we have the chance to talk again."

"Perhaps," Jan said. She disappeared through the office's outer doors and into the hospital's depths.

Ruth clucked as the doors closed behind her. "Don't worry, young man. She has that effect on most men."

Bill turned back toward Ruth. "Excuse me?"

"Jan. She has that effect on every man she meets. Too bad, though. She's so into her work, she seldom takes time to date. If I had her looks and her age, I'd be stepping out with every man who looked my way. I'd always be busy."

Bill chuckled, in spite of the heat he felt spread across his cheeks. "Was I that obvious?"

Ruth reached out and patted his coat sleeve, her voice a whisper. "I could give you her office number, if you like. I've been trying to get that girl to go out with someone for the last five years. Work, work,

work. That's all she does. She needs to get out and kick up her heels."

Bill's response was cut short by the arrival of a balding man of short, rotund proportions. The man stepped from the CEO's office and, without waiting for an introduction, moved between Ruth and Bill and pumped Bill's hand in an arm-jerking shake. "Bill, Bill Deming. Waiting for you all morning. Come on into the office and have a seat. Ruth, get the man a cup of coffee. Make it that espresso stuff you guys like so much. I'm a tea drinker myself. Get me some tea, Ruth, will you?"

Ruth squared off with Sterling, her bony hands clenched on her hips. "Mr. Sterling, in this day and age, I would think you'd know better than to ask a woman to…"

Sterling waved a hand at his office assistant. "Yeah, yeah. Please, get us something to drink. Is that good enough?"

Ruth harrumphed and headed off to the coffee machine. "The nerve of the man…" The words faded as she moved off.

Sterling's words came rapid fire as Bill followed him into his office and settled into a rich leather chair. The man was nervous, apprehensive about this stranger about to dig through the guts of his operation and pass judgment on what Sterling might consider to be his life's work. Bill had seen it before.

Sterling shifted uncomfortably in his chair and Bill let him stew in his nervousness. It was always good to keep the management team that he was auditing off guard. It tended to make them more spontaneous, more revealing. The oversized, high-backed chair made Sterling look like a munchkin, and with his flushed cheeks, the effect was intensified.

Sterling cleared his throat and then started in on the speech that Bill was sure the man had rehearsed for hours before his arrival. They always did.

"It is our hope that your audit will conclude quickly so we can move on with the ground-breaking for the new cardiac wing. It will be quite a boon to the community."

"I will complete the job as quickly as possible. I anticipate taking about two weeks."

Sterling's pasted-on smile drooped. "We'd hoped it wouldn't take so long. We already have the contractor on board to begin excavation next week."

Bill rose from his chair and walked over to a bank of floor-to-ceiling windows that offered a picture-postcard view of Mount Rainier. The mountain stood tall and regal in the distance, the purity of its white snowfields and glaciers contrasting with the intensely blue sky. A small plume of white mist drifted from the summit and smeared the sky to the north.

He faced Sterling. "I'll do everything I can to expedite the process, but you were made aware of the rules of this game before I arrived. The anonymous donor has come forward and offered your facility eighty million dollars to help with your project. The first increment of that donation, approximately twenty million, is the exact amount I believe you need to get your project off the ground, but I will need the full two weeks."

Sterling shifted uncomfortably. "We have an excellent reputation. That should account for something. We sent you all that advance information. Couldn't you use what we sent you and abbreviate that part of the audit?"

Bill shook his head. "I'm surprised you'd ask such a question. My client is a professional philanthropist who spends much of his time and a considerable portion of his wealth assisting institutions like Wilkes Memorial. He demands and deserves that hospitals such as Wilkes meet a rigorous test of their solvency and good management. I can skip nothing for the sake of expediency, for you or anyone else."

Bill ticked off points on his fingers. "First, the hospital must be independent of larger corporations or holding companies for a period of at least five years. The hospital must be not-for-profit and it must withstand a complete audit of its financials, management processes and records. Wilkes Memorial has already met the first three criteria. The final test, which includes a review of the financials, your management policies and procedures, and a records review, is where I come in."

Bill raised a hand to stave off what he knew would be Sterling's next words.

"I know how arduous this process can be, but it is a requirement if Wilkes Memorial wants the funding my client has to offer. No audit, no money."

Sterling sank back into his chair with an audible sigh.

"On the good side, I can tell you that it was the considerable positive publicity received by Wilkes' transplant program that drew my client's attention; that, and your exceedingly high level of charitable donations from the local community. I need to see files, policies and records that describe and support those operations."

Sterling sat forward in his chair. "Much of what you ask for is highly proprietary. We guard the information surrounding those programs as our most precious commodities."

"It's your choice. Provide what I need to complete my audit, or tell me to leave. It makes no difference to me but will make all the difference in the world regarding my client's funding of your construction project."

"You'll have access to everything you need," Sterling said after a long pause. He rose from his chair, came around the desk and offered Bill his hand. Bill set his coffee aside, stood, took Sterling's hand and the two men sealed their agreement with a brief shake.

"Great. Now, if you can show me to the office I'll occupy for the time I'm here, I'll get started. If things go well, this shouldn't take any more than the two weeks we've allotted for the task."

"I'm counting on it," Sterling said, and escorted Bill out of his office and back to Ruth's desk. "Anything I can do to help, you have only to ask. If I'm not around, just ask Ruth to put you in touch with the Assistant Administrator. She can get you anything you need and speaks for me when I'm not around which, I'm afraid, is all too often with the demands of the Board, community and all."

"I understand," Bill said.

"Ruth will show you to your office. I'm due to meet with the Board in five minutes. They've already got their shorts in a wrinkle, agonizing over the outcome of your audit." Sterling stepped past Bill and hurried out through the administrative suite's main doors.

Ruth looked up from her computer terminal and gave Bill a knowing look. In the filtered light of the office florescent fixtures, her eyes actually glittered. "So, did the munchkin set you straight on everything?"

Bill let loose a low laugh, then coughed and covered it with the back of his hand. He elected to avoid answering the question and tried another tack. "Jan said that you're the one who actually runs things around here. In every hospital I've visited, it's been that way. The boss's assistant is the one person who can be counted on to know everything and run things behind the scenes."

Ruth blushed and dropped her eyes to her desktop.

"I'm sure you're wrong. Mr. Sterling is the boss."

She looked up and her smile had a disarming effect on him. "Ruth, if you were twenty years younger ..."

She laughed and handed him a neatly folded piece of paper. "Try thirty, sonny. And here's a phone number for you. It's for Jan's desk in the Nursing Tower. You could get it off the hospital roster, but I figure it's about time she stepped out and did something other than work. She needs a boost."

Bill started to refuse the offer, but she cut him off.

"No, you take it. You impress me as a nice young man. I think you'll enjoy each other's company. Promise me you'll give her a call."

When Bill attempted to refuse again, the crafty old meddler cut him off immediately.

"You call her and I'll show you to your office, and even help you with your audit. You don't and you can just find your office on your own. Now promise you'll call Jan. What's it going to hurt?"

Bill thought back to the effect that Jan had on him when they met in the hospital's lobby. The impact had been like the fabled lightning strike, reducing him to the level of smitten adolescent. Any woman who could have that sort of impact on a man would be worth calling.

He took the paper from Ruth's hand.

"Okay. I won't promise anything, but I will call her. Maybe we can have coffee."

Ruth rose from her desk. "Good. Now let's get you started. You're all set to meet with Dan Hickman, the comptroller, right after lunch. That'll give you time to drop your things and for me to give you the nickel tour."

Bill waved a hand toward the door. "Lead on."

Ruth inclined her head regally. "Gladly."

As they left the admin wing, Bill gestured toward the hospital's ancillary wing down the left hallway. "Could you help me get data regarding the hospital's transplant program? Mr. Sterling said he would make the information available and my client has a particular interest."

Ruth paused mid-stride and gave him an intense, searching glance. The look sent a chill racing up his spine. Then, just as quickly, the expression on Ruth's face transformed and the calm smile returned.

"Of course. I'll see what I can do."

Bill smiled his gratitude, hoping the look came across as genuine. Ruth, because of her position, could be invaluable to his work. He couldn't afford to lose her confidence.

As they neared the next set of doors, Bill reached for the door's crash bar and nearly fell through as it was jerked out of his hands.

Carole burst through in a flurry of file folders and trailing assistants, and they collided, spilling a stack of paperwork from Carole's grasp. Bill instinctively draped an arm around her waist to keep them both from falling.

It took Carole a second to change gears and recognize the man who was holding her. When Bill dropped his arm and she finally stepped away, she gave him one of those lopsided smiles that he remembered so well. "I guess that's twice you've tried to run me over in the last couple of days. Hello, Ruth. Giving our visitor the VIP tour?"

Bill noticed that much of the warmth had left Ruth's expression. "You know our Assistant Administrator, Mr. Deming?"

Bill made a deliberate show of shaking hands with Carole.

"We go back a ways, yes," Carole said. "He told me that he would be doing our audit when we ran into each other yesterday, but with everything else going on, I guess I'd put it out of my mind."

Carole stepped closer to Bill's side and looped an arm around him. It was a familiar gesture that Bill remembered from yesterday and twenty years before. Carole always needed that physical contact.

"I have a day full of meetings, but could you drop by later if I gave you a call? Perhaps I could fill you in on a few things," Carole said.

Bill noticed Ruth's tight-lipped expression in his peripheral vision, so kept his voice carefully neutral as he said, "Of course. I've got appointments all day, but I'll swing by later when things slow down and see if you're available."

"For you, I'll make myself available." Then Carole purposefully glanced in Ruth's direction and added, "For old time's sake and on a purely professional level, of course. See you then." Carole stepped around Bill and rushed toward the office adjacent to where Bill had met with the CEO. Her assistants followed like so many well dressed baby ducks.

Ruth reached for the door this time, and opened it for Bill. "You know our resident whirlwind, I gather?"

"Yes, I do, but from another time and another life."

Ruth's eyes crinkled at the corners. It reminded Bill of his mother's expression when she'd caught him doing something particularly bad as a child.

"You're an interesting man, Mr. Deming. Having you here should prove to be very eventful."

Bill frowned. "Let's hope not. In my line of work, interesting is not always a good thing. In two weeks; not one day more or one day less; I plan on being in my car and headed back to California."

Ruth smiled as Bill turned his back to her and lead the way out of the administrative wing. "We'll see, Mr. Deming. We shall see."

Chapter 5

The chief surgeon finished his search for any blood vessels that might have been nicked during the long surgical process they had just completed, and withdrew his hand from the body cavity. "So, are you enjoying your residency, Dr. Young?"

Brahms echoed softly in the background.

"I was lucky to have been chosen for the position, Dr. Harrison. I've learned a great deal. I'd enjoy it more if you'd let me close, like the other residents' preceptors."

The young surgeon-to-be was in his late twenties. A shock of brownish hair peeked out from under his surgical cap. His eyes were clear, blue and intense as he watched the senior surgeon, his instructor this day in the OR, reach for the rubber duck. Dr. Harrison jammed the flat, heart-shaped piece of flexible latex into the body cavity like he was stuffing cornbread into a turkey and drew it up tight against the outer wall. It would serve as a protective platform against any suture needles taking a wrong turn and probing too deeply into the patient's abdomen.

Surgical Resident Rick Young was always amazed when he watched this part, in spite of how much he wanted to do it himself rather than act as an observer. His preceptor today was an artist, with a strong and sensitive hand, and yet with a casual air about him that made everyone in the OR feel comfortable and at ease.

Across the table, Harrison considered his resident's comment. The boy was talented, but there were some things he simply liked doing himself. He glanced up in a rare gesture of confidentiality and met Young's eyes. "I kind of prefer doing this part, myself. Suturing is an art form and I take it as a personal challenge to do a precise, clean job for my patients. No matter how much we cut them open, no matter how ragged the incision, I believe that if you take the time to do it right, you can minimize the scar tissue. Some people prefer staples, but I'm for the old fashioned method. The scar you leave is your worst or best advertisement once the patient has been discharged from the hospital. You'll just have to be patient, doctor. Soon, you'll be a full-fledged surgeon and you can close all the cases you like."

Harrison flashed a grin at the resident and smoothed the duck atop the patient's internal organs, then accepted the suture and needle from the OR nurse. He inserted several strong stitches at the top of the incision to start the procedure. The resident watched in awe as Harrison's fingers flew down the incision in tiny, almost microscopic steps.

When the incision was a third of the way closed, Harrison reached in with his fingers and checked the top stitches. They held firm. Pleased with his work, he tugged the rubber duck down a few inches toward the base of the opening. Another few minutes and he had a clean line of stitches in place along the full length of the original incision, with only an inch-long slit remaining. The resident could see the shiny beige surface of the rubber duck, still in place beneath the hole. Harrison gave it a tug and it folded in on itself and slipped through the tiny hole. Harrison held it up to the light and smiled.

"Not a drop of blood on it. We've got a clean one here, boys and girls."

The head OR nurse whispered a soft, "Yea!"

Everyone in the OR chuckled and Harrison looked over at the resident. His broad grin was evident through his surgical mask and face shield. "Want to finish this last little bit of suturing?"

Young was already taking the next suture and needle from the OR technician. "You bet."

"Then get to it. Use the stapler if you get in trouble, but try not to.

I've got my signature on this one and this DaVinci doesn't want his work blemished."

Harrison glanced at the clock above the OR door. "Two and a half hours. Not bad for a busted spleen. It was a messy one at that. Nice job, all. See you in the break room for the post-op brief in a few minutes. We'll try to keep the case review short. Maybe we can have you out in less than an hour."

In one voice, the resident, anesthesiologist, nurses and technicians groaned and replied, "Yes, doctor."

In the physicians' locker room an hour later, Harrison hummed a snippet from an old 1960's folk song as he stripped off his surgical gloves. He tossed them into a garbage bin, found a bench, and allowed himself a few minutes of satisfaction. He was pleased with his team's performance on both of the cases they'd handled this morning. He'd worked with the same head nurse for more than two years, and she had brought her collection of technicians and OR nurses to peak performance in that time. After more than two hundred and fifty procedures, from the simple to the vastly complex, their dedicated crew had the lowest complication rate of any surgical team in the facility. That's why when Dr. Augustino entered the break room a few minutes later, Dr. Harrison was in great good-humor. He greeted the middle-aged epidemiologist from the comfort of his bench without bothering to get up.

"My illustrious Dr. Augustino. How goes the world of infection control?"

"I need a word, Luke."

Harrison sat up in his chair. Ignacio Augustino was normally a man of buoyant good cheer. His proclivity for practical jokes and mild-mannered jesting was legend at Wilkes Memorial. He seldom started a conversation with anything less than a smile or friendly chuckle.

"No knock-knock jokes this morning, Iggy? Something wrong?"

Augustino rubbed the palms of his hands against the thin fabric of his scrub pants like he was trying to get something off of his palms, but couldn't. He looked up at Luke and frowned. "That spleen of yours, this morning?"

Harrison nodded. "Sure. We finished that one hours ago. It was routine. We had a clean entry, got the spleen, and got out. It was a righteous procedure."

"Maybe not so good, Luke. There were post-op complications."

"Iggy, by my calculations, the patient should be leaving Recovery by now. It couldn't have gone better."

"Did you close, or did someone else?"

"I did, all but the last inch. I had a resident finish that. Why?"

"The patient arrested a little bit ago. We couldn't bring him back. It looks like there might have been a major bleeder deep in the body cavity. There was extensive blood loss."

Harrison lunged to his feet and slammed a fist against the nearby row of lockers. "He died? Why wasn't I called? I should have been called immediately. He was my patient!"

Augustino held up a hand to fend off his friend's ranting. "You were called. I was told they couldn't find you. The resident on call in Recovery handled it. I can't remember his name, but you can check the record if you want to talk to him. They called me as I was passing that area of the hospital, so I was there when the patient crashed. It wasn't pretty."

Augustino checked his watch. "We lost him a half hour ago. As you might guess, the family's a mess and the lawyers are already circling, waiting to pick the bones."

Luke's brows knit into a thick, intense single line above his eyes. "The only thing that could have gone wrong would be if we'd left something inside when we closed. I personally checked every inch of that body cavity, so I know that didn't happen."

Harrison scrubbed his forehead with one hand, and then dropped back onto the locker room bench. "There were no bleeders. I ran the colon."

Augustino nodded. "It looks like you missed something, Luke."

"That's impossible. My crew accounts for every instrument and bandage wrapper, every time. When I pulled the duck, there wasn't a fleck of blood on it. I ran the bowels myself and there wasn't a bleeder in that patient."

Dr. Augustino sighed and laid a hand on Harrison's shoulder. "Something went wrong, Luke. The family's in the waiting room, outside Recovery. You want me to talk to them, or do you want to do it?"

Luke brushed Augiustino's hand off his shoulder and turned

away. "But it's just impossible, unless…"

"Unless what?"

Harrison found he couldn't meet his old friend's eyes as he considered the one possibility that made sense. He and Iggy had worked together for over ten years, had consulted when Wilkes was being built, and worked as a team to put together the money and staff that ultimately turned it into one of the Pacific Northwest's great hospitals.

When Harrison didn't reply, Augustino said, "My friend, there is always an 'unless' in these situations."

Harrison's voice was a low growl when he finally turned his attention back to his friend. "I'll talk to the family. And thanks, Iggy. I appreciate you bringing this to me yourself. When will it go up for review?"

Dr. Augustino stepped halfway through the door leading out of the locker room and paused. "I expect the Case Review Committee will convene first thing tomorrow. Peer Review will be just before that. I'm not sure who'll get that task, but we generally jump on surgical deaths pretty quick. Give me a call and I'll let you know the results. Get your case notes to transcription as soon as possible, so that we can put this behind us."

Luke waited until the door closed behind his friend, and then picked up the phone and dialed a number on the hospital intercom. The musical voice of a trained medical receptionist answered at the other end. "Internal Medicine. May I help you?"

"This is Dr. Harrison. Put me through to the chief, immediately."

"I'm sorry, Dr. Harrison. The Chief of Internal Medicine is in conference."

Harrison growled his next words. "Interrupt that conference. Tell him he'll talk to me now or I'll come down there and bust down his door."

The voice on the phone jumped an octave. "Right away, Dr. Harrison."

The strains of an oldies station came over the line briefly as the receptionist transferred the call. Olivia Newton John was cut off mid-chorus as the other end picked up seconds later. The voice at the other end sounded short-tempered and angry. "This had better be good. I've got a major donor in my office."

"I'll just bet he's going to donate a pile of money, now that you've harvested my patient. We didn't agree on this one and we're supposed to agree on each of them before we take a patient down. This was a routine case. I like to be known for saving the routine ones, at least. Now, there'll be peer review, case review, and maybe a law suit. This could bust things wide open and we can't afford that."

The voice at the other end of the phone shifted from edgy to soothing tones. "Calm down, Luke, calm down. I talked to the Director and got approval before I moved on this one. Sorry I didn't have time to tell you. You know there won't be any tracks leading to you. After all these years, we're very good at these things, as you well know. Besides, no matter how good you are, complications happen all the time, so write off the experience to that. We needed this patient. The donor in my office has over one million dollars on the table. That's enough to get a start on renovating one of the operating rooms, the outpatient procedure room in Family Practice, and leave something for us." The voice hesitated. "And as for your reputation: you continue to support the Director's goals in our little venture and your reputation will be just fine. To do otherwise might stimulate release of some information that neither the Director, you, nor the hospital would like to have get out."

Harrison slumped back onto the edge of the bench. "You just don't understand, do you? Everyone on my team observed this case. It was routine. We all cheered when we were done. What are they going to say when the Committee meets and asks them about it? In the past, we've only harvested borderline cases, ones that could have gone either way. This one wasn't even close."

"Luke, Luke. As I said, complications happen all the time. Maybe this one wasn't the best candidate, but we needed her liver. It'll mean a lot of money for the hospital, and the residuals for the team will be substantial. She was an organ donor, after all. Her life will go for the greater good."

"And for your checkbook balance."

"Yours won't suffer, either, Luke."

"I still don't like it. What about the Case Review Committee?"

"Lester Williams heads it. I've known Lester for years and he's taken money from me before. I'll talk to the Director again, and then I'll speak with Lester. You and your OR crew don't have to do anything but tell the truth. The case went well and you expected a full recovery. Something happened and you can't explain it. It's the vagaries of medicine. It'll remain a mystery indefinitely."

"And if the family sues?

"The hospital will write a check. I'll have our lawyers approach them tomorrow, early, and offer a very generous settlement with six digits. We'll still make enough for us and the hospital, considering the donation the organ recipient's father will make to the hospital's building fund. Now, I really do have to go. Relax, things will work out fine."

Harrison exhaled deeply and returned the telephone to its cradle. He knew he should trust his friend. They'd been together a long time and involved in this particular scheme for years. So why was he so worried now?

He grabbed the front of his scrub shirt, pulled it over his head, tossed it into the corner of the room and then let a long, loud sigh blow through his lips. Maybe it's time for me to get out of this business; maybe become a simple family doctor in some small town in Wyoming. Things are getting too complicated.

He pulled on a fresh set of scrubs and headed back to the OR.

Chapter 6

Walking back to his office from the last scheduled interview of the day, Bill felt good. The first day on the job had gone very well. Nothing terribly exciting had come up and he considered it a good omen for how the rest of the assignment would go.

He wanted to look through the last of two stacks of paperwork that he'd left on his desk before leaving for the evening. He'd only made it through one of the piles so far, and had counted on a late night. Then Carole showed up at his door just after noon and asked him out for dinner. He'd accepted at once. While dating an executive from the firm he was auditing might be considered bad taste, what guy wouldn't be tempted by a rematch with the woman who'd been his first love? Opportunities like that didn't come along every day.

So why did he have this queasy feeling in the pit of his stomach? He paused mid-stride and chuckled. Probably first date jitters – the second time around.

He lifted his eyes in time to see someone step from his office and quietly close the door behind them. He or she, he couldn't tell which because of the long green surgical smock and cap the person wore, hurried off in the opposite direction as he approached.

"Can I help you?" he called.

The person disappeared around a hallway corner without a reply.

Bill followed, but when he rounded the same corner, there was no one in sight. He shrugged and retraced his steps to his office. Probably someone leaving him a note or some information Ruth had arranged for him to receive.

He hadn't bothered to lock his office, which had been a mistake he wasn't proud to admit. The first rule of auditing was to safeguard your data. He'd let thoughts of the date with Carole distract him. He'd be sure to fix that and get his head back into the job. He had a reputation for his staid, predictable, methodical approach to work, and he didn't want to change that now.

As he entered the office and closed the door behind him, Bill did a quick visual search of the room. Nothing looked out of place, except for one small thing: a bright turquoise file folder tucked in among the other files stacked neatly on his desk. That hadn't been there before.

He sat down, pulled the file out of the stack, and flipped it open. He did a quick scan of its contents. The file was full of surgical reports, pieces of medical files from a half dozen patients, and clinical notes. This definitely hadn't been here before.

A piece of paper fell out of the file, slipped off the edge of the desk and floated to the floor. He picked it up. It was one of those pink telephone message forms, about three inches square. The words were printed in green block letters, with the lingering scent of felt-tip pen.

"Mr. Deming. Since you are here to audit the hospital's records, you should know what is really going on."

He'd seen more than one note like this before. Some conspiracy nut would learn that he was around and try to co-opt him into their crusade to save the world from the evils of their hospital's management team. Mostly, they turned out to be quacks, disgruntled workers, or worse.

He read on.

"The papers in this folder are extracts of patient files where a patient died. In each case, the patient should have recovered. In each case, the patient's organs were harvested for transplant. Someone is killing patients to steal their organs. It has to stop!"

The note was unsigned.

Bill read the message several times before he set it back on the desk. As skeptical as he was, a cursory review of the contents of the turquoise folder suggested just the slightest ring of truth.

His curiosity piqued, he decided to dig a little deeper, and examined the file's contents in closer detail. The first item was a photocopy of documents from a patient record, copied, and then stapled together. No attempt had been made to hide the names or social security numbers of the patients, which was a major breech of patient privacy laws.

The record was for a Mr. Robert M. Cummins. It was dated one year before. He had been a twenty-five-year old male, in excellent health, who'd taken a fall off a horse. The injury put him into a vegetative state, but the physician's record identified no major brain damage. The initial diagnosis was that Cummins would eventually come to and recover fully.

Once in the Intensive Care Unit, Cummins took a turn for the worse, sinking deeper into the injury-induced sleep. A few days later, all brain activity ceased and he was pronounced dead.

A living will was in place requesting no heroic measures once brain function had stopped. The family had agreed to pull the plug on his respirator. A scribbled physician's note at the bottom of the page indicated that Cummins' heart had been harvested for transplant. The recipient's name was listed and Bill recognized it from an article he'd read in that day's morning paper: a prominent local businessman who controlled a major software company in Tacoma, just north of the capital.

Something he'd read earlier in the day tugged at the back of Bill's mind. He rooted through the stack of folders on his desk and found the one he was looking for. It was a list of major contributors to the hospital's general fund. The heart recipient was prominently featured. The gift had been more than eight hundred thousand dollars.

Bill set aside the files and leaned back in his chair to consider. This was all very interesting, but was not an indication of a conspiracy in and of itself. Grateful patients frequently offered gifts to the hospital that saved their lives. It was human nature and he'd seen it a million times.

He picked up another stapled packet of documents from the turquoise file. This record also indicated that a patient had died unexpectedly, also under questionable circumstances. This one happened only one week ago. The patient arrived at the Emergency Room in a commercial ambulance, the victim of a multiple car pile-up on Interstate 5. There had been broken bones, a serious head injury and the possibility of internal injuries. The brief OR report from a subsequent exploratory procedure reported no internal injuries but considerable potential for brain damage.

The patient died on the operating table during a second procedure aimed at resolving a cranial hemorrhage. The cause of death was listed as complications arising from anesthesia. What caught Bill's attention was the piece of a living will that had been included with the file. It had been signed by the patient's relatives and authorized the harvest of his organs. A third copy appended to the page identified the recipient of the patient's liver and lung as the son of a prominent state politician. An article in the morning's paper suggested the man might be running for governor in the next election.

Bill switched his attention back to the list of financial patrons and found the senator's name. This donation was followed by six zeros.

Bill found that his stomach was churning. There was too much of a pattern apparent in the evidence for his liking, and as an auditor that one thing he knew about was trends. On the other hand, it could be a series of innocent coincidences. The one thing that he was sure about was that he didn't know enough about the situation to be able to call it either way. Until he could reach a conclusion, objectively and through cold reasoning and evidence, he had to maintain his perspective, remain objective. Unless he came across more evidence, these records wouldn't even be a note in his report. They had been provided to him against medical policy, and outside the laws governing patient privacy.

Besides, it was common for a family member to be grateful when a surgeon saved a relative. That frequently meant a sizeable donation to the hospital. Perhaps it was only coincidence that an organ donor was immediately available, who was a perfect match for the recipient when a patient died.

Perfect match …

He rolled the words around in his mind. He was no physician, but he knew that organ transplants were a tricky business. Blood and tissue matches had to be nearly perfect for the recipient not to reject a donated organ, even with the new anti-rejection drugs on the market. How rare a perfect match was, he had no way of knowing.

And then there were the waiting lists for transplant recipients. They were sometimes years long and governed by rigid state and federal guidelines. Where were these recipients on those lists? He would check that in the morning. The answer would be telling.

He read through the remaining stack of case reports in the turquoise file, and found another that had been documented in the last few weeks. Again, the patient had been expected to survive her injuries, but died of complications resulting from a medication error. The hospital had settled out of court with the family, writing a check within a week of death.

Several of the deceased woman's organs were donated to people who would have otherwise perished. This time, he didn't recognize the recipient's name.

Bill scanned the file but could find nothing more. No financial donation was listed as follow-on to the procedure in anyone's name. Here was an instance where someone in the community was confronted by a significant loss, and no one from the hospital benefited but the organ recipients. This one looked normal. So why was it in the file, if whoever delivered this information to him wanted to send him a message? There must be more to this one than was obvious at first glance.

Bill stared out at the trees and fountain in the garden beyond his office window. A breeze shuffled the branches overhead and they fanned their green boughs over the garden's scattered boulders and ferns. A junco, with gray wings and buff colored body, and black covering its head like an executioner's hood, clung to the swaying branches, undaunted by the wind.

Who had left these documents? If they actually felt there was a problem, why didn't they take the information to the police?

In his heart, Bill doubted there was any substance to the conspiracy claim. Too many times these anonymous warnings were simply crackpots with a desire to be David to their employer's Goliath. It was sad that patients died, who might have otherwise lived, but the simple truth was that sort of thing happened in hospitals. Some people got well and some died. Hospitals did their best, but sometimes that simply wasn't enough.

Following an impulse, he picked up the phone, punched in a number and waited. The call was answered on the second ring.

"Comptroller's office. This is Williamson. Can I help you?"

"It's Bill Deming, the visiting auditor."

Bill could feel the frost that clung to the woman's voice at the other end. Their appointment, earlier in the day, had not gone well.

"What can I do for you, Mr. Deming?"

He gave her the last name of the person listed on that last patient record in the turquoise file. "Can you take a look at your patronage list and tell me if this individual's made any substantial donations to the hospital in the last while?"

"May I ask the purpose of the inquiry?"

Why, indeed, Bill wondered? Was he on a wild goose chase, wrapped up in a conspiracy theorist's warped leanings, or was he simply doing his job? If there was something wrong and he didn't uncover it, he'd surely lose his job.

He forced his voice into its usual calm monotone. "Wilkes has a great patronage program and I'd like to document it for my report. To do that, I need to substantiate receipt of the donation. It might help my client support his decision to make the contribution he's considering if we can confirm a few things regarding the other people who give to the hospital."

Her response was flat, grudging in its acceptance. "Hang on a moment. I have the file right here in the computer."

There was a pause while she called up the information.

"Here it is. Yes, we just received the cash transfer to our charitable account, from his bank."

"May I ask how much he gave?"

"I'm sure that would be all right. Since he is a senator, it is a matter of public record. He donated one point two million dollars. The gift has been designated for the hospital's geriatric program."

Her voice brightened noticeably. "I'm sure your employer will be happy to hear that."

"I'm sure he will," Bill said and hung up.

As he replaced the phone in its cradle, he returned his gaze to the small stack of papers in the turquoise file. Three out of three. The trend was hard to deny. All of the cases listed in the file involved influential people, and each of the transplants was followed by a significant donation.

What now? Perhaps he should go to the police. No, even with what he had, he wasn't sure he had enough to take to the police. The three cases with suspicious outcomes were not enough, and what he had was based on a lot of supposition.

There were two places he could check to confirm or disprove what he'd seen in the turquoise file: the Transplant Program Management Office and the pathologist's reports for the patients who had died. The first would give him a complete record of organ recipients he could compare against the list of the hospital's financial patrons. The second would help him to confirm the legitimacy of any organs being harvested.

He closed the turquoise file and pushed it away, to the far side of the desk.

Of course, he could always just ignore the information; pretend that he'd never seen it in the first place. He could quietly complete his audit, head back to the sun and warmth of California, and resume his quiet, predictable life. The thought was enticing. His first career as an Army Medical Service Corps and Medical Intelligence Officer had offered more than enough excitement for one lifetime. Getting shot at was over rated, even if your job was to help wounded soldiers in the process, or seek out information that might save them from getting sick or wounded in the first place. He'd promised himself that this, his second career, would be different and considerably less exciting.

He drummed his fingers on the top of his desk and rubbed at an old scar on his left shoulder. That bullet had been way too close, and after over ten years and a full recovery, it still pained him.

On the other hand, that built in desire to find answers, to develop solutions to complex problems, is what made him good at his job. He'd be less than true to what he was if he didn't at least take a look into this. What he really wanted to do was talk to the person who'd delivered the file.

Bill glanced at his watch. It was already after five and his date with Carole was at seven. He needed to get back to the hotel, walk Alex, shower and get a change of clothes.

The idea that patients, people who surrendered total control over their lives might have been betrayed for something as base as money nagged at him. It prodded at his deep need to see things orderly, neat, and each fit into its nice little box. Healthcare workers killing patients just did not fit well at all.

He stared out the window again. The junco was gone and the ferns were still.

Chapter 7

Dr. Ian Farley sat across a small interview table from his old friend and offered the man his most sincere, concerned expression. He held his hands out wide to his sides. "I certainly understand, Morgan. Who wouldn't? But there's simply nothing I can do."

Secretary of State Morgan White was a bear of a man, well over six feet tall and two hundred pounds. Some of the once massive chest and shoulders had settled into a comfortable pot above his belt, but the well-cut, thousand-dollar suit hid most of that. On most days, he was an imposing figure of strength and power. Today was not one of those days. He looked wizened, run down, an old man. A tear traced its way down a weathered, creased cheek and dropped to the surface of the tabletop.

It broke Farley's heart that his oldest, dearest and most powerful friend should be reduced to this, but there really was nothing he could do. The decision simply wasn't in his hands.

Morgan finally looked up after several long moments of silence. "We've known each other for what, forty years, Ian? I'm the one who bankrolled you when you set up your first practice. You and

I grew up like brothers. Our kids grew up together."

Farley nodded. "Grade school together, then junior high and high school. The only time you and I have been apart for any length of time was when I went to med school."

The Secretary stared intently into his friend's eyes. "In all that time, have I ever asked that you do anything for me? But I've helped you anyway, right? You and this hospital of yours?"

Ian shifted uncomfortably in his chair.

"Well, I'm asking now," White said. "My son may well die in the next few months if he doesn't get a heart and lung transplant. Wilkes is one of the few hospitals in the region that can do that operation."

White paused and then dropped his eyes to his hands again. "Help me, Ian."

Ian blew out a heavy sigh and raised his eyes to the ceiling. They'd already covered this ground, several times. He'd been this man's friend for so long he felt like he could actually feel Morgan's pain. He reached out and took his friend's wrist in his hand, squeezed it.

"Eric is my godson. You know how much I want to help him, but the fact is he's number sixty on the waiting list for that combination of organs. I checked the state register myself. There are a lot of worthy recipients in front of him on the list, who are in the same situation. Many of them have parents who feel exactly as you do."

Secretary of State White looked up and met the doctor's eyes again, and his expression tore at Ian's heart.

"I'll beg, if necessary," White said.

Ian slumped in his chair and let his hands fall to his sides. "You know how I feel about you and your family, but as your friend, I have to be honest with you. There's very little hope that Eric will get a transplant in time. Too many people are ahead of him, even if we could find a good tissue match with a donor. It's a very complicated situation."

Ian had gone to the "Director" himself—and she'd told him to drop the issue. The combination heart and lung transplant was too high visibility to keep quiet within the hospital, the city, and the medical community. Not many had been attempted, let alone completed successfully.

She'd shut down his request before he'd even had a chance to spell out the details: how much money Morgan was willing to donate to the hospital; the fees his old friend suggested he would be pay for the operation. The Director had been right, of course. The operation would be too visible to the public, impossible to keep under wraps.

Ian shook his head as he examined the top of the bowed head across the table from him. Maybe it wasn't impossible to keep the operation quiet. Maybe it was just very, very difficult.

"Even if your son were to somehow move up on the waiting list, finding the right donor is often more a matter of luck than anything else. People aren't exactly standing in line to give away their livers and lungs. Have you considered what the media would do to you and this hospital if we jumped the chain to take care of Eric?"

White came halfway out of his chair and slapped the flat of his hand on the tabletop. "Damn the media! And you can have my political career, for all the good it will do my son. He's my only child ..." His voice trailed off and he slumped back into his chair, his head hanging between his outstretched arms.

Ian waited as White collected himself. He watched as tired, old eyes filled with tears and lifted to meet his once more.

It was then that he made up his mind: he would do something to help Morgan and his son, no matter the cost. Their friendship went back too far; their bond was too strong for him to endure his friend's agony as his only son faded away.

He would take matters into his own hands, regardless of what the Director said. The "informal" organ program that he'd been involved with for the past three years had helped innumerable people from the ranks of the rich and famous, so why not his friend Morgan White? The Director had already said no to the project, but the director wasn't the one who was out on the line taking all the chances. After three years, it was time that he called the shots once in a while, and there was a lot that his friend could do— had already done—to help the hospital. It was the right thing to do, no matter how you looked at it, wasn't it?

Ian sucked in a deep breath and then exhaled. "Maybe there is something I can do. If there's any way I can make this work, it'll happen. You have my word."

A hopeful smile formed on White's flushed face. "I know you can do it, Ian. No matter what it costs, you set it up. I'll pay any price."

"I know you will," Ian said. "I just hope that price isn't too high for all of us."

Chapter 8

Bill opened the door to his hotel room. The room was warm and smelled like dog breath. He glanced to the sofa, where Alex lay with one eye cocked open in his direction. Just the tip of the dog's tail waved left to right as Bill made contact.

"Don't get up for me," Bill said as he dropped his briefcase next to the sofa and gave Alex's ears a thorough scratching.

The phone's message-waiting light was blinking, so he crossed the room and picked up the handset and dialed in the code for his messages. The recorded voice at the other end was Carole's.

"Sorry Bill, but I'll have to cancel tonight. Something's come up. We'll reschedule. See you soon."

"So much for the fantasy date," he said aloud.

Alex grumbled in response, eased his heavy body off the couch, stretched, and walked over to the door.

The evening air outside was clear, with just a hint of moisture. A soft breeze shuffled through the parking lot, scattering bits of paper and dried leaves across the pavement. The tall fir trees that flanked the hotel on all sides whispered and sighed as the cool breeze shifted their limbs. Bill absorbed all this like a cleansing draught and marveled at how much he'd missed this aspect of the Northwest's weather.

Alex appeared unfazed as he hunted the perfect spot for evening toilet.

"Practically a perfect evening for a Monday, Alex," Bill said. "Except when you consider that I'm a single man in the prime of my life, and I'm headed for another night alone with my dog."

Alex looked up, wagged his tail, and then bumped his head against Bill's leg.

"Not that you're bad company. Compared to the hospital's comptroller, you're amazing."

"That's not what I heard. Word was that poor Ms. Williamson was smitten when she met you and was crushed when you didn't reciprocate."

Startled, Bill turned on his heel to see Jan McDonald-Sanchez striding across the parking lot toward him. Her hair was tied back in a thick black braid that flipped behind her as she walked. Her deep brown eyes and trim, athletic figure stirred something inside him that made Bill feel vaguely unsettled.

"Jan. This is a pleasant surprise." He held out a hand in greeting. "I realize that I forgot to thank you for your help earlier, but I had no idea you'd track me down to solicit an apology."

"Hope you don't mind me showing up uninvited. I got your hotel from Ruth."

Bill chuckled. "From the matchmaker, herself?"

Jan laughed. It was a soft, delightful sound, and Bill forced himself not to stare. What was the effect this woman had on him, after only two meetings?

"So, you've gotten to know our beloved Ruth, then?"

"She made me promise I'd call you, or she wouldn't show me where my office was," Bill said.

"You didn't call. I'm crushed."

"I'll just bet. Besides, I am the evil auditor and the last thing you need is some door-to-door consultant begging for a night on the town."

Jan walked over to where Alex had resumed his snuffling investigation. Bill assumed the dog was about to engage in yet another call of nature, when Alex's attention suddenly shifted and focused on the new arrival. His tail beat frantically at the air as Jan approached. When she reached out a hand to greet the dog, Alex dropped to the ground and rolled over on his back, so his belly could be scratched.

Bill laughed. "Alex is usually friendly, but never this friendly. I suspect you have an admirer."

Jan squatted down next to the dog and gave Alex's chest a vigorous rub.

"I don't mind. Guys always react to me like that, or so Ruth says. I'm quite certain that's why I was sent to meet you today, to distract you with my feminine charms."

She finished scratching Alex and stood up.

"They sent you to distract me?"

"Exactly. It was the last stunt I expected my friends at the office to pull, and I apologize for their behavior. I hope you don't hold it against the hospital. It's actually a great place to work, does a lot of good for the community. The hospital and the community shouldn't suffer for the narrow-mindedness of a single individual like our CEO. I tracked you down tonight to apologize for them using me like that to distract you, although I must say that meeting your wonderful dog is a bonus."

As a professional, he should have been outraged, but frankly, he found he didn't much mind the opportunity to meet Jan. She'd impressed him when they'd met earlier, and she was definitely attractive.

"What they did certainly wouldn't disqualify them from receiving the donation from my client, but it sure could color my perspective," he said. "They're not the first to try and divert an auditor's attention from a project. I admit that when I met you, I had thoughts along those lines, myself. Since you've offered your own version of things, I can keep my guard up for other tricks that the illustrious Mr. Sterling might try while I'm here. I'm grateful that you came to me like this"

He paused and grinned. "And here I thought you came to see me tonight because you were suitably impressed, maybe even liked me."

He noticed the sudden color rise in her cheeks, and her reaction confused him.

"I don't dislike you," she said. She stood, and then reached down and smoothed the wrinkles from her skirt.

Bill laughed again. "If that isn't a vote of confidence, I've never heard one. How about having a cup of coffee with me, by way of apology?"

Jan cocked her head to one side and considered the offer through half-closed lids, her long lashes momentarily hiding her wide brown eyes. "I guess we could do that. It'd have to be Dutch, of course. I wouldn't want you to think I'm trying to distract you from your work."

Too late, Bill thought. "Now that all the cards are on the table, a little coffee couldn't possibly hurt anything. It just so happens that my social calendar is empty for the evening."

"I'll wait out here while you take care of your friend. We can take my car. I've got a place in mind. It's a little bistro in the lobby of one of Olympia's oldest downtown hotels. Good atmosphere."

Bill nudged Alex toward the hotel room with his foot, trying to excavate him from beneath a rhododendron where he still lay, ever hopeful for another belly rub.

"Shameless dog," Bill said.

Behind them, Jan laughed.

They ended up at the Urban Onion, a quiet little restaurant, located in the old part of town that specialized in vegetarian food. It was a small establishment, with less than twenty tables and soft lighting. Bill sipped a glass of Riesling and considered a menu that he had no hope of understanding. He hadn't realized how hungry he'd been until they'd stepped into the restaurant and the fragrant aroma of cooking overtook him. Thoughts of coffee quickly receded from his mind and they both agreed that dinner might be a better idea, as long as it was Dutch.

"I've never been big on vegetarian food, so I have no idea what some of this stuff is," Bill said.

Jan set down her menu. "I'm sorry. We can go somewhere else if you like."

Bill held up a hand. "I didn't mean it like that. In fact, I've had vegetarian meals before and liked them just fine. It's just that this menu is almost entirely vegetarian and I have no idea what I'm getting into. What does tofu taste like, for example? And what are all these other odd names? I'm out of my element, here." He gave up and set the leather-bound menu aside.

Jan touched his hand as she laughed. It was a casual gesture, but her touch sent a jolt of electricity ripping up his arm.

"They're mushrooms, and tofu is a sort of vegetarian staple. It's like a hard custard, and tasteless," she replied.

"If it's tasteless, why serve it?"

She grinned at his comment.

"Why don't you order for both of us?" he said.

"A man who's willing to let the woman order his meal," she said. "How very progressive for a man in your profession."

That snapped Bill's attention back. "My profession?"

She nodded. Her face was serious, but even in the dim light of the restaurant Bill could see the glint of humor in her eye.

"You know—accounting," she added.

"Ah. You mean I'm rather progressive for some staid, old auditor. Everyone knows we auditors normally work in dusty, file-filled rooms."

Bill's voice became a whisper, with a tinge of conspiracy to its tone. "They only let us out of our rooms once or twice a year and we try to make the most of it."

He took a sip of wine, and held the glass up so he could admire the liquid's crystal clarity in the candlelight from a sconce that hung on the wall above their table. "Actually, I am a little staid when you get right down to it."

They both laughed.

"I imagine life as a nurse and life on a reservation would probably be a bit more exciting than mine."

Jan shook her head, and her thick braid of ebony hair slid forward over her shoulder to bisect her bust line. Bill found it hard not to stare as she casually flipped it back into place behind her.

"Believe me, life on the reservation is anything but exciting. It's not like you see on television, with lodge gatherings and dancing all the time. The people of my tribe live pretty much like the rest of the world: work, family, school. Actually, I don't live on the reservation any more. My brother still lives there, but I moved off years ago." She shrugged.

"By and large, we're just regular people—as boring and staid as the next person... or should I say auditor."

They laughed together again.

Bill wasn't sure if it was the wine, or Jan's company, but his attitude was dramatically improving by the minute. Thoughts of the broken date with Carole were all but forgotten as their meal came and they both dug into bowls of French Onion soup, followed by entrees that did not disappoint.

The evening went too fast, in Bill's opinion. Jan turned out to be easy to talk to, with a quick mind and an easy sense of humor. Immersed in their conversation, he lost track of the time until the last glasses of Columbia Crest Riesling were poured to accompany a dessert of creamy chocolate mousse and strawberries.

They lingered over the remnants of the thick confection.

Jan set her near-empty glass aside after a long, comfortable silence and lifted her eyes to meet Bill's. "So, how's the consulting going so far?"

"As of about an hour ago, I'd say very well."

"I meant the work."

"You pumping me for information?"

"Hardly. It's just conversation."

Bill felt his mood shift suddenly, his guard going up. He set his own glass aside as he considered her question. "I guess there's no harm is saying that things are going pretty well, with maybe one exception. I can't really go into detail, and I'm sure it will turn out to be nothing in any event."

"That doesn't surprise me."

Jan folded her hands in her lap, and then rearranged her napkin on the table. Her discomfort was apparent and it made Bill wonder at the sudden shift in atmosphere. Maybe she wasn't so innocent of her administrator's attempt at manipulating him. It was pretty convenient that she showed up at the hotel when she did. She'd agreed rather quickly to have dinner with him when he'd made the suggestion.

When she saw his expression change, Jan quickly added, "What I mean is that we went through an accreditation survey not too long ago. There were a few minor questions regarding some of the patient outcomes in the OR and ER, but nothing of consequence. We passed with flying colors, and got a three-year accreditation."

Bill lifted his own napkin from his lap, folded it neatly and placed it on the table. He signaled for the waiter to bring the check. "I really don't think there's much to worry about. The rate of medical misadventure at W.M. is right on the benchmark for an organization of its type. In fact, it's almost too perfect. In any event, I generally don't worry about that sort of thing. I'm mostly financial and process-oriented."

It was only half a lie, but he was uncomfortable with the questions she was asking and felt no guilt.

The thought came to him then that perhaps she could help him. If she was going to pump him for information, why not turn the tables around and do some of his own digging?

He leaned forward. "What do you know about Wilkes' transplant program?"

Her brow furrowed. "Anything specific?"

"As a rule, I look at an organization's major programs, and my employer has a specific interest in transplant programs. Today, I studied some records from transplants. It all seemed pretty routine, but I've got some questions."

"If you're interested in finding out more, I could direct you to our patient records clerk. She might be able to clear things up for you. She's kind of shy, but I've known her for years and I'm sure she'd help you out," Jan said.

"That'd be great. I'd like to talk to her."

Jan pushed her chair back from the table. "I guess we should free up this space for someone else. It gets pretty busy here, even on a Monday."

As he rose, Bill felt the disappointment wash through him. The evening had been so warm until the questions began to flow. Up to that point, he hadn't felt this comfortable with a woman in a long time. He looked up to see Jan's face shift from thoughtful consideration to a cheerful brightness that captured his heart completely.

"You know, if it's not too late for you, there's a great coffee bar a few blocks over," she said. "It's right on the water. Sometimes I go there just to watch the people and the boats go in and out of the marina. The latte isn't the best in town, but the place is always interesting."

Bill matched the stack of bills Jan laid on the check and helped her on with her light jacket. She reached up with one hand to flip her long braid from beneath her collar. She turned toward him and hooked her arm through his. "Good conversationalist and a gentleman, too. If you cook, you're the perfect man. Ready to go?"

As much as the tone of the evening had changed, what else was he going to do tonight? Maybe her questions were innocent, and he was just being paranoid.

"Sure. Why not? You lead. I'll follow."

They left the restaurant and walked out into the cool evening air. This close to her, his senses were full of her scent, which seemed to lack any sort of perfume and was more like the fragrance of fresh rain or clean linen.

They made their way through the dark streets of downtown Olympia in comfortable silence and along the short walk that led to the port area. He paused as they rounded a corner and he caught sight of the waterfront, the lights from the far shore reflecting on the smooth, dark surface of the bay.

She glanced over at him when he paused to take in the view. "Everything okay?"

Bill smiled as he gazed up into the clear evening sky as he considered the question. He hadn't felt this comfortable with anyone in a very long time.

"I think so. In fact, everything seems pretty darn good," he said.

She squeezed his arm and he felt a warm glow settle over him.

"Think you can forget your audit for the next little while? Your mood changed pretty dramatically when I asked about it back there in the restaurant."

Bill shrugged. "It's just an audit. What can happen?"

Chapter 2

Nurses, doctors and technicians moved through the ER's hallways and exam rooms. It was another busy day in the trauma suite and Claire Fairweather paused in her routine of paper shuffling to examine the terrain around her.

Two ambulances were pulled up to the ER's wide, sliding glass doors, unloading patients. Beyond them, at the far edge of the tree-lined circular drive, another rescue vehicle wheeled toward the hospital, the passenger-side door already ajar as the Emergency Medical Technician prepared to leap from the vehicle.

She sighed, praying silently that the EMT would have the sense to let the vehicle come to a stop before charging out the door. Just last week, one of their technicians had broken a leg when he jumped from a vehicle in his haste to help the injured patient inside.

She snorted. "Kids. Nothing but a bunch of kids."

Inside the ER, the pastel green corridors were jammed with the ebb and flow of patients, staff, and family members reacting to real or perceived crises.

Today was a busy day, for sure. Two car wrecks on Interstate 5, a boiler explosion at the old Stadium High School in Tacoma, several dog bites, a playground casualty, and the usual load of social visits from elderly pensioners with nowhere else to go. In Claire's understanding of busy days, today was shaping up to be a challenging one.

Room 2 was particularly tragic. A young man in his twenties, with severe neck trauma and multiple fractures to all limbs had been racing his daddy's Fiat and lost control. The police who met the parents in the ER said there wasn't much left of the car, except the hood ornament, which they pried from where it was imbedded in the tree's trunk. They found the mangled, dead body of a large German shepherd some distance off the road. Dog, Fiat and driver all came out the worse for wear, given the outcome of their meeting.

Only the tree survived, and the prognosis for it was not good.

Claire sighed and glanced down at the three-inch pile of forms on the reception desk. So many people, so much paperwork. She squared up the stack of paper and placed it neatly in the gray metal inbox at the side of her desk.

It was time for a coffee break.

"Dr. Samuels, there must be something you can do," the forty-something father said.

The doctor closed the cover on the patient chart and hung it on the end of the exam table.

Samuels had worked in the Wilkes Memorial's ER for the better part of five years. He'd started here right out of his residency at the University of Washington Medical Center. After all the years, and all the twelve-hour days, the place practically felt like home. The people he worked with were like family, but days like today, even that could ease the strain of life in the ER.

The long days weren't the problem. He could handle long hours. It was the intensity. At medical school, his professors had talked about the intensity of the work, but words could never prepare a person to deal with the constant flow of hurt and maimed patients, the relatives and loved ones in crisis.

All his life, he'd wanted to be an emergency doc. Lately, he wasn't so sure.

Dr. Samuels brought his attention back to the father of the

unconscious boy who lay on the table. Now and then a soft moan would leave the young man's lips.

Two nurses and a technician scurried around the prostrate form. They rigged the tubes and probes necessary to support the boy's life and monitor his vital signs during transport to the Intensive Care Unit. The patient's father rubbed at the shoulders of a small woman who would have been pretty, even elegant, on any other day. This afternoon, she sagged like a crumpled rag from grief over her wounded child.

"There's not a lot anyone can do, Mr. Stephenson. Bruce is a young man, so he might pull through, but I'm afraid it's all up to him. The broken bones will knit. Even the damage to the back will heal. There isn't any spinal cord damage that we can detect at this point. It's the blow he took to the head that's the trouble. When he was thrown from the car and struck the tree, it was head-on, and the blow fractured the skull near the frontal lobes of the brain. He's sinking into a coma, at this point. The good news is that going into a coma is the body's way of shutting down so that it can repair itself, although there's no good bet when it comes to brain trauma of this magnitude.

The mother sniffed loudly and squared her small shoulders. "Isn't there anything we can do?" she asked

"You can stay with him, read to him, and be by his side. Sometimes comatose patients come out of these things surprisingly well. The body has a great affinity to heal itself, in spite of what we think we know it can or cannot do."

Dr. Samuels laid a hand on the father's shoulder and steered him toward the door. "Dr. Michaels will meet you in the ICU when your son is settled in. He'll be taking over care of your son and will answer all your questions. It will take a while for them to move Bruce upstairs and get him comfortable, so why don't you two go down and get a cup of coffee in the cafeteria? Then you can head up to the ICU and Dr. Michaels will be ready to meet you."

The father's face flushed. "You offer us coffee? Our son is in there dying and you offer us coffee?

The man's wife laid a hand on her husband's sleeve. "Thank you, doctor," she said.

The Stephensons walked out of the exam room.

Samuels sighed as Bruce Stephenson was rolled out of the exam room, and then noticed that there was another patient on a gurney right outside the door. A housekeeping attendant dashed in ahead of the patient, hastily wiped down the exam table with disinfectant, and the patient was rolled in. An ER nurse supervised as the patient was lifted from the gurney to the table, and it all started again.

Samuels squared his shoulders as he glanced at the chart an EMT handed him.

"Another vehicle accident. Looks like a one-on-one between one of the new VWs and a semi," the EMT said.

"Do I need to ask who lost?"

Sarah Laughlin clung to the edge of her desk, the knuckles of her right hand white with strain. She'd just received an electronic copy of the chart for a young man who'd been in an automobile accident and noted a single line of script at the bottom of the page, "Approved organ donor."

She flipped through the chart. The physician's notes indicated a modest chance for recovery and extensive testing that was due the following day. Only the patient didn't make it, dying an hour after admission to the ICU, and kept on life support for several more hours after that so that his organs could be harvested. And here was a note clearing the patient for harvest. Was this yet another case of murder? If so, it was the sixth one this year.

She ran her fingers over a small stack of data-covered spreadsheets. Last year, if her data was right, they'd taken fourteen lives. She reached up to pluck away a long, wispy strand of auburn hair from her pale face. Her large blue eyes reflected the intense conflict churning inside her as she caught her reflection in the glass of the picture hanging over her desk. Beneath those eyes – ones she'd often been told were pretty – she could see the dark bruises of worry. For someone so young, she thought she looked very old.

Had she done the right thing, delivering copies of her files to that auditor? Would he believe her and get the information into the right hands? Should she approach him and talk to him?

She had so many questions, but who could she ask for guidance? If anyone found out she'd given him the files, maybe she'd be the next victim.

Patients were dying at Wilkes Memorial—people who shouldn't

be dying. As the hospital's patient records clerk, it was her job to review the records for deceased patients, to ensure they were in top form for the post-mortem review board. What she'd found a few months before, while preparing for the hospital's semi-annual retrospective case review, were cases where the patient's death had been questionable. The clues had been subtle, but it was to her credit that she'd been alert to inconsistencies in the physician reports. That was the purpose, after all, of the retrospective review – to uncover problems before they became litigious for the hospital.

She shook her head and again her long, straight hair fell down over her face. Absently, she tugged a bright green elastic band from around her wrist and used it to pull her hair into a ponytail.

She was only a records clerk. It wasn't her job to act like a detective. Maybe she should let the issue go, let someone else worry about it.

As soon as the thought entered her mind, she dismissed it. More lives might depend on what she did with the information she'd uncovered. She couldn't just sit and pretend it wasn't happening.

She didn't claim to be a woman of the world and many things about life confused her, but one thing she did know was paperwork and statistics. Her superiors had told her that she had a natural affinity for numbers. If analyzed from the right perspective, numbers could reveal things that people often couldn't see with the naked eye. Combine that information with descriptions written in records, and it was almost like putting together a jigsaw puzzle. A picture formed if you did it just right.

She hadn't liked the picture that she'd put together in this latest case; not one bit.

Sarah tapped the edges of her reports together so that they made a neat pile in the center of her desk.

She'd look at her data again. Maybe she was mistaken. Maybe she missed something important, something that would clear it all up. She'd give it one more week.

"Did you hear what happened, Dr. Samuels?"

It was late in the day and the young ER doc was within an hour of his shift's end. He still had a dozen reports to dictate and sign, and he didn't have time for idle gossip. It had been a rough day, and when he did finally get to go home, he still had to try to be a father to his two children and husband to his wife. Today was a soccer match for his youngest, and a concert at his son's grade school, so it would be a busy afternoon.

Mostly, what he wanted to hear right now was the sound of his own snores.

He shook the cobwebs of self-pity from his mind and twisted on his stool to face the ER receptionist. "I'm sorry, Claire. What did you say?"

"Bruce Stephenson, the young man you treated this morning? The one who drove his sports car into a tree ... He died this afternoon, right after we admitted him."

Samuels swiveled back around and returned to the open patient record.

"Bummer. I was pretty sure he wouldn't make it, with that massive bump on the head. His stats were pretty low and there was no way to know the full extent of the intra-cranial damage."

Claire nodded and sniffed.

That caught Samuels' attention and he twisted around to face her. He'd known Claire for all five years at W.M., and he'd seldom seen the tough old bird moved by the loss of a patient, not outwardly, anyway.

"I've known his parents for years," she said. "My daughter went to school with the him, although she's a few years younger. His folks are pretty sensitive people, with a close bond with their kids. When they left the hospital they thought their son had a chance to pull through. What's worse is that Mrs. Stephenson is the type to take something like this to court."

"I did what I could, Claire. There was nothing else to be done."

Samuels swiped a hand at the fatigue that had settled across his vision. "Lawsuits are always a risk in this business, Claire, but that boy was a mess. I even thought I could save him, but... We all did what we could."

"I suppose."

Samuels paused with his pen suspended above the signature line of the chart he had completed and considered what Claire had said. He scribbled the necessary signature, tossed the record aside, and took a form from a cubbyhole in the reception station's hutch. The form was titled, *"Risk Management Assessment Report.*

He looked over his shoulder to where Claire wrestled with the keyboard of a computer that didn't seem to want to cooperate. She cursed softly. "Whoever invented these things should be hung. Why ever did we leave manual records and bring these electronic devils into our homes and offices?"

"Claire?" he said.

When she lifted her eyes in his direction, he continued. "Thanks for the heads-up. I'll get a Risk Management file going on the Stephenson case right away, and I'll make sure it gets to administration."

The receptionist gave him a small smile and then pointed a long-nailed finger his way. "About time you young pups started listening to us clerks. There may be hope for you yet, Dr. Samuels."

"A lofty compliment, indeed," Samuels said

Claire retrieved a copy of the Stephenson record from the central database and handed it to Dr. Samuels, printed and ready for review.

As he filled out the required squares and blanks on the topmost form, he considered the timeliness of the Stephenson boy's death. Many patients in his condition hung on for days, even weeks before their body gave up. It was odd that he had expired so quickly, without any of the usual signs: irregular heart beat; labored breathing. He would check the chart again, later. Maybe he'd missed something.

He'd have to call his wife and tell her he'd be late for the soccer match.

Chapter 18

During the days that followed his date with Jan, Bill saw her only occasionally. He spent the time prowling Wilkes Memorial's halls, interviewing staff and sitting in on meetings of the hospital's numerous committees.

There was a certain amount of tedium to what he did, digging though reports, interviewing an endless list of staff, but he truly liked his work and found it interesting enough on most days. The only parts that he found difficult to deal with were the sometimes long, boring meetings that he routinely had to sit through to find what he needed for report. It was at those times that he occasionally found his mind wandering between person he might be interviewing, and the way Jan had tucked a strand of ebony hair behind one ear as they'd talked at dinner.

As much as he found thoughts of Jan intruding upon his work, contact with her since their date had been practically nonexistent beyond a casual "hi" as they passed in the hallway. In truth, he hadn't made a serious attempt to contact her as he tried to focus on his work. Intellectually, he knew that not talking to a person for a week or so after an initial date was not unusual. It happened all the time in his world, where work took a priority. It was only when he remembered the warmth of her touch or the depth of her eyes in the evening light that it gnawed at him.

Occasionally, his thoughts would wander to memories of his time with Carole, and how they'd met that first night in town. She hadn't called, either. Carole was a busy woman, and he had no doubt that she'd pushed him out of her mind. She wasn't the Carole he'd known so long ago. She was more self-possessed, seemed more worldly, a successful businesswoman. He doubted that she seriously entertained the thought of getting together.

He glanced at the turquoise file that lay in his briefcase, half open on the floor near the base of his chair. And then there were those patient deaths ...

Bill frowned out the window of his small office at the birds that flitted about the garden beyond.

He scrubbed at the top of his head with one hand. "I haven't got time for this. I've got work to do. I don't have time for women *or* half-baked conspiracies."

He turned back to the stack of paperwork and dragged a thick file across the desk. It was a marketing package that he'd requested from Carole's administrative assistant the day before. He picked up a glossy brochure and flipped through it, searching for background information that he could use in the introduction section of his final report.

He found what he wanted on the inside flap of the first page.

Wilkes Memorial was located in the heart of the Pacific Northwest's South Puget Sound region, in the state's capital. With three hundred in-patient beds, eight operating rooms, two of the most modern intensive care and cardiac care units in the nation, W.M. was a shining star in an otherwise struggling healthcare community. Average patient census was 250 in-patients, filling more than eighty percent of the hospital's beds on any given day. The OR routinely worked at capacity, with little patient backlog.

He grunted at the implications. In a time when most hospitals were lucky if they filled fifty percent of their beds and had barely enough staff to keep their operating rooms going, Wilkes Memorial was in an enviable position.

He skimmed the rest of the material and took notes whenever he came across an interesting fact: It was hard not to be impressed.

"Hey, stranger."

Bill looked up as Carole slipped through the door and kicked it closed behind her. She carried two steaming cups of coffee.

"Thought I might drop in to see how you're doing. I'm not interrupting, am I?"

Bill pushed his chair back and accepted the cup of coffee. "You're never an interruption," he said. She folded her long legs into a wingback chair across from his desk. A satiny sweater hugged her trim, athletic figure and silk slacks clung to her hips in ways that he found unsettling.

He sipped the warm brew, feeling awkward. "Thanks for the coffee."

Her smile was broad; her head slightly cocked as she watched him and seemed to enjoy his discomfort. "I lifted it from the little bistro in the lobby. Have you been there? Their latte is the best in the city. They give it to me free for letting them have the space for their little shop. I didn't have any say in the matter, but they don't know that."

Bill picked up the marketing blurb he'd been reading and waved it at her—anything to avoid meeting those eyes of hers. The thought of it started a warm churning in the pit of his stomach, and sent a surge of weakness through his extremities. "If I believe what's written here, it seems you've aligned yourself with one great hospital."

Carole's eyes lighted at the compliment. "Does that mean we get a good report?"

"I can't reveal my findings at this point, but I can't see why the hospital wouldn't do well." There was that awkwardness again. He felt like he needed to impress Carole with something, anything.

Bill wiped his hand across his eyes. What was happening to him? He wasn't some hormone-plagued teenager. First Jan, and now Carole; his responses to them were way out of line.

I have got to get my mind back in the game, here.

He cleared his throat. "I've got a few things to check on, but I should be able to wrap things up by the end of next week. Your financials are particularly impressive. Your support in the community, your internal operations, all seem to point toward a prosperous, well-run operation. Your patronage program is almost too good."

He toasted her with his coffee cup. "All of this is due, I'm sure, to your keen leadership abilities and business acumen."

She raised her own mug and returned the salute. "Obviously."

Bill picked up the transplant file that he'd set aside Monday. "This program, for example."

Carole's eyes narrowed as she focused on the file.

"It's summary data from your transplant program." Bill held up a hand to forestall her concern. "Like everything else at Wilkes, it seems like a stellar operation. In fact, you have a greater success rate with your transplants than any facility on the West Coast: fewer rejected organs, faster response to organ requests, and quicker turn-around for procedures. The two physicians most involved in this program are Doctors Harrison and Farley."

Carole leaned forward in her chair, her gaze intent on the file in Bill's hands. Her hair fell forward and its tips caressed the softness of her blouse. His heart skipped a beat.

"Do I detect concern in your tone?" she said.

Bill dropped the file in the center of his desk. "Not really, but you could help me resolve a few questions that I have about the program. Transplants, like cardiac work, are of particular interest to my client."

Carole settled back into her chair. "We're proud of that program. A lot of those recipients come back to us with solid donations. It keeps us moving forward as a hospital."

"Then maybe you could point me toward Sarah Laughlin. I'm told she's one of your authorities on the program and patient records."

Carole sipped the last of her coffee, her brows knit into a frown.

"Sarah is one of our lead patient records clerks. You don't need my help to find her. Just follow the signs to the far end of the admin wing."

She rose from her chair. "I actually came by for another reason. I felt bad about canceling our date the other day. Any chance of a rematch? Maybe tonight? I planned to cook in: lasagna."

Bill considered the pile of work on his desk, and then glanced up at Carole. Past memories hit strongly as his eyes ran over the neat feminine package before him.

"I'd planned to work late, but how can I say no to lasagna?"

"Great. I'll email you directions. Be there at seven. Dress casual. Around here, that means jeans."

After Carole's visit, it was a struggle to get back into the data he'd been working on. He finally gave it up and pushed the stack of reports aside. He couldn't seem to get rid of the very sensual image of her sitting in his office chair. Neither was he willing to fend off memories of that first love. There was no way he could focus on work now.

He pushed back from the desk and made his way toward the car. He'd pick up Alex from the hotel and go for a run.

As he walked, his mind drifted back to the first time they'd really been together. Where had they been when it had happened and was it really more than twenty years ago? They'd been down by the docks at Steilacoom, a little town at the edge of Puget Sound.

Could that same sort of spark be rekindled after all these years?

His thoughts drifted back to the evening with Jan. *What about her?*

He pushed the thought from his mind. He'd only dated her once, and she hadn't made any effort to contact him since. It was only one date. There was no commitment there.

The thought of Jan reminded him of what she'd said about the patient records clerk, the one with information about the transplant program: Sarah Laughlin, the lady in charge of those records.

He glanced at his watch. It was early enough that he could look Sarah Laughlin up on the way out, before he headed back to the hotel. If he could talk to her, dispose of the issues she'd raised, maybe he could dispose of the whole conspiracy concept and close out the audit. Maybe he'd be home early, away from the confusion and uncertainty that seemed more and more to engulf him, the longer he stayed. Murdered patients, his past and renewed relationship with Carole, the disquieting effect that Jan had on him... It was pretty hard to take it all in at one time. This was not the quiet and predictable assignment that he'd anticipated it to be.

He shrugged into his jacket and headed for the door. With any luck, he could wrap up this transplant thing and spend an evening with Carole.

An evening full of possibilities.

Chapter 11

Bill entered Sarah's office to find her sitting at a small, tidy, single-pedestal desk. Large blue eyes watched him take a seat opposite her. Donald Duck and Mickey Mouse memorabilia littered the desk. A painting of large daisies the same color as her wispy burnished blond hair dominated the wall next to her desk. Pictures of two cats and a small dog sat next to her phone.

"Hi, Sarah. Thanks for meeting with me on such short notice. I hope I'm not interrupting your work unnecessarily."

"I have no idea why you'd want to talk with me, Mr. Deming," she said.

Sarah's pale complexion and large eyes gave her an elfin look. Thin lips and firmly set chin revealed an intense anxiety.

Sarah fidgeted the open file and reports into a neat stack in front of her, like a protective wall separating her from this intruder. Her fearful gaze spoke volumes.

Whatever it was that she was worried about was real enough to her.

"You like animals, don't you?" He nodded towards the

photographs.

Sarah brushed her hand across the top of the photo of her dog. "They're my family. I don't have anyone else, except my sister, and she lives a long ways away."

"Have you had them long?"

"Willy—he's the dog—he died two months ago. I thought about getting a puppy to replace him, but it's hard to replace an old friend. He was thirteen when he died. I call the cats Tom and Jerry. They're pests, but I love them anyway."

"I'm sorry to hear about the dog. I have a dog named Alex. He goes everywhere with me. He's at the hotel right now."

"You leave him at the hotel? Aren't you afraid he'll get lonely, or destroy something while you're not there? Willy would raid my closet and chew up my shoes if I didn't get home from work on time."

Bill took out a picture of Alex running on the beach with two adults in hot pursuit. "Alex is a real gentleman, and too lazy to go to all that trouble."

She laughed. It was a soft sound, like a tiny wind chime pushed lightly by a breeze. "Maybe I could meet Alex some time?"

"That's my mom and dad. They're why I chose to live in California, and took my current job. After all my years in the army, I wanted to be close to home after I retired." He leaned back in the chair. "Do you like your job here?"

Sarah handed the picture back and returned her hands to her lap. She nodded, and the bun at the back of her head slipped a little to one side. She patted it back into place and secured it with a bobby pin.

"It's a good job and it can be challenging. All patient records have to be organized, checked for completeness, and summarized for several of the hospital's committees."

Bill placed the turquoise file on the edge of Sarah's desk. "Like the information in this file?"

Her cheeks flushed a light shade of rose. "I'm sure I don't know what you mean."

He tapped a finger on the file folder's rigid front. "This file was left anonymously on my desk. It contains incriminating evidence of falsifying records. If what's in this file is correct, people are losing their lives unnecessarily. It amounts to murder, Sarah. You understand that I must find out if this record is true or false." He spread his fingers over the file. "Tell me the truth, Sarah. Did you put it on my desk?"

Sarah straightened her back and squared her shoulders. "Of course not. State and federal law protect patient records. I would never do such a thing."

Bill was sure he'd hit a nerve, and was certain he'd come to the right person.

"Don't play games with me. If I'm going to do anything with this information, I must see the source files." He tapped the file again. "If what's in here is true, it's a matter for the police. The fact that my employer intended to donate a large amount of money to this hospital doesn't enter into this."

Sarah ran her fingers along the edge of the files next to her phone. Her defiant gaze met Bill's. "I know nothing of this ..."

Bill lowered his voice. "I've been in the hospital business for more than twenty-two years. No matter where you work, in a federal hospital or a private facility, there's one constant: all patient records go through the records clerk. That's you. You have to know about the information in this file." He wasn't about to let her get away with denying knowledge of the file. "You're one of only a few people in this hospital with access to this information. If you really care about what's happening at Wilkes, you'll show me your source material so I can do something about it."

Tears glistened and spilled over her pale cheeks. Bill reached into his pocket and offered a handkerchief. She waved it off and pulled a handful of tissues from a box in her desk drawer. Her hands shook as she wiped her eyes and blew her nose.

"I'm afraid of what they'll do if they find out."

"Who?" Bill asked.

Sarah ignored his question. "They've killed people. They've taken the lives of patients who shouldn't have died," she said.

"Who are 'they' you're talking about?" He could almost feel her fear.

"They're the most important people in this hospital. Do you understand what I'm saying? These are powerful people. They have access to everything that goes on in this hospital. They control patients' lives and my job." She stood and turned away only to whirl back. "Who's to say they'll stop with killing patients and not go after me? Who's to say I won't be fired! That's just about as bad as being murdered. I need this job to live."

Sarah scrubbed at the tears on her cheeks and dropped back into her chair. She studied Bill's face for an instant, and then reached into the bottom desk drawer and removed a stack of patient summaries. She handed them to Bill.

"Maybe these will convince you that I'm not just a weirdo, dreaming up conspiracies."

"I didn't say..."

She pointed at the files. "Read," she said.

Bill flipped through the files, one by one. Names and circumstances on each report supported the information that had been left on his desk.

He sat back and whistled through his teeth. This was not the delusional thinking of a warped mind but was stark fact. She had a right to be afraid. It frightened *him*.

This was cold-blooded murder. Patients that should not have died were murdered and their organs harvested for a favored person not listed on any official organ donation waiting list. Or if they had been listed, there was no way they should have received their organ donations before others ahead of them on the priority list. Each of those questionable transplants was followed by a substantial donation to the hospital. There was no avoiding the link between them; little possibility that the association could be written off to coincidence.

Bill forced his mind to slow down, to deal with one thing at a time. First, he had to validate the information in his possession. It could be misrepresented in some way, and he didn't want to overreact to a falsely represented situation.

If her information was correct, police would, of necessity, become involved. Not only would it complicate his audit, he would become involved with the police investigation. His experience in the military, when he'd been attached to medical intelligence to investigate claims of medical abuse, had turned into witch-hunts that had taken months, years, even. Bill passed both hands over his face. If a police investigation failed to find concrete evidence of a conspiracy, he and his employer could become targets for litigation just for raising the issue. Slander and liable did not sit well with hospitals, where good will and the confidence of the public were paramount to success or failure. The healthcare community was a small and close-knit group, and a black mark on his company's record in that sort of situation could mean being black-balled from further business for a long time to come.

He had better be sure of his actions before he raised this issue to anyone. He'd have to do an investigation of his own, and gather more facts.

"Give me your source data," he said. "I'll keep your identity confidential until I've confirmed what you've said. I won't point a finger in your direction until it's absolutely necessary."

A tentative smile touched her lips. "I don't want to lose my job. It's all I have."

"I'll keep you out of it as long as I can, Sarah, but if the police investigate, you'll have to cooperate with them."

She nodded. "I understand."

"Right. Now, about those records?"

Sarah reached into a drawer, pulled out a large sheaf of papers and handed it across. "That is all of it. All the details are there. I have another set of those documents—photocopies—at my house. I know that's a breech of patient privacy laws, but I believe this is important enough to break the rules." She spread her fingers over the files. "You'll see what I mean. I've found twenty cases in the past year or two. Who knows how many more there have been?"

Bill tucked the files under his arm and stood up to leave. "You've done a lot of work, so it shouldn't take long for verification. I'll get on this right away and give you a call on Monday."

Sarah rose from her chair as Bill reached the door. "Thank you for listening, Mr. Deming. It means a lot to have someone take me seriously. I approached the CEO and Assistant Administrator about this when I first discovered it. They said they would look into it, but I don't think they ever did."

Her last statement made Bill pause. Why wouldn't Carole or Sterling look into something like this? The CEO seemed like the consummate politician, and would have done anything to protect his hospital and his own reputations. Carole... she was aggressive about everything and he felt certain that she'd do just about anything to protect her job. He found it hard to imagine her not charging headlong into any investigation of wrongdoing in her hospital. It just didn't stack up.

Unless they were both part of a conspiracy.

He put that thought aside. He'd had the concepts of ethics and integrity pounded into his brain by the military and couldn't imagine someone in Sterling or Carole's position violating such a trust.

Bill thanked Sarah for her time and headed back to his office.

The voice at the end of the phone line was strong, male, and carried a decided tone of authority. "You say you met someone who has found out about our program?"

The other voice was softer, female, yet still carried a marked tone of confidence and assertiveness. "Not us as individuals, perhaps, but yes, I'm certain he knows something is going on. His name's William Deming. He works for a consulting firm out of California. He could have uncovered something incriminating."

"Get closer to him. Find out exactly what he knows. Too much is at stake to let this slide."

"Getting close to him won't be a problem. Finding out what he knows may be another issue. He's a professional, and I doubt he'll reveal anything until he's dotted the last 'I' and crossed the last 'T' on his report."

The man's tone edged up a notch, and tension underlined his words. "That may be just as well. We don't need anything leaked right now. The timing would be bad."

"I understand. I'll keep you informed."

She was confident that she could stay close to Deming, and wasn't at all sure that she minded the possibility. On the other hand, finding out exactly what he did or did not know could be difficult. .

She squared her shoulders as she stepped from the cramped phone booth. She'd have to figure out something. Fortunes, careers, and maybe even lives, depended on her actions.

Chapter 12

Bill's mind was a jumble. Shifting concerns and issues charged in and out of his thoughts like the wind that whipped through the evergreens. A storm was brewing, with a wind strong enough to break branches and splinter wood. A branch crashed to the ground nearby as he took Alex for his evening walk.

The dog tugged his way toward an interesting shrub and ignored the fact that Bill was running late for his date with Carole.

"Come on, Alex. I'm on a schedule, here."

"Give the dog a break. He's been inside all day and this is the highlight of his day."

Bill turned. Jan leaned against the driver-side door of his Supra in the parking lot outside the hotel room. In spite of the surprise of her arrival, the sight of her made him smile.

"He knows when I'm on a tight schedule. He does this to torture me."

She smiled and brushed away a strand of hair that had escaped from the thick braid slung over her right shoulder. The soft blue cashmere sweater clung to her lean, angular body, and snug fitting jeans hugged her hips like an invitation.

The corners of Jan's mouth curved. "Sounds like you have plans," she said.

"Actually, I do."

"Too bad. I'd hoped otherwise – maybe for a rematch from the other night. I had a great time. How about the next couple of days? Any free evenings when Alex can spare you for a few hours for dinner out?"

She really had amazing eyes. While his attention was on Jan, Alex tugged hard on the leash, and Bill nearly lost his balance. He swore under his breath.

Mission accomplished, Alex trotted happily over to bump his head under Bill's hand. Bill rubbed the dog's brow.

"I can make time," he said. "Come in while I put Alex up. I've got a few minutes."

Alex noticed Jan nearby, and his heavy tail pumped back and forth against Bill's leg. Jan squatted down to greet him and gave Alex a hearty scratch on the chest.

"Now he's stealing the girls."

"He's sweet," Jan replied. "You're not planning to keep him locked up in the hotel room all evening while you go out, are you?"

She scratched Alex behind both ears. The dog dropped his rump to the pavement and thumped one leg as Jan's fingernails dug into a good spot.

"My car's great for two people, but the back seat's a joke. Alex wouldn't be comfortable if I could get him back there in the first place. The hotel's a better option."

"So who's the date?" Jan said.

It was really none of her business, so why did he find the question so disturbing? "I'm meeting a woman I went to high school with."

"Ah."

As they walked toward the hotel, Alex stayed glued to Jan's side.

"Alex is smitten." Bill fished his hotel room key from his jacket pocket.

"You think so?" She gave Alex another fierce scratch along the base of his long spine. "That's wonderful."

"He is a dog of discerning taste," Bill said.

"I'll take that as a compliment. Why don't I take him home with me? I have a fenced yard, five acres of land, and I'm off tomorrow. I'll keep Alex and you can pick him up tomorrow after work. That will give you some extra time with your old high school buddy. When you come over to retrieve him, we can go out and get something to eat."

Bill stared down at Alex "So this is what it's come to. You picking up strange women, going home with them, and abandoning me for an easy belly rub?"

"I'm hardly what most people would refer to as strange, and I'd rather enjoy having Alex over if you're willing to trust me with him. My dog died a couple of years back and I've missed him. It'll be fun for me."

Bill unlocked the door to the hotel room

"If you're sure it's no trouble." He paused.

Jan shook her head. "I'll wait out here. You've got to get going and I don't want to keep you. I just dropped by to say hi, and see if you were free."

"I'm glad you stopped by. Sorry I didn't call you at the office. It's been a busy week." He hesitated, and then thought: What the heck? Might as well ask.

"Have you ever been involved with the organ transplant program at Wilkes?"

Jan's expression didn't change. "I've been in intensive care for years, so I've seen a few transplant cases. Wilkes has an excellent reputation for that sort of thing. Anything in particular you'd like to know?"

"Wilkes does nearly twice the transplant cases each year as other facilities in the region. Olympia is a big city, but Wilkes is on par with the largest of Chicago or New York hospitals."

"I'm new to the business side of things at Wilkes, so I'm probably the wrong person to ask. Carole, the assistant administrator, is more familiar with that phase of the organization."

Bill handed Alex's leash to Jan and their hands touched. Her fingers were icy cold.

"The transplant program brings in a lot of revenue. It's good business – that much I know. And with the trauma unit constantly busy, Wilkes is exposed to a greater number of potential organ donors than other hospitals in the area. That's why our hospital appears to handle more than other facilities."

"I'm sure you're right, although the hospital's revenue and cash flow both look good enough without the transplants. Patronage plays an amazing role at Wilkes, in direct cash donations as well as estate trusts. I've seen few communities as grateful to a hospital as this one."

Jan scribbled her address on a scrap of paper and handed it to Bill. "We all work hard to serve the community. It's one of those corporate culture things that hospitals strive for. When you succeed in that arena, I suspect it's kind of natural that you'd get a lot of donations."

She led Alex towards her car. "You be good, Alex," Bill said. The dog didn't even look back. "Hey, don't you want his dish, food, and his toiletries?"

Jan laughed. "He'll be just fine," Jan said. "I have everything he'll need to be comfortable at home. We'll see you tomorrow night, at my place."

Bill watched Jan's retreating form until she climbed into her car and drove away.

An hour later, Bill stood before the large, polished mahogany front door of an expansive house overlooking the waters of the Puget Sound. With immaculate gardens, abundance of dormers adorning a towering façade, and the predominance of red brick and bay windows, it was an impressive place. Tall, full rhododendrons, holly and a carpet of flowers skirted meandering slate walks and a smooth, asphalt drive. An island of grass in the center of the front yard glowed with chemically induced vigor and a conspicuous absence of dandelions.

He felt a little school-boyish, standing there in front of the big door, holding the bouquet of flowers he'd picked up at the Safeway on his way across town.

Carole opened the door a second after his knock and ushered him into a foyer that dripped with chandeliers and Italian marble.

She posed just inside the doorway, one arm stretched high along the corner of the entryway, lips curved into a sultry grin. Light from broad patio windows filtered through the shadows of her wispy, translucent blouse and breeze-blown hair.

The obvious staging indicated a woman planning a seduction. "Some things don't change," he said.

Carole moved to Bill and molded her body to his, and he was sure his toes would have curled if they hadn't been locked in tight-fitting dress boots. The passionate kiss sent a flood of warmth through his body. He dropped the flowers and ignored them as they scattered across the floor.

Carole stepped back and smiled.

"That's quite a welcome for an old friend," Bill said.

"You're a very special old friend."

She knelt down to collect the flowers. Her blouse floated open at the neck to reveal ample cleavage and the fact that she was wearing no bra. His pulse jumped. His report and how it might affect Carole's position at Wilkes Memorial was the furthest thing from his mind.

It was an effort to draw back and think straight. He concentrated on something else. "Is that lasagna I smell?"

"As promised." She didn't appear affected by the blatant kiss. "I took off early from work today and threw a little something together."

"I should have picked up a bottle of wine."

She set the flowers on the kitchen counter. "I have a very good wine open and breathing in the dining room."

Carole walked away and returned with two wine glasses and an open bottle. She offered him a glass and raised it in a toast. "To very old, very good friends, and a renewed relationship," she said.

"Is that a toast or a warning?"

"You decide."

Carole came around the counter, took his glass from his hand, and set their drinks aside. An electric sensation shot up his arm and into his stomach as she led him toward a curving, pine and maple staircase.

"We've got an hour before the lasagna is ready. Why don't I give you a tour?"

She led him upstairs, unbuttoning the front of her blouse as they went.

An hour later, Carole slipped from the large four-poster bed. Bill propped himself on one elbow to watch her sleek, naked form glide across the room toward the attached bathroom.

"Is this the way you always greet old friends?" he called after her.

A few minutes later, she strode back over to where he lay and took his face in her hands. "Only the ones who steal my heart in high school and return for a rematch."

Bill sat up and swung his legs over the side of the bed. She lowered herself into his lap and his arousal was fast and hot.

"You weren't the only one to have a heart pilfered that night near the Steilacoom docks. Quite an event for both of us."

She snorted and kissed him, her lips lingering, savoring.

She pulled back. "We were both quick studies."

Just when Bill thought things might get interesting, Carole jumped up and hurried off across the room.

"Hey, what's your hurry?"

She disappeared through a set of wide double doors and returned wearing a sheer robe that clung to her body in ways that Bill found most alluring. She ran her fingers through her shoulder length hair and patted it into place. The tussled look made her look more desirable as she smiled wickedly at him over a cocked shoulder.

"I thought we'd taken care of anything urgent an hour ago," Bill said.

"We worked at it, but there's a pan of overcooked food in the kitchen that needs attention. There's cold water in the bathroom for whatever's smoldering. Our dinner is a few seconds away from becoming cinders. I will not spoil one of my finest kitchen creations, even for all you offer."

Bill climbed out of the bed once she'd headed downstairs.

He hadn't realized how long it had been since he'd been with someone like Carole. She was at once both tender and aggressive, and had definite ideas about what she wanted from a man.

As he dressed, Bill let his gaze wander about the room. Carole hadn't given him a tour of the house. It seemed to reflect her character, with its feminine appeal, yet lack of frilly, stereotypical female accoutrements. The bedroom might have been called Spartan, with its absence of mirrors, fluffs and frills. The furnishings were sturdy and made of heavily grained oak.

He slipped into his shoes and headed downstairs, finding his way to the kitchen by smell. Carole was slicing French bread. A freshly tossed salad sat on the counter next to her.

"Anything I can do to help?"

She continued sawing the skinny loaf with an oversized knife. "You can have a seat and talk to me. "

He pulled a bar stool up to the breakfast counter that separated the food prep area from a small dining space, and reached for the wine.

The kitchen was large with a wrap-around counter of heavy, gray-speckled granite. Every surface was covered with stainless steel devices of all shapes and kinds. If there was a logic or order to the kitchen, he couldn't see it, but it felt comfortable. Overhead, the copper bottoms of heavy, commercial grade, copper-clad cookware hung in neat order, with the bottoms showing not a single brown blemish.

"You have quite a place," he said.

"I got most of the furniture from the divorce," she said. "The house came later, after I landed the job at Wilkes. It's been a real boon to my life – working at Wilkes I mean. It's made a difference. I feel more complete, I guess. I have a good job, respect, the money I never had before Kurt and I split up. If there's one thing I learned from the divorce and the destitution I lived through afterward, it's that while money may not be everything, it sure makes happiness easier. I wasn't about to be one of those single women, out there looking for a long-term financial arrangement that meant servitude to some money-making, insensitive guy."

"That's a little extreme, isn't it? I know a few single women who do very well without a man in their lives."

"My point exactly," she said. "You can't understand what it's like to be a woman cast adrift by a man. I was totally dependent on him one day—blissfully happy in my self-imagined cottage life—and then had that bliss ripped away by the crack of a judge's gavel."

Carole turned and faced him with her hands on her hips, the bread knife hanging loosely from her fingers.

"I thought we were happy. I took care of the house and Kurt talked about having a baby. Then, out of the blue, his lordship walks out, takes everything, and moves in with some chick he met during night class at the university.

"He took our money, my pride, and ten years of my life. I didn't fight back when his lawyers showed up with documents for me to sign. I was numb. I didn't think to read what they put in front of me. I just signed. One day I was in our happy little home. The next day, I was in an empty building with a 'for sale' sign out front."

"I've been gone a while, but I still know that in Washington, a person can't do that to their spouse," Bill said. "It's a community property state, and you have to show proof of being represented during a divorce. His lawyers couldn't get away with treating you like that; of taking advantage of your state of mind to suit his needs."

"Exactly. A few weeks later, I was destitute and literally running out of the means to buy food and the barest essentials for myself. That's when I finally woke up and called a friend of mine, a woman who had handled a divorce for a mutual friend. I'd always considered her something of a vulture, someone who made her living off the misery of others. I found out later that she'd been through the exact same thing as I had a long time before we met, and had come by her trade the hard way.

"She filed to reopen the divorce proceedings and we took my loving ex-husband for everything he had. Hence the furniture you saw upstairs. I don't like some of it, but I keep it as a kind of reminder of what I went through. I'll never make that mistake again."

"Getting married?"

"I mean I'll never let myself become that dependent upon anyone. I come first, now. Any man in my life will have to understand that going in."

She turned back to the counter, picked up a jar and then smacked it on the counter with a crack. "I will never allow myself to be abandoned and hungry again, not for anyone."

Carole slid a tray of sliced bread into the oven to warm, and moved to a second oven. She removed a steaming platter of lasagna. The aroma made Bill's stomach growl loudly. Carole must have heard his stomach growl, because she lifted the golden brown platter of lasagna before her like a trophy. "I'll take that gastric applause as a sign of approval."

"If that tastes as good as it smells, you can. When do we eat?"

"Patience, dear boy. Some things are worth waiting for." She headed around the counter and towards the dining room.

"I'm glad we got together, for a lot of reasons," she said. "It's wonderful seeing you again. It's like we picked up where we left off, years ago."

"I'm nearly finished with the audit. I'll be heading home to California before too long."

"I'd think it would take more time to audit a facility as big as Wilkes. Have you found anything interesting in your diggings, or are we just another well-run hospital at the precipice of healthcare excellence?"

"You have a great organization, and I'm not quite done yet. In fact, I just tripped across something interesting that I need to wrap up before I can close out my report."

Carole rested her elbows on the table, her gaze fixed on Bill's face. The front of her robe fell open and Bill found it difficult to focus on his food.

"And what could be so interesting, besides the hospital's attractive and sexy assistant administrator?"

Bill reached across the table and slipped one hand around the back of Carole's neck, pulled her towards him and into a deep kiss. She sighed and his libido came wide awake.

"The perks of the assignment aside, I'm caught up in some issues related to the hospital's transplant program. Your huge patronage program and the transplants seem tied together. It's an interesting relationship that I've seen before, but never to this extent. In any event, I need to document the details for my client, who has a particular interest in that sort of thing."

Carole frowned.

"The transplant program is our signature effort. If anything were to happen to it, the hospital would be in a bind ... I'd be in a bind. With patient privacy legislation in place, you digging into the program's records could be risky for your employer and us. If something negative were to turn up, were to leak out, it would be disastrous."

"I've touched a nerve? I'm sorry. I really shouldn't be talking about this."

She waved his comment away. "Do what you have to do. Just be careful."

She traced a complex pattern on the back of his hand with a long, manicured fingernail. "What do you say we forget about work for the rest of the evening? I'm hungry again."

Bill smiled. "I gather you're not talking about lasagna."

"It'll reheat."

Chapter 13

Bill stifled a yawn and reached for the phone. It had been a long morning in the office.

The CEO's assistant answered. "Wilkes Memorial administrative offices. Ruth, here."

Bill stretched and swiveled in his chair to gaze out at the gray-shrouded skies beyond the office window.

"This is Bill Deming." He stifled a yawn.

"You sound tired, Mr. Deming. I understand you and Jan have a date tonight. You should be rested."

"Did Jan tell you that?" When Ruth didn't immediately reply, he continued. "We're getting together, yes, but I doubt you'd call it a date."

Bill imagined the smile on the old matchmaker's face. "A rose is a rose, and I'm just glad to hear she's going out with someone. That girl …" She cut herself off and cleared her throat before continuing. "So, what can I do for you, Mr. Deming?"

"I need to meet with two of your physicians. I need to talk to them before I wrap things up. I'd hoped that perhaps you could expedite the meeting."

"My, what confidence you have in me." Bill could hear the rustling of papers in the background. "Who exactly is it you want to meet and what shall I say is the topic?"

"Doctors Harrison and Farley. They're big names on your patrons' acknowledgement list. The topic is the hospital's highly successful transplant program."

There was a long silence at the other end of the line before Ruth replied. "I see. You want to see Harrison and Farley: our chiefs of Surgery and Medicine, respectively. They can be hard men to latch onto. Give me a few minutes while I see what I can do."

Bill waited.

"The schedule in my computer says that they're both right here in the conference room this morning," Ruth said. "They came in for a meeting before I arrived at work and should be done any time now. I don't know what their schedules are for the rest of the morning, but if you hurry you might catch them before they leave."

Bill hung up the phone, stretched again, and headed for the administrative offices. He arrived at Ruth's desk just as two physicians in white doctor's coats stepped from the conference room. One was tall, immaculately groomed, and had a tan that was too even to be natural. Bill pegged him as the surgeon. The other was short, balding, paunchy, with a gut hanging over the waistband of carefully tailored Armani slacks. With his bland expression and pasty complexion, Bill guessed the man had to be a *flea*, industry slang for Internal Medicine physician.

Ruth stepped out from behind her desk to intercept the physicians and make the introductions. Bill was impressed with her smoothness as she interposed herself between the men and the door and redirected their attention. Apparently, when Ruth spoke, everyone paid attention.

"Gentlemen, this is Mr. William Deming. He's the auditor who was sent to pave the way for the donation that could get our latest project on track. Mr. Deming, this is Dr. Harrison, our chief surgeon and Dr. Farley, chief of the Department of Medicine."

Bill noticed that the two men visibly tensed when they heard Bill's name, then quickly regained their composure as they each offered a brief handshake. Harrison's grip was firm and warm; Farley's cool and slightly clammy.

On first impression, Bill sized Harrison up as a naturally pleasant man with a cheerful disposition and ready smile. Farley appeared to be trying to duplicate the other's calm demeanor, but his piggish, closely set eyes were out of character and the attempt failed. His nervous hands were in constant motion, and betrayed his discomfort and nervousness.

This was their first meeting, and Farley was obviously nervous about it. Why? Bill filed that question away for later.

"Gentleman, if you could spare a moment," Bill said. "I'd like to get some information from you that could help me wrap up my audit."

The men hesitated and glanced at each other.

"It could have a significant impact on the award of the funds to the hospital, by the person I represent," Bill said.

Both physicians looked at their watches, but Harrison spoke first. "I could spare you a few minutes, but I've got a case in the OR in half an hour."

"I guess I can give you ten minutes," Farley said. "I understand how important all this is to the hospital."

"And make sure you give us a good report!"

Bill turned toward the familiar voice as a third person emerged from the conference room. Carole paused next to Bill and touched his arm. Her voice was low and conspiratorial. "Watch these two, Bill. They're shifty bastards."

All three men smiled, with Farley and Harrison's smiled looking decidedly forced.

"Stop by later, if you have a chance. There are a few things I'd like to go over with you." Carole squeezed Bill's arm, stepped away and disappeared through her office door. The wink she gave him as she departed left little doubt about what she wanted to discuss.

Bill followed the two physicians into the conference room, where they all took seats around a large oak table. Expansive plate glass windows looked out over the hospital's parking lot and to a dense stand of trees beyond. The first drops of rain dotted the asphalt outside as Bill started the meeting.

"Gentleman, during the course of my audit, I've studied the extensive patronage program the hospital enjoys within the community. In the past year, W.M. has received more than ten million in donations, an amount that exceeds industry standards for a facility of its size. In fact, that amount is more than double that of what its counterparts in the region have received in donations. Your names continually pop up in association with those donations."

Bill placed a slim file folder on the table before him and folded his hands over the top of it. It was an old consultant's ploy: make a person think you have a file with all the information and they either relax and spill what they know, or their curiosity gets the best of them and they reveal themselves through the questions they direct toward the file. It was human nature, and the trick seldom failed.

"My question is simple: how do you do it? What makes this hospital so important to the community that they'd offer such an amount? It's a remarkable feat."

Harrison started to reply, but Farley raised a hand to cut him off. "I suggest that the level of donations that we enjoy at Wilkes is simply a result of the exceptional level of care we offer, and the influx of wealthy people we've enjoyed in the geographic area as a result of the technology explosion. They get sick; we heal them; they're grateful; Wilkes Memorial reaps the benefits."

Bill removed several sheets of paper from the folder and pointed them at the two doctors. It was a copy of the data he'd received from Sarah the day before.

"I have some information that links the majority of the hospital's donations specifically to the transplant program. I noticed that you, Dr. Farley, have personally placed a large number of the transplant recipients onto the hospital's priority list and that Dr. Harrison has been presiding surgeon on the majority of the cases where large donations were involved."

Harrison shifted his gaze out the window, and then turned slowly back to Bill as he responded. His broad smile showed too many teeth for Bill's satisfaction.

"We both make a point of playing a big role in the program. We know that a little extra special service for a potential patron might ultimately benefit the hospital in a variety of ways, so we give them the extra attention when we can. We're all proud of the transplant program at Wilkes. If you know that, then you also know that we have a higher rate of turnover for our transplant recipient list than any other facility in the Northwest, maybe on the west coast."

Bill nodded his agreement.

Dr. Farley picked up the lecture when Harrison paused. The expression on his face suggested feigned tolerance, as though he was instructing a child who didn't know better than to ask stupid questions.

"The transplant program is one that both Luke and I are very proud of, and the donations associated with the program have been a boon to our hospital. If you need any of the details, beyond the patient records themselves, I would be happy to direct you to my clinic administrator. She has all the facts."

"I don't think that will be necessary, Doctor Farley, but thanks for the offer. I think I have all I need. One other question before you go: Who keeps the organ transplant priority list for the hospital, both the regional and federal lists?" Bill asked.

Farley's eyebrows cocked and his mouth broke into a thin-lipped smile. "That would be my job. My administrator actually keeps it, but I'm the lead on the project."

"Great," Bill said. "Then perhaps I should meet with your assistant."

Farley waved away Bill's comment. "Nonsense. I'll have a copy of the lists and the associated hospital policies delivered to your office this morning."

Both physicians rose and headed for the door. Bill took the cue that the interview was over and thanked them for their time.

Farley smiled as warmly as his piggish face and darting eyes would allow. Harrison's pasted-on smile remained strongly in place as he nodded in Bill's direction and followed Farley out.

Dr. Harrison's voice was barely a whisper as the two men stood in the doorway to the OR locker room.

"He's getting too close," he said

"You worry too much." Farley pushed the door open and led the way inside. He leaned against the door jam and considered his options as Harrison opened his locker and dressed for surgery.

"But he's already connected us with the transplant program."

Dr. Farley frowned. "He could get that information from a variety of places, not the least being the patient records, themselves. It's not public information, but an auditor like Deming has access to that sort of thing. It's not a problem, I tell you. He's applauded our program, not challenged it."

Harrison shrugged into scrub pants and slipped his feet into a pair of florescent green clogs. "I've seen that look on your face before. You trying to convince me, or yourself?"

Farley waited until Harrison had pulled his scrub top over his head before responding.

"It's only natural that someone would link us to the transplant program. You're the chief surgeon for heaven's sake. I'm a prominent Internist, who deals with the older portion of the population, the people who can afford the procedures and are most likely to need them. He's not a detective who is trained to ferret out this sort of thing. He's just an auditor; he's a bean-counter."

Harrison sat on the bench in front of his locker and stared at his feet. "What if he is a detective? Maybe he's a cop working under cover, and the police are closing in? You'd better hope he doesn't find anything more, or we're cooked. That last patient from the OR was a bad call. She should have survived, and everyone knew it. The same for the one in the ER. We're walking a fine line now, Ian, and we could go to jail if we get caught."

"You're just paranoid. And as far as those last cases go, you have nothing to complain about. They were the most lucrative ones we've had all year. Collectively, we netted several million dollars for the hospital, not to mention what we and the rest of the crew bagged for ourselves. You want to return the quarter million that you got?"

Harrison shook his head, then rose and headed for the scrub sink. "No, you know I can't. I've got three kids in college, a mortgage the size of the national debt, and a wife who spends what's left like politicians spends tax money."

Farley reached up and placed a small, pallid hand on his friend's shoulder. "We're in this together, Luke, from the team on up to the Director. Don't crumble on me. We can't afford it. Another couple of cases and we can tone it down for a while if you like. Our special list of recipients only has a couple more names on it, so we should be able to wrap things up soon, maybe put the program on the shelf for a few months and let things cool down."

"The heart-lung case and the kidney?"

"Yeah, looks like those two will do it. The first one could be the biggest cash cow we've seen yet. The kidney isn't any big deal, but is a complicated cross-match. The patient has a rare blood type. You were there when we decided to move ahead with those two. We've got to get both of them done this month or the money will go elsewhere. They could head to South America and get the same service for a lot less money. We need that business."

Harrison thumped the kick plate near the doors with the toes of his clogs, and the heavy, sealed doors leading into the OR swung open. "We should get those over as soon as possible. And Ian..."

"Yes, Luke?"

"Be a little more careful this time when you pick the donor. You walked the line with those last two. The relatives could still cause trouble. You need to check out the family before you make a decision. You should have considered that before you acted."

Farley shrugged, the movement causing ripples in the layers of jowls under his chin. "I didn't make those calls. She did ... the Director, I mean."

"We know that she's not even a physician..."

Farley held up a hand. "She's got us this far, hasn't she? We all agreed to defer to her for important decisions. She's in a better position to see the bigger picture than we are."

"I don't like it. I just don't like it," Harrison said as he stepped through the door and into the OR.

"But you do like the money, you old fool. You always have." Ian spoke softly to his friend's back as the doors closed between them. "You just try living without the money you make from this and see how you feel."

Farley turned and headed back out, into the main corridor. Maybe his old partner was just a little too worried. Maybe he was becoming a liability.

This would take some thinking.

Chapter 14

Bill unlocked his office door and looked up when he heard footsteps. *Oops,* was his first thought when Jan smiled a greeting.

"Hope I didn't catch you at a bad time," she said. She was dressed casually, in snug jeans and a Washington State University sweatshirt. Her hair was pulled back in a long, thick ponytail and the sun's filtered rays glancing across her face gave her skin a golden, luminous glow.

Bill felt a flush of guilt as she brushed by him and walked ahead of him into the office. *Why do I feel guilty?* He had no clue.

"No intrusion at all," he said. "But I thought you were at home today, spoiling my dog."

She tucked her legs beneath her in one of the chairs that fronted his desk. He sat down heavily in the other.

"Alex is fine. He's a wonderful dog and is comfortably curled up on my couch. You didn't tell me he was so well trained, to hand signals and all. I had a lot of fun working him around the yard today."

"Usually, it takes dynamite to get him to do anything other than nap."

"My brother used to be on the K-9 detail for the Olympia PD," she said. "And I'd watch him work his dog. I tried a command or two on Alex, just for fun, and he responded. He's pretty bright."

"Alex is also good at not paying attention when it serves his purposes. Those hand signals go back to our days of competing in dog agility trials. He was doing well until my constant traveling got in the way. He has his titles in two different organizations, including AKC and the North American Dog Agility Club. He was quite the speedster. Now, I'm afraid he's just a lazy old coot."

"Don't cut the boy short. You should have seen him chase a stick this morning. You'd think he couldn't get enough of it."

"Chase a stick? He never does that for me."

Jan pointed at a brightly colored file folder that lay on the floor next to Bill's chair. "Did you drop that?"

Bill reached down and retrieved the transplant file.

"Anything important?" she asked.

"I'm not sure, actually. Just something I have to check out."

That file had been in the center of his desk when he left. He was sure of it. How did it get on the floor?

Jan held out a hand. "Mind if I look?"

Bill hesitated, and then handed her the file. Maybe trusting her wasn't the smartest thing to do, but he had to have someone on his side. At the least, he needed another person to validate his concern over patients who should not have died of their injuries.

Jan flipped through the pages in the file and Bill saw her eyebrows shoot up. "This is serious stuff," she said.

"I talked to the person who gave me this. People who bring this sort of thing forward to strangers like me are usually pretty harmless, but may be a little off in their perspective. At least that's my experience. I don't generally trust their conspiracy theories. On the other hand, in this instance, I think the concerns may have merit."

Bill watched the color drain from Jan's face as she thumbed back through the documents and reread the first, second, and then third report. Bill could see the concern clearly etched on her face as she finally raised her eyes to meet his.

"I assume Sarah Laughlin gave you this. That's why you asked about a records clerk the other day. She's the only one who would have access to all the information in this file. Others might have access to individual pieces, but Sarah's the only one who could get to all of it."

Bill didn't see the need to reply and simply waited as Jan continued to read. He turned his gaze toward his office window. It was still gray outside, but the rain had stopped and the sky was showing signs of brightening.

"If what she says here is true," Jan said. "It's possible that she's not delusional and has a right to be concerned. I'm no expert, and there may be good reasons for what she found, but what I see here is very alarming. The initial attending physicians predicted that at least two of the patients should have recovered completely from their injuries. A third is more iffy, but questionable enough to make me think Sarah is on to something."

Bill took the file from Jan and laid it on his lap.

"Did you notice that in the first case, the post mortem showed more organs missing than those designated for harvest for an approved recipient?" Jan asked.

He flipped to pathologist's report for the patient that Jan indicated. Then he turned to the last page of the file, a copy of the transplant office's log. The log showed no record of the additional organs. It might have been a clerical error, but the extra organs never made it into the hospital's records.

He slipped the papers back into the folder and rubbed at his temples, trying to ease the headache that was forming behind his eyes.

"No, that's a twist I hadn't seen before. This may be nothing, but Sarah did say at one point that she thought there might be black marketing going on. Do you think that's possible?"

Jan reached up to brush a long strand of ebony hair behind one ear. "I've read articles about organs being harvested in the States and flown by private jet as far away as South America. People there are willing to pay a high price for smuggled organs. There is a lot of money down there."

"You may be right, but it's hard to imagine doctors doing such a thing. Did you notice the patient that was Jewish?"

Jan shook her head. "I didn't see that."

"I missed it the first time I reviewed the file, too. It's a subtle note, in the bottom corner of one of the patient profile pages.

"It's my experience that Jewish families become extremely concerned about the integrity of the body when it is to be buried," he said. "Hospitals don't make that kind of omission from the records easily. The family would not have allowed the body to be desecrated in any way. 'Desecration' would be their word for removal of any body parts of the deceased."

Bill slapped the file against his thigh, stood and paced over to the windows behind his desk. Conflicting thoughts battled in his head. Maybe there *is* something wrong at Wilkes Memorial. The deceased patient's religion was listed as Jewish. Assuming that his parents were Jewish, as well, they would not have allowed the organs to be harvested. In the Jewish religion, that was tantamount to desecration of the body, and not allowed. The newest medical student, fresh out of training, would have caught this one. It had to be more than an administrative mistake.

But murder? He found it hard to believe that people would go so far.

He rubbed at his temples again. The ferns beyond the window were still dripping from the last rain. Bill watched a goldfinch, a bright splash of yellow and black, zip from branch to branch, and then settle on the ground at the base of the window. The bird was oblivious to the presence of murder and conspiracy on the opposite side of the glass. It was a lot like the patients who would be arriving at the hospital today, unaware that they might never leave again if there was a market for their organs.

"If what's in these records is correct, this is appalling. It needs to be reported to the police," Jan said.

Bill turned back to face her. "I certainly can't afford to dismiss this as someone's warped imaginings. I have to investigate this thoroughly. I feel like I'm holding dynamite in my hands when I look at this stuff. On the other hand, if it is all simply a case of misguided conspiracy fantasy, and maybe some administrative error, then a single word about it could end up in litigation and embarrassment for everyone involved. I've got to be careful how I handle this."

"Good point. Maybe you should sleep on it before you do anything more. You could talk to Sarah again. Discuss it with her, bring up all the pros and cons of such an accusation that involves the integrity of dedicated doctors and the reputation of the hospital itself."

Jan's comments and her presence were quieting, comforting. It wasn't like the feeling he'd had for Carole last night. That was lust, basic and simple. This was something far more complex, and a little more disturbing. He'd been a bachelor for too long, seen too many relationships come and go from his life to get caught up in something that a person might label as love. On the other hand, there was a sense of warmth and trust when he was with Jan, and talking to her seemed to anchor his thoughts. The lust was there, too, but this was more involved in that.

Yep, "complex" was the right word for his feelings for Jan, and he wasn't all that sure he was ready for that right now.

He shook his head to clear the thoughts. Now he was the one with a warped imagination. He'd just met her a week before. If he'd had those feelings for Carole, whom he'd known since high school, that would be one thing. Jan was almost a stranger.

"Sarah is quiet, very bright, and I have to admit that she made some good points," Bill said. "You're right. I'll talk to her again and see if she has any additional input."

Jan stood and moved towards the door.

"Be careful," she said. "If there's a criminal element at work here, you could be in serious danger. If they find out that you're onto them, that you're a threat, they might want to eliminate that threat. They've already killed patients. Who's to say they'd stop there?"

Bill slid into his desk chair. "I've had pretty much the same thought. So much for completing my report this week."

Jan paused with her hand on the doorknob. "See you tonight? Remember, I have your dog hostage."

"Can I bring anything?"

Jan shook her head, her long ponytail swishing behind her. "Just yourself."

She pointed at the file. "If you want, we can talk about that some more. Maybe some of my ICU experience would help when you have to dig any further into the medical aspects of the patient deaths listed in that file."

"Thanks, I have a feeling I'll need all the help I can get."

Once Jan had left, Bill headed down the hall to Patient Administration. When he pushed open the door to Sarah's office, it was empty. He stuck his head into the adjacent office and asked the man sitting there if he'd seen her.

The young man shook his head without lifting his eyes from a tall stack of reports. "She left around nine this morning. She'd gotten a phone call from a family member and had to leave. She said she'd be back in an hour."

Bill checked his watch. It was after one. He asked the clerk to give Sarah a message, then thought better of it and scribbled one of his own on a pad and left it on her desk. By mid-afternoon, with no call from her, he went back to Sarah's office and checked on her again. The clerk in the next office, whom he now knew as Roger, shrugged when Bill asked after Sarah.

"It's not like her to be away so long. She's very punctual and really committed to her job. It's all she talks about."

Roger's eyes grew wistful. "A girl like her should have more in her life than just a job, I mean."

Bill headed for the cafeteria to grab a sandwich, even though there was a churning in the pit of his stomach that threatened to displace the hunger. Where was Sarah?

He thought of the patient files she'd given him. *If what she'd concluded and passed onto him was true, and if someone had learned that Sarah had given him the file, she could be in danger.*

That last thought surprised him. If he thought she might be in danger, then he was accepting the possibility that Sarah was right, and that patients were being murdered at Wilkes Memorial. And if that was true, how far would the killers go to protect themselves?

Chapter 15

After a miserable bowl of tepid soup and soggy crackers, Bill's mood was in the hopper and his outlook for the rest of the week was even worse. *I should just close out my report and get out of here. There's more than enough information to write a good report. It wouldn't be the first time a consultant did a less than thorough job, and I could be down the road and halfway to California by morning. I'm no cop. I've no business investigating things like this.*

As soon as the thought crossed his mind, he dismissed it. There was a chance that people were dying here, for no good reason other than someone's greed. He couldn't live with himself if he just let it go.

He swiveled his chair to face the office window and small woodsy garden, beyond.

Things were complicated. That was the best word for it: complicated. The theorized murder of patients was more than he'd ever imagined dealing with as a consultant, and now there was this thing between him and two women at the same time.

He'd hardly had two dates in the last six months and now he was involved again with a Carole that he hardly knew, and Jan. On a good day, he would be lucky to successfully navigate a normal relationship with a single woman, let alone two. And to top that off, the two women were co-workers.

Last night had been an exciting time with Carole. He hadn't been with a woman like that since, well... actually, the last time Carole and he had been together, and that was over twenty years ago. Rekindling a romance with your high school sweetheart was the sort of thing a guy read about, fantasized about, but never expected to experience in real life.

And yet, as much as they'd been together back then, Carole was different now. Last night, she'd been an aggressive, enthusiastic lover, just teetering on the edge of domineering. He wasn't all that sure what that meant in terms of any sort of long-term relationship, or that he would even want to hold onto someone like the Carole he'd been with yesterday. She was an overly complex woman and carried a lot of baggage from her divorce. Recollections of the night slid through his mind. She had been very, very affectionate.

And then there was Jan.

He barely knew Jan, but each thought of her caused a pleasant flutter in the pit of his stomach. There had been moments last night when it had been Jan's face that he'd seen in his mind, and it confused him. Even though he had only talked to her a few times since their impromptu date, she'd remained in his thoughts.

The two women were different in every way. Carole was all physical attraction, quick emotion, and spontaneity. Jan was soft spoken, understated, with a wry sense of humor. The memory of her holding his hand or touching his arm still sent a pleasant warmth shooting through his body.

He ran a hand through his thick mane of hair. Why was he spending all this time worrying over a couple of women? He had murders to worry about.

He turned back toward his desk, eyes drawn immediately to the brightly colored file. *Better to put my personal life on hold for a while and focus on business.*

In his past life as a medical intelligence officer in the Army, he'd dealt with unexplained human death. To be dealt with effectively, even death had to be evaluated objectively, researched, and tracked to the root cause. Sadly, there was nothing objective about how he felt about the current women in his life. They had managed to get him off track, something he would have to remedy. He scrubbed his forehead with his palms. This was getting way too complicated.

There's that word again: *complicated*. His life was normally so simple, predictable, manageable. He liked things that way, but nothing about this trip back to his home state, about this job or the people he'd met had been any of those things.

The door to his office creaked, and he spun his chair back around to face it.

"Hey fella. Got a minute for a girl? You look like you could use a break."

He stifled a groan. "Carole. As if on cue ..." he said.

Bill swiveled his chair toward her as Carole came around the desk. She gave him a lingering, warm kiss that took him deeper than he needed to be taken just then.

"Nice to see you, too," she said. She backed off and gave him a quizzical look. "Something wrong?"

"I'm sorry," he said. "It's this audit. I thought I had it all wrapped up, but now it looks like I've got loose ends. Hard to tell when I'll be finished, or when I'll get to head back home."

"Good for me. How about a rematch tonight, at my place?"

He hesitated.

"Or your place. I'm flexible."

Her hands felt warm and he was tempted to take her up on it. But there was his date with Jan... He didn't want to hurt her by breaking their date.

"I'm sorry but I'm busy tonight. Maybe a rain check?"

"Sure. No problem." Carole stepped away from him. She waved at the pile of folders on his desk. "Anything I can help with?"

"No, but thanks. I have to wade through them myself. It's one of the burdens I carry on these assignments." As he said the words, it occurred to him that he wasn't totally sure if he was referring to the files or her.

It was only partially a lie. He did plan on talking to Jan more about the transplant program, and he was uneasy about discussing Sarah's information with Carole. There was a feeling behind the latter point that he couldn't quite put his finger on, so he let it go.

"Some of the patient deaths shown in the records, where the deceased became an organ donor, concern me," he said. "I'm sure it's nothing, but the chart indicated that a single organ was harvested from the body. The post mortem indicated that more than one organ was missing from the body when it was autopsied."

"It's probably a paperwork error. Who did you get the information from? Did you confirm it with our pathologist?" Carole asked. She fished a small pad and pen from the pocket of her pants suit. "Tell me who you need to talk to and I'll arrange to have you see them this afternoon."

"I've already tried. She's away from her office – I left a message."

"Her? Our pathologist is a man. I figured that's who you'd want to see."

Bill mentally slapped himself in the forehead. He'd read the organization chart and both the pathologist and his assistant were men. He'd nearly exposed Sarah's identity to a member of the management staff.

Wait a minute! He'd totally overlooked Carole as a potential member of the patient death conspiracy that might well be going on at the hospital. She was a key person on the hospital management team. Where better to ramrod a black market organ program than from right next door to the CEO's office?

As soon as the thought crossed his mind, he dismissed it. He'd know her for over twenty years. He knew her well enough to know that she wasn't capable of taking another person's life.

He sucked in a deep breath to regain his composure. "Actually, I think that talking to your path expert might help. It'd be great if you could set up the meeting."

"I'll set up the meeting."

Carole rose from her chair, came over to him again and wrapped her arms around his neck. She placed her cheek softly against his and whispered, "Now that we've taken care of that, how about reconsidering tonight?"

Bill took her by the shoulders and moved her to arms length. "I really can't."

Carole's eyes narrowed. "Another woman?"

He'd always been a terrible liar, so he opted for the truth this time around.

"Another woman, yes, but not in the way you think. I made the date before you and I got together last night. It would be wrong for me to back out. Besides, she has Alex."

She released her grip around his neck and stepped away. "Alex?"

"My dog. He travels with me."

"Ah. Never really liked dogs. They drool a lot and get the carpets dirty."

Bill laughed and got up from his chair to escort her to the door. He kissed Carole lightly on the forehead before she turned to leave. "You'd love Alex. Everyone does. Anyway, this woman kept him for me last night, so you can't begrudge her my visit. Without her, I'd have had to leave your place much earlier than I did."

"There is that." Carole reached for the door. "Give me a call later and let me know how things are going. I'll call the pathologist as soon as I get back to my office and set up your meeting." She closed the door quietly behind her as she left.

After Carole left, Bill checked his watch and called Sarah's office, without result. As the day wound to a close, he walked down to her office. It was still empty. The man in the next room, Roger, had left for the day, as well. It was common for patient records clerks to leave early, with the standard nursing shift change at 3:30 pm. It kept the people who maintained the patient records closely linked to those who used them the most, the nurses.

Bill walked into Sarah's office and closed the door behind him. He did a quick visual inventory of the room, to get a feel for where she might have stored reports or information that could help him with his research. Among the stacks of paper neatly arranged on every surface was an old-fashioned Rolodex. He flipped through it and found Sarah's home phone and address, along with several passwords for computer programs and bank accounts.

"Trusting soul, aren't you, Sarah?" It was the mark of an organized person and one who didn't expect anyone to go through her things when she was gone.

He was now one of those people who did go through other people's things. He comforted himself that he might be investigating a murder.

He was closing the address file when he spotted a folder tucked under the edge of a desk blotter. He examined the protruding edge of the file and saw his name printed in large, block letters on the exposed edge.

He slid it free and flipped through its pages. They were much the same as what he'd seen before, only this file had more cases in it, going back three years. There were extracts of patient records, autopsy results, death certificates, and log entries from the transplant program.

Bill tucked the file under his arm and slipped out of the office. There were soft footsteps behind him and he turned in time to see Luke Harrison approaching from down the hall. The man was freshly scrubbed and dressed in formal evening attire, his hair slicked back to perfection and the omnipresent toothy smile firmly in place.

"Mr. Deming, right?" he said as he approached.

The man's cheerful attitude felt slightly slimy, but Bill returned it as he shook his hand.

"Dr. Harrison. Nice to see you again."

"About to get started on the weekend. How about you?" Harrison asked.

Bill nodded. "Just a little more to do and I'm off for an early date."

"Ah yes, I remember the dating life. Been married twenty years, myself. Couldn't imagine what it'd be like to have to hit the dating scene again."

Bill laughed. "It can be rough."

Harrison's smile never faltered, but his expression was flat, like someone who was engaged in a conversation but wanted to be anywhere but there. "It's good I found you. I'd hoped to invite you to join me for a drink after work, before I remembered a dinner outing that my wife had scheduled. A few of us from the hospital usually meet at Dirty Dave's Pizza and Brew for a beer, but there's a charity fundraiser that the little woman and I have to attend tonight. If you're here next week, perhaps I can get you to accept a rain check."

Bill had to wonder how much Harrison's wife would enjoy hearing herself referred to as the "little woman." He'd heard his father refer to his mother that way, once, and then bore the bruises from her reaction for more than a week afterwards.

"Thanks," Bill said. "But with any luck I'll have my work here wrapped shortly and will be on my way back to California by then. No offense intended."

Harrison headed off down the hallway and waved over his shoulder, the smile never faltering. "None taken. Such is life. If that date goes south and you've got a suit and tie, you can always head for the Performing Arts Center. The Cancer Society will be glad to take your money. It's downtown; a few blocks off Capitol Way."

Bill checked his watch and headed for his office to pick up his briefcase and coat. He was running late. It was nearly five and he had to be at Jan's by six. She'd promised him dinner and a tour of her place. It sounded like the sort of evening he needed: laid back, relaxed, a chance to sort through the things he'd discovered with someone he felt he could trust.

When he got back to his desk, he tucked the new file into his briefcase. As an afterthought, he gathered up the rest of his notes pertaining to the transplant program and stuffed them into the briefcase, too. He might have time this weekend to sort through the material again. This last batch of information was particularly interesting, suggesting a trend of unreasonable patient deaths that went back for years. Perhaps he'd give Sarah a call at home, let her know he'd found the file and ask to meet her. It'd be interesting to hear her conclusions regarding this new information.

In the hall outside Bill's office, a man waited behind a partially closed door, watching as Bill closed and locked his office door. When Bill was out of sight, and clearly headed for the outside door, the man stepped across the hall and picked up the receiver of a house phone on a nearby wall. He punched in a number and waited as the call went through.

"He's left his office."

He paused.

"Hey, I know this is an emergency phone, but they don't record the calls during shift change. I checked. Yes, it looks like he's gone for the day. You want me to check the office? Yes, I have the keys. He may have taken something from the patient admin clerk's office when he went in there, but I couldn't get close enough to be sure."

He paused again.

"Okay, I'm off the clock, then. Remember, you said I'd get those medications. Can I pick them up before I leave? Good. My wife's in a lot of pain and this will help."

Chapter 16

When Bill pulled into the hotel parking lot, remnants of the sun peeked through the crimson-fringed clouds gathered on the horizon. Itinerant raindrops spattered his shirt and jacket as he walked from the car to his hotel room, his mind on a dozen things other than the weather.

When he unlocked the door to his hotel room, and pushed on it, it wouldn't budge. It felt like something was braced against the door, on the other side.

Using main force, he managed to lever the door open a crack and saw the edge of the bed's box spring leaning up against it on the other side. He pushed the door open further and got his head through so that he could see inside. The whole room was trashed. The sheets were torn off the bed and scattered. His suitcases were strewn across the floor, half open with the hinges destroyed. Shattered dresser drawers lay atop the couch and chair, and all the cushions had been slashed.

His stomach churned. Who would do such a thing? He had nothing of value. He glanced down at the briefcase in his hand. Unless the intruder thought he might have left something very important in the room.

He felt a cold chill creep up his spine as he got the door open the rest of the way and stepped through the rubble to the phone. He called the front desk and reported the incident. The phone was slippery in his hand, from the sweat that had formed on his hands. This sort of thing happened to other people, not him. Even in the Army, when the danger had frequently been all too real, he couldn't recall being this shaken or angry. Angry? He was furious.

He swore under his breath. He had touched the phone with his bare hands. He knew better than to do that. He should have gone to the hotel office and left things alone. The police wouldn't be happy with him. He'd messed up any chance of getting prints off the instrument.

Careful not to touch anything else, he sat down on the battered, sliced couch and waited for the police to arrive.

Whoever had done this had been thorough.

The police arrived fifteen minutes later. The officer in charge was a tall, bored looking man with a small pot riding over his glossy black utility belt. He took notes as Bill related what little he could.

"There's been a rash of burglaries in the area lately," the officer said. "You find anything important missing? You involved in anything that might cause someone to want to get into your room?"

Bill wasn't sure if he should mention the file Sarah Laughlin had given him. He decided against it, and shook his head. He still didn't know enough about that situation to be sure someone would go to this extreme to protect themselves. The patrolman gave him his card and then snapped shut the notebook he'd been using.

"Looks like petty burglary to me. Sadly, it's not uncommon at hotels. We'll keep an eye on the place for a while to see if the perp makes a return visit, but I wouldn't hold out much hope. Meanwhile, if you think of anything, give me a call at that number. I'll make the report later this evening, back at the station, so you and the hotel can file your insurance claims. I doubt if you'll be bothered again. The sorts of petty criminals who do this don't usually show up again at the same place for a long, long time."

When the cop had departed, Bill remembered that the message light had been blinking on the phone when he'd arrived. The possibility of someone calling him at the same time as the room was being ran-sacked seemed almost humorous. He glanced at the closet. At least his clothes hadn't been damaged. Once the hotel got the room back into shape, he'd be able to pick up where he left off without too much trouble.

So why did he feel so angry? It was like he'd been personally violated, even though the room wasn't his, and nothing of his had been seriously damaged.

He called the hotel desk to let them know that it was okay to send in a team to clean up the room, and then checked his watch. He was already late for his date with Jan.

There was a loud knock at the partially opened door to his room as he waited for the desk clerk to answer. Juggling the phone in one hand, he made his way to the door and opened it again. A half dozen maids and workmen had already arrived, and judging by the tools and buckets in their hands, were ready to clean up the mess. He hung up the phone and glanced again at the blinking message light. The voice mail would have to wait.

He let the work crew into the room, grabbed his jacket and headed for the car. It wasn't until he'd climbed into the Supra and kicked the engine to life that he realized his knees were shaking. He felt vaguely ashamed. Not that long ago, he'd been through combat, with the bullets flying, and he hadn't been this shaken up. Had he changed that much is such a short time? He'd been retired only a few years.

He'd brought the briefcase with him and stashed it on the floor behind his seat. Could the information in that thing be that damaging that someone would break into his room to find it?

His mind went back to Sarah. She'd been gone from her office nearly all day. Her co-worker said that wasn't like her to just disappear. Bill found himself suddenly worried about the girl, and oddly convinced that her suspicions were somehow justified

No. He shook his head as if to clear it, and pounded a fist on the steering wheel. No. Now he was the paranoid one. Sarah could have just been off with friends. Her office mate said that she'd gotten a call from a family member. Maybe that was it. There'd been a family emergency and she'd left suddenly to take care of it. Maybe she was playing hooky. Young girls did that sort of thing

The burglary probably just had him riled. That was why he was so out of sorts about Sarah's absence. In fact, the more he considered the whole situation, the more surreal it seemed. That was the stuff of movies and novels, not real life.

Bill slid into the Supra's driver seat, started the car, and started to back it out of the hotel parking space, when a midnight blue Lexus pulled up behind him. Carole stepped from the car a moment later.

Whatever happened to calling before you show up? On the other hand, maybe she was the one on the voice mail

He put the Supra in park and got out to meet her. "Carole. This is a surprise. Everything all right?"

She stormed up to him, eyes ablaze with anger, her face mottled and pale. Her hand lanced out and slapped him hard across the face. The blow stung like fire.

Bill reached up instinctively to block the second swing and grabbed her wrist.

"Whoa! Wait a minute. What's going on?"

She struggled to free her hand. He let go and she lunged at him again, but he caught both her hands this time and held them fast to her sides. She squirmed and struggled. She was strong, and it took a major effort for him to keep her from lashing out at him again. She still hadn't said a thing.

"Tell me what's going on," he demanded.

"You're going out with that McDonald woman tonight, that's what's going on."

She spit the words, eyes awash with barely contained tears. "You think I wouldn't know about it? I'm the assistant administrator at that place where you work right now. I know everyone and everything that goes on there. Jan and I eat lunch together several times a week."

She mocked Jan's lower pitched voice. "Oh, have you met the new auditor? Bill Deming? Isn't he a nice guy? We had dinner the other day…" She glared. "After all I've been through … I trusted you … I told you … we were lovers, and now you're going out with *her*. I thought we were together … You're just like Kurt, just like all the others."

"Jan and I are friends," he said. "Last night with you was wonderful, but I didn't realize we'd made any sort of commitment. If anything, I got the impression that you didn't want anything to do with any man on a permanent basis. After everything you said about Kurt …"

She shrugged out of his grip, and Bill let her go. He stepped back a pace, just to be sure.

Carole stood her ground, still glaring at him with those intense, lovely eyes. "You think I sleep with any man that comes along? I have standards, and I thought you did, too. Now I know differently." She turned away abruptly and he reached out a hand to touch her shoulder.

"Carole, don't leave like this. We go back too far. Let's talk it...."

She spun back around, knocked his hand away and landed a second wide-handed slap across his face. The blow connected like a rifle shot and drew the attention of a couple getting out of their car a few yards off.

He stepped back, one hand raised to the welt that was forming on his cheek. "One more time and I'll forget I'm a gentleman. Neither one of us said anything that would give the other the idea that we were exclusive."

Carole's voice took on a low, dangerous tone. "I gave myself to you, Bill, just like before. You let me down this time, just like you did twenty years ago. Nothing else needs to be said."

Bill felt his own temper rise. She'd started all this, a long time ago, and continued it last night. He should have known better.

"If being together meant that much to you, you would have waited for me after college," he said. "It was you who broke off our relationship to run off and get married as soon as I was out of sight."

Carole dropped her eyes and her voice softened, although Bill could see her face was still creased with anger.

"When you showed up, when you seemed so happy to see me, I thought we could pick up where we left off. But I was wrong." She lifted her eyes to meet his once again, and the intensity there made Bill take a step back yet again. "But you remember this, Mr. Bill Deming: I gave myself to you then, and again yesterday. That may have been a mistake on my part, but you made the biggest mistake of your life when you accepted what I offered, and then threw it back in my face. I will never forget what you've done, and you will pay for it."

The pain in her voice made his heart sink. Maybe he had judged the situation totally wrong, and was partially responsible for what had happened. Maybe he'd been insensitive. He'd let himself get washed away in the passion and romance of being with a woman who'd haunted his memories for more than two decades. He suddenly felt sick, felt the need to ask her forgiveness, but the words wouldn't come.

She misinterpreted the look on his face and waved a careless hand at him, even though her complexion was still a deep shade of scarlet. "Don't worry. I'm not going to slap you again. I'm in control now," she said. "In fact, I am in control of a lot of things around here that you may not be aware of, and should have considered before you did certain things.

"And as for college, you betrayed me when you went off to college, not the other way around. You left me, when we were supposed to have gotten married and had a life together. I had it all figured out, and then you turned everything upside down. Kurt was there for me, when you weren't.

"And then Kurt betrayed me, too, when he left me for that young bitch he married. And you're doing the same thing with one of my own friends? You will pay for this, Bill. Mark my words. This isn't the end of the story. There are things you don't know, things that can hurt you. Don't come to me for help when they wash over you and take away what's important to you."

She climbed into her car, slammed the door behind her, and laid a long patch of smoldering rubber as she sped away.

Chapter 12

The drive to Jan's house took thirty minutes, but seemed like an hour.

How could he have read things so wrong, to go from the luckiest guy in the world one night to an insensitive bum the next? Had he been so busy enjoying the excitement of being with Carole, the big stud returned from her past, that he forgot to be sensitive to her needs and feelings?

As he made his way north through the city, past brick cottages and quaint farmhouses, he rubbed the side of his face where he could still feel the sting of Carole's hand. No, it was hard to accept full blame for what happened last night. Hadn't she been the pursuer when he'd shown up at her door?

Carole was a key figure at Wilkes Memorial, and what had happened between them put his project at Wilkes at significant risk. She might well want him out of the building, and out of her sight after what he'd done—what she'd accused him of doing. If she did that, it would never hold up with the CEO. The hospital needed the money that would result from his report. On the other hand, the situation was bound to get sticky, and news of it would get back to his boss in California. That would be a tough one to explain. No, no matter how he looked at it, he'd screwed things up pretty good this time. He should have seen it coming.

He was on a long, narrow gravel road well into the country before he finally spotted Jan's name and address on a mailbox. He turned the Supra into the driveway between two ancient cedars. The winding drive took him through a dense stand of fir and cedar and emptied into open meadow that was surrounded by a wall of twisted Garry oak trees. The Garry oak was unique to the South Puget Sound area, he knew from his days of living in the area. His mother had been an avid gardener and loved the trees. In the center of the meadow was a small house, so pretty it could have been taken from a postcard. It was a Cape Cod-style building, with a red brick front, tiny front porch and high dormers along the roofline. If he had imagined Jan standing in front of a house, it would have been this very style.

In fact, Jan was standing on the front porch as he drove up, hugging a tall young man. Alex sat on the step below them.

Bill felt the jealousy rise as he pulled the car to a stop in front of the house and climbed out. The emotion felt grossly out of place after what he'd just been through with Carole. After that performance, he had no rights on any woman, least of all Jan.

Bill stepped from the car, and Alex bounded off the porch and raced over to greet him. The dog jumped up and lashed a wet tongue at Bill's face as Jan and the man she was with stepped off the porch and walked over to meet him, arm in arm. Jan's broad smile lit up her face as she stepped close enough to plant a soft kiss on Bill's cheek.

"You're late," she said.

Bill shrugged, unsure of how to respond. Silence seemed the best bet.

Her companion hung back a step, grim-faced and obviously uncomfortable with the situation.

Jan took Bill's hand and beckoned to the other man. "Bill, meet my brother, Jake Williams. Don't let the last name fool you, he really is my brother."

Bill stuck out a hand and Jake took it in a firm grip that was strong, but not bone-crunching.

"Nice to meet you," Jake said, although his tone was anything but sincere. Bill felt the distrust reeking from the man. Overly protective brother, or something else? It made Bill wonder.

Alex distracted him from his consideration of Jan's brother, demanding attention. Bill reached down to scratch the dog behind the ears, but managed to keep on eye on Jake as he attended to Alex's needs.

Jake was taller than Bill by a good three inches, and looked to outweigh him by fifty pounds. Judging by the cut of the blue suit that he wore, the man was an athlete, sharing his sister's angular features and trim frame. He had dark brown eyes and thick black hair parted in the middle that hung long over his ears and down the back of his neck. His nose had been broken more than once, giving him a look of rugged competence.

Bill looked from Jake to Jan and back again. The resemblance was striking. There was an innate intelligence in both of their faces that was hard not to notice.

"Jake's a cop," Jan said.

"Investigator," Jake corrected.

"He works special cases for the State Bureau of Investigation, the local version of the FBI."

The comment forced a smile from Jake's lips, something Bill bet didn't happen too often.

"Actually, we're better than the FBI. We actually do get our man, or woman, as the case may be." The last comment brought a broad grin from Jan.

"Jan tells me you're auditing her hospital," Jake said.

Bill leaned back against the side of the Supra and nodded. "I'm about done, but it's been an interesting job."

"Actually, my little sister likes to think of me pounding a beat. It makes her feel better to imagine me walking the streets of Olympia in the rain and cold, suffering as much as possible."

Jan punched his shoulder. "Like you really suffer … Jake's on a case that involves Wilkes. After you shared what you'd found with me the other day, I thought it might be all right if I passed the information on to Jake. He thinks you might have found something important to his case."

Jan reached over and took Bill's arm, pulled him away from the car, and led the two men toward the house. Alex nudged in between Bill and Jan as they walked.

"I'll be glad to discuss the case with you, Jake," Bill said. "As long as it doesn't compromise my employer. You have to appreciate that any information you might want about the firm that employs me, or about the person who's commissioned the audit, would require a warrant."

Jake waved the suggestion away as they stepped into the house. "I'm not after your employer or the hospital's prospective patron. I'm investigating the death of two patients. I'm not even sure that I have that much of a case. We're looking into the two deaths at the request of a state representative who's suggested that at least one of the deaths was unwarranted and benefited a political enemy. It's a sticky situation, at best, but we have to investigate. The idea of a major political figure being involved in a patient murder is a little hard to fathom. In this case, it's the Secretary of State, and the voters think the man's a saint."

Bill remembered reading that the son of a prominent state politician had received a transplant. The note was in one of the files that Sarah had given him. The briefcase with that information in it was still in the car.

"I know about that one," Bill said.

That comment got Jake's attention. "Do you think there's anything to it?"

"Maybe, and there's more that may be related to it. Maybe we should go over what I've found. As an investigator, maybe you can tell me whether I'm being paranoid, or if there's a basis for my suspicions."

An hour later, over a hastily prepared dinner of spaghetti, French bread and salad, they finished going over Bill's findings regarding the Secretary of State's son, and the other deaths that were described in Sarah's file.

Jake and Jan sat across the room on a long, overstuffed couch. The room was furnished in a comfortable hodge-podge of styles; the new recliner with its tasteful, soft brown upholstery and dark oak trim across from a couch of plush velvet in deep gold. Several oak occasional tables and side chairs were scattered around the room. In one corner stood a small entertainment center with a Bose stereo system that Bill had coveted for himself for years. The walls were painted soft beige and covered with a mixture of modern and Native American art. It was a comfortable, pretty room and matched his image of Jan.

"I wrote Sarah off as just another kook conspiracy theorist at first.

I occasionally run into them in this business," Bill said.

He took a long swallow of the beer Jan had produced a few minutes earlier. Not normally a beer drinker, he was surprised by how good it tasted after the way his day had gone.

"Whenever I audit an organization, I can generally count on someone coming forward like Sarah did. Usually it's a disgruntled employee who wants to get even with his boss. I'm someone who's not familiar with the organization's past, so that sort of person sees me as approachable. Sometimes, it's someone with serious interpersonal problems. Less often, I learn something critical to the study I'm involved in.

"Sarah approached me anonymously. That's usually a bad sign. You can't confirm or refute the offerings of a 'Deep Throat' because it's hard to find out who they are and discuss the issues directly."

"You're lucky it wasn't a letter bomb," Jan said.

Bill laughed. "You're probably right, but some days, it just wouldn't matter either way." He reached up to touch the welt on the side of his face.

Jake hoisted his bottle. "That's quite a mark. I can count all five fingers."

"I've definitely had one of those days, but it gets worse. My room at the hotel was broken into and torn apart while I was at work today. Alex was here with Jan, or I'm sure it would have never happened." Bill glanced to the rug next to the kitchen stove, where Alex snored softly and they all laughed.

Jake slid forward, his gaze more intense than before. "You think it's related? That's not much of a leap, actually. If you *are* onto something, I doubt that someone who's killed patients would think twice about rifling your room to find the evidence. Did they find anything?"

Bill set the bottle of beer aside. "Nope. I had all my important papers with me at the office."

"What about this Sarah woman? Jan's mentioned her to me before, but I've never been able to talk to her. If I'd tried, it would have exposed our investigation. Do you think she's legit, now that you've had the chance to do a little digging?"

"I'm pretty sure she's on the level, but before I could make any sort of definitive finding, I'd want to interview some more people at the hospital to be sure; maybe some of the folks in the ER and OR.

Jan took the empty beer bottle from Bill. "I may be able to help with that. If you give me a list of names, places or times, I can check the shift logs in the ER and OR and get a line on who you want to see."

"That would help."

The beer and the feel of Jan's small, comfortable home were loosening him up, and Bill felt like talking. He'd kept his concerns about the deaths at Wilkes to himself for so long, that it felt good to be able to discuss it out in the open.

"It was the depth of the information in Sarah's file that caught my attention. The reports were put together in detail. When I finally located Sarah, she gave me even more information, including the photo-copied log from the transplant office."

"Jan's described some of that to me," Jake said. "Much of it could still be written off to simple coincidence."

Bill took a second beer from Jan as she returned from the kitchen. He set it aside without drinking, scooted forward on the chair, and lifted one of the reports for emphasis. "If I were Wilkes Memorial's CEO, that's just the approach I'd take to explain this away. Things happen in a hospital the size of Wilkes. Ten or fifteen deaths over a year, when the average patient census is more than two hundred patients a day, nets a statistic that's well within industry standards. On the other hand, I recently came across two cases that crossed that line. One involved harvested organs from a boy whose parents would never have agreed to the procedure. That case, more than any other, suggests that the patient's records were falsified, and that the organs were taken without consent. The record modifications were subtle and well done. If Sarah hadn't dug up that case, no one would have ever known."

"I would think the pathologist would discover that sort of thing during the post mortem," Jake said. "Does the pathologist do the autopsy? Doesn't he just get tissue samples from the various organs? There would obviously be some missing."

Jan leaned back into the couch's deep cushions and hugged her arms across her chest. "Not if there wasn't an autopsy, which happens a lot. And what if the pathologist was in on it? If the corpse were loaded with any sort of weight, the funeral home would never think to question it. I've read about morticians who do that to flesh out a body that's been destroyed, to make it appear more normal when there's to be an open-casket ceremony for the deceased."

"Okay, I'll accept that as possible," Jake said. "Maybe all this does tie together into a murder-for-money scheme, but we need hard evidence to be able to take action against the hospital. Right now, we don't know who's in on it. The cases you've seen, Bill, involve reports and no actual bodies or hands-on evidence linking all this to someone, or some set of 'someones'. What you've found parallels SBI findings, but we need something conclusive that will let us shut down this murder for profit operation."

"Why don't you explain to Bill what you need, specifically?" Jan said.

Jake took a long pull on his beer and set aside his empty beer bottle.

"I'll start with some background to bring you up to speed: We opened the investigation into Wilkes Memorial and a couple of other hospitals a few months ago. The State Attorney General received an anonymous letter indicating that people were dying to provide an organ harvest for the black market, somewhat as you've described. The A.G. was recently in the hospital, herself, and while she was there, asked us to investigate," Jake said.

"We looked into the complaint for several months and came up with zilch. No leads, no names, nothing. That's when I asked Jan to help out. I actually had her deputized."

"No Deputy Dog jokes, please," Jan said. "I've heard them all from Jake and his wife, ever since I agreed to help."

Jake grinned, and then continued. "Officially, she's a volunteer police reservist who keeps an eye on things for us at the hospital. Up to now, all she'd found were irregularities that pointed to something happening, but no concrete evidence."

Bill reached into his briefcase and lifted out the last file that Sarah had put together, that he'd taken off her desk earlier that afternoon. "Then you're going to love this."

He handed it across to Jake. Jan scooted closer to her brother to read over his shoulder. When they were done, Jake let out a long whistle and leaned back in his seat. "For this, I'm going to need another beer."

Jan took the file from Jake's hand. "This is exactly what we needed two months ago. What you've got is a coroner's report identifying missing organs. Before Bill got this, all we had were suspicions and what could have been written off as coincidence."

Bill cut her off with a raised hand. "On the other hand, how this information came into my possession is questionable. Wouldn't it normally require a warrant to get this sort of thing? The courts would challenge much of it under patient privacy laws."

"Not true," Jake said. "I've checked state and federal law on this. In the event of a patient's death, where that death is suspected as being the result of foul play or conspiracy, the patient's records can be released as a part of an ongoing investigation with or without a specific warrant."

"But still, this information was given to Bill inappropriately. Are you sure it would stand up in court?" Jan said.

Jake and Jan argued the point, and Bill found himself distracted by the striking beauty of the woman who sat across the room from him. As she threw argument after argument at her brother, Bill could see something more, an intelligence and wit that said volumes about her keen mind and compassion.

"So, will you do it?" Jake said.

Jake's question snapped Bill back into the conversation. "I'm sorry. Do what?"

Jan gave Bill a searching glance. "Seems as though our consultant's mind was wandering."

Jake's eyes narrowed. "I'll just bet," he said.

Jan laid a hand on Jake's arm. "Now's not the time for the protective brother."

"I need someone with access to this information to help me out with our investigation," Jake said. "If you can dig up just a little more information, I think I might be able to get the warrants we'd need to probe deeper into the hospital's records, to find conclusive evidence. It'll increase our chances of busting this group."

Bill leaned towards Jake. "Wait a minute. I work for an anonymous donor who's recruited my employer to audit Wilkes. I'm not supposed to be working with the police to dig out murderers."

Jake rose and paced across the small living room. He stopped near the room's natural rock fireplace and turned back toward Bill. "I understand your hesitation. On the other hand, you wouldn't have to do much. If you could just keep us apprised of what you found as you continued your own digging, it might still do the trick. If this Laughlin woman passes you any more information, you could simply hand a copy off to Jan and she would see that I got it. At some point, we'd bring Sarah in for questioning. With any luck, you'll find enough hard stuff that we can use her and the records as the crux of a solid investigation."

"That could be a problem," Bill said. "Sarah left the hospital unexpectedly this morning and hasn't returned to work. Her office mate says it's not like her. I didn't attach much significance to her not being at work for a day until my room was broken into. If someone knows that Sarah gave me evidence that would link them to the patient deaths, Sarah could be in real danger. Whoever's doing this ... How far do you think they would go to protect themselves?"

Jake grunted and sat back down. "They've already killed. In my experience, when a person has killed once, it gets easier for them to kill again. Sarah would be a primary witness against the murderers, and if they know that, they could be hunting her right now."

Jan shook her head. "Maybe we're making too much out of this. What if she's just ill or off visiting a relative?"

Jake ran a hand through his thick hair. "You may be right, but just to be safe, I'll have a cruiser sweep by her house a couple times a day starting this evening. If we see activity in the house, I'll come up with an excuse to pay her a visit to satisfy all of our concerns. You two can keep an eye out for her at the hospital."

"I didn't agree to work with you."

This time it was Jan's eyes, and her eyes alone, that locked with his and Bill felt his heart sink. "People may have died because of what's going on, for no better reason than to pad the hospital's coffers and a few wallets."

Bill lifted the beer bottle to his lips and drained its remaining contents in one swallow. When he was done, he set it the empty aside with a sigh. "I guess I don't have much of a choice," he said, his eyes never leaving hers. "I just hope we're all wrong about all of this."

Chapter 18

Bill and Jan stood side-by-side in the doorway as Jake's dented Ford Bronco bumped its way across the front yard and down the long driveway. Alex shuffled over from where he'd been sleeping to stand between them and Bill ruffled the fur on the back of the dog's neck.

"What have you done to Alex? You've only had him a day and his ribs have disappeared. I see a lot of jogging in your future, old buddy."

"He looks unimpressed," Jan said. She turned and headed back inside.

Bill followed her through the house and into the kitchen. She took a beer from the refrigerator and handed it to him.

Bill popped the top off the bottle as they leaned against opposite kitchen counters in companionable silence. Like the rest of the house, the kitchen was an eclectic accumulation of neatly arranged furnishings. Scattered on the walls was an equally diverse assortment of Native American and contemporary art. On one wall was a unique ink drawing of a rainbow trout, framed in a simple, glossy black frame.

Jan sipped her wine and smiled as he examined the picture. "It's an original," she said. "Made by a local person named Jan Bieber. Friend of a friend."

"The detail is amazing. How'd the artist get it so accurate, so exactly right?"

"It's not a drawing. The artist actually dumps the fish in ink and then makes the impression on the paper using the fish, itself."

Jan crossed the room, stood beside Bill and traced the fish's outline with a long, slender finger. "It fits in with the rest of my messy approach to life."

"I like your place. It's comfortable."

Jan grimaced. "Ouch. Comfortable is not the best word to use to describe a girl or her house. Exciting, alluring, almost anything would be better than comfortable."

Bill mentally kicked himself and decided to head the conversation in another direction. "Thanks for taking care of Alex last night."

"Did everything go well with your date?"

Bill felt the heat rise under his collar. Maybe this wasn't the best way to steer the conversation. "It was all right," he said.

Jan let the issue drop. "How about a tour? I can show you my menagerie before we lose the light outside."

"Menagerie? It's getting a little dark for a tour outside, don't you think?"

She flipped on a switch that bathed the area behind the house in bright light as she headed out the door. Bill followed her out, Alex at his heels. He hadn't been able to see behind the house before, but what he saw now amazed him: Row after row of covered pens stretched away from the house for fifty yards toward the south. Surrounded by a wall of tall, old growth fir and pine, the place looked every bit the sanctuary that it apparently was. The walkways between each cage were closely mowed and gave the place a park-like appearance."

As they approached the cages, Bill spotted two bald eagles, remarkable for their brilliant white head and tail feathers. There were also several large hawks, assorted pheasant, quail, two Canada geese, and a variety of other birds he couldn't identify. To the left of that was another, shorter row of cages made of sturdier material that housed a stocky-looking bobcat that gave a low, throaty rumble as Jan approached. A raccoon and several balls of fur that looked like smaller, sleeping versions of the same, occupied adjacent enclosures.

"This is amazing."

Jan smiled. There was no mistaking the fondness she felt for the animals as she trailed her hands along the front screens of the cages. "I've got a license from the state to foster and rehab injured animals. Chester, the bald eagle you saw in the first cage, flew into a lookout tower and broke a wing six months ago. He'll be ready for release back into the wild soon. The other eagle, and the rest of the birds and animals that I have here have similar stories. I work pretty closely with the State Fish and Game folks. They help with the food and seem happy for the assistance."

Bill stared, turning on his heel to examine every cage. "It's like your own private zoo."

Jan's face creased into a frown. "It's not a zoo. Each of these animals will be released back into the wild when they're well enough to care for themselves. As much as I get attached to them, I make a point of not making them house pets."

"What about that bobcat? He seemed pretty excited when you approached his cage."

"That's Barnacle. That growl was actually his version of a domestic cat's purr. He's been with me the longest and is the exception. He was rescued from a house in town, from owners who abused him. He's pretty tame, but I still hope to turn him around and eventually either set him free or find a habitat where he can live out his life."

Bill stopped in the middle of the walkway, and turned a slow circle, his eyes taking in the cages, the animals, and the surrounding trees. "This is wonderful."

She nodded. "It keeps me off the streets. It's one of the reasons I don't date much, and why Ruth is always on my case."

They continued their walk in silence, Bill examining the collection of birds that occupied each enclosure. He noted that the wings of several birds were splinted or wrapped in white bandages. One raccoon had a leg in a cast and hobbled around its cage with an oddly humorous gate, like a three-legged pirate, mask and all.

"How official is your work with Jake and the police?" They strolled past the raccoon and into an area that housed smaller, more docile animals.

"Not very." She paused at the fence to crouch and examine a pair of Bobwhites huddled in a pile of straw against the cage's outer wall.

"He asked me to keep my eyes open. I didn't find much, at first. Then you came along."

"So, I was invited here tonight because of my value as a witness?"

"Not entirely." She looped her arm through his as they walked on. He found that he enjoyed the warmth of her touch, and wondered at the contrast between this strong, caring, and beautiful woman and the aggressive assertiveness of Carole. How could he be attracted to two such different women?

"I asked you here because I enjoyed our time together last week and thought it would be nice to see you again."

They walked in comfortable silence as the sunset beyond the trees to the west and darkness overtook the land, lingering in the yard a while before returning to the house. She paused on the step of the back porch, standing slightly above him, and then turned and drew his lips to hers. She slipped a hand behind his neck and drew him closer to deepen the kiss. The kiss washed through him like a soothing wave. His hands slipped around her slender waist as the softness lingered, the tender passion of their embrace strengthening.

She released him and stepped back, a glow in her eyes as she met his gaze. Her smile and the pleasant flush of her cheeks sent another warm flush through him and stole away whatever words he might have said.

"So," she said. "Do you still think I invited you over just so you could talk to my brother?"

Alex bounded up suddenly and wormed his way between their legs, breaking the moment. They both laughed.

"No, that was pretty convincing. However, I may need additional evidence before I can make a definitive ruling."

Jan reached for the screen door and stepped inside, leaving him on the porch with Alex. "Ha. I'm not that easy."

Bill joined Jan back in the living room a few seconds later. He looked at his watch. It was nine-thirty, and he wanted to be at the hospital early the next morning. Saturdays were good days for writing reports and he wanted to be at his desk and on the job before seven. As much as he hated the idea of leaving just as things between him and Jan were getting interesting, if he was going to leave at all, he needed to head back to the hotel now.

He said as much, hoping for a protest, but receiving none. She just nodded her understanding and led him to the door. Slightly disappointed, Bill left Jan on the front porch after another long, lingering kiss and headed for the car, Alex on his heels.

He'd romanced his share of women in the past, but seldom had a single kiss had such an affect on him. As he steered the Supra down the dark, gravel stretch to the main road, Alex once again slumbered peacefully on the passenger seat.

"We've got a problem, Alex, and it has nothing to do with the patients dying at Wilkes. I'm falling for that woman."

Bill glanced briefly through the rear-view mirror as the dark shadows marking the tops of the trees surrounding Jan's house disappeared from view.

"Falling for a woman? That hasn't happened to me in a very long time."

Alex twitched an ear, and kicked several times with his hind leg, hot in pursuit of dreamland prey.

What a night. In the few short hours he'd spent with Jan, he found himself enrolled in a murder investigation, and falling for a woman he had known only briefly.

And if I'm falling for Jan, then what about Carole? The thought sent a cold sensation creeping up his spine.

Chapter 12

"This is Dr. Farley."

The chief of Wilkes Memorial's Department of Medicine spoke into the phone with the curt, clipped tones of a man too busy for interruptions. Today was Saturday, and ever since the hospital's administrator had demanded that his clinic be open for patients on the weekend, he'd found it difficult to be civil during the day. Saturday was a time for relaxing with the morning paper, not wiping the drippy noses of geriatric cases.

Already late for his first appointment, he was not in the mood for idle chatter over the phone. The patient was an elderly gentleman he'd been seeing for more than a decade. The old coot was filthy rich, had battled leukemia and diabetes for more than a decade, loved Farley for what he'd done to ease the man's pain, and could one day prove to be a source of considerable contributions for the hospital. He'd have to play nice when he saw the man, no matter how he felt.

When he heard the voice at the other end of the line, his demeanor changed dramatically. The voice was feminine, so the words cut through any pretense of gruffness he might have mustered for anyone else.

"We have a problem," the voice said.

The Director. What could she want? Farley ran through the events of the past few days in his mind. What could have happened? Could she have found out about the boy they'd harvested without her approval?

"What type of problem? The transplant for the Secretary of State's son went well. The experimental drug that we used all but eliminated the possibility of rejection. We stand to receive a large donation for both the hospital's building fund and ourselves. I don't see any problem in that."

There was a lengthy silence. Sweat beaded on the back of Farley's neck and dampened his collar, and he felt compelled to defend himself. But against what? What could she want? She usually worked through Harrison. She'd never called him directly before. Maybe she did find out about the ER case.

"Is it the FDA's approval of the drug?" He couldn't think of anything else that might upset her. "The release by the FDA isn't official yet, but I was told they'd give us the okay for controlled experimentation. That will keep us in the clear if we do the paperwork right, backdate a few things. I don't see how any of us, or the hospital, could be at risk. We've stretched things further in the past."

"You told me last month that we'd have unrestricted approval by now."

Farley had bent the truth on that point, and he knew it. He'd needed the infusion of funds the last transplant had provided, for personal reasons. He'd already lied to her once, and he couldn't get caught again. The woman ran an illegal organ transplant program. She'd called the shots on dozens of patient deaths over the last couple of years. There was no telling what she might do if she found out that he'd been freelancing in the ER, calling for a patient death and transplant, without her okay. He could become the next organ donor, if he wasn't careful. He would have to improvise.

"I talked to the FDA last week. The approval's tied up in committee, but we should get what we need in another week. My contact will fax a copy of the papers as soon as it's signed," he said.

"We pay your man enough that he ought to be able to fabricate what we need right away."

"He can only do so much. They have an extensive bureaucracy."

Farley's voice cracked as he spoke those last words, and he cursed under his breath. He knew that he had a tendency to reveal himself through his voice. Even with his patients, particularly the terminal ones, his inability to lie convincingly had always felt like a major drawback. He brushed at the long strands of hair that he combed over his expanding bald spot, and then rubbed hard at his temples.

"I want you to make sure that you stay on top of the FDA issue, but that's not why I called you. One of the hospital's employees is suspicious of our program. She's put together a package of records and provided them to a man who's auditing the hospital. You spoke to him the other day."

"I remember the man, but I don't understand your concern. We've been careful to cover our tracks."

"*Careful* is not enough. The woman's name is Sarah Laughlin. You've met her. She's the patient records clerk who reviews all the case write-ups for Surgery. She gave the records to Deming, the auditor, a few days ago. I'm not sure what he'll do with the information, but Miss Laughlin must be dealt with. She's dangerous and has to be stopped."

As the meaning of the Director's words sank in, Farley swallowed hard

"What can you expect me to do? If you mean …" He paused, afraid to say the words. "If you mean that I should arrange for the Laughlin woman to disappear, you've got the wrong man. I'm a doctor, not a kidnapper nor a murderer. If things are that bad, maybe we should shut down the operation for a while."

The Director laughed. "You know that's not an option. Besides, at the least, you're already guilty of conspiracy to murder, so don't even pretend to play coy about that issue. If I tell you to dispose of Miss Laughlin, you will do as I say. In Washington State, you can go to jail and never see the light of day again for what we've done, and you're in this up to your eyeballs. In another state, you might even get the death penalty.

"But I can't…"

"You will do as I tell you, and we're not shutting down the operation. If we suddenly stopped doing transplants, people would get suspicious. The legitimate side of our program is world-famous. If it suddenly ground to a halt, people would ask questions. Even if you did manage to escape the law, you wouldn't be able to show your face in public again, much less practice medicine. You'd live in fear of being arrested for the rest of your life. There isn't a court in the country that wouldn't label what you've done as murder."

"I won't be a part of a cold-blooded killing."

The Director chuckled, and Farley reached for the bottle of Mylanta that he kept in his top desk drawer.

"Don't you worry yourself about it. I know you haven't the spine for that sort of thing. I'll take care of Miss Laughlin, but don't you get too high and mighty about being a doctor. Who was it that administered the overdose to that boy in the ER? Did you think I wouldn't find out about that? How long would it take before someone remembered that the Chief of Medicine was present during several of the cases where a patient died of questionable causes? And I have copies of all the records to prove your relationship to what happened. It would not take much for me to let those records become public."

Farley felt the sweat begin to dampen his armpits, the back of his shirt. She was threatening him. What information did she have? He had covered his tracks so carefully. He decided the best option was to ignore the threat, hope it would never come up again. "I still think that we should cancel the next few procedures, hold off until after that auditor leaves."

"Out of the question. The next case is an easy one, and means too much to us. You only have to get a kidney. Yesterday you said you had a perfect tissue match and things were all set. How often does that sort of thing come along? A perfect match is hard to find. The man whose son needs that kidney is one of the richest men in the state, so we are going to help him. Then he's going to help us by making us all a little bit richer."

"If that Deming man goes to the police with the information the Sarah Laughlin woman gave him, we're in big trouble."

"You take care of your end by getting that kidney. I'll take care of everything else, including Deming. Ms. Laughlin will be out of the way shortly. As far as the hospital is concerned, she left work on Friday and has not been seen since. Maybe she ran off with some young man, chasing love and happiness. Doesn't that sound romantic?"

The Director's laugh wasn't pleasant. A chill climbed Farly's spine, one vertebra at a time.

Farley shook the Mylanta bottle. It was empty. He slammed it against the top of his desk. What had he gotten himself into? He'd been a good doctor once.

"Don't worry about it, Ian. Haven't I always taken care of nasty details, things you and Harrison don't have the stomach for? I'll take care of things this time, as well. Plans are already in motion."

"But what about ..."

"Stop whining, Ian. I said that I'd take care of things."

There was a painful finality to the click of the connection being severed as she hung up.

Farley gently replaced the telephone receiver in its cradle. It felt like the temperature in his office had just dropped ten degrees. He'd have to call maintenance and have it checked.

Chapter 20

The Intensive Care Unit was short-staffed and overrun when Jan checked in for her shift as head nurse of the unit. She barely had time to strip off her coat before she was shoulder deep in IV lines, O^2 monitors, and injections already late for administration.

Of the fourteen beds available, all but one was filled with terminal geriatrics and post-surgical cases that hadn't gone as well as expected. *The three coronary bypasses will be the toughest*, she thought as she scanned a chart during shift change. The previous shift's head nurse waved another chart at her, calling Jan over so they could do the shift-change briefing.

"My name's Gwen. Welcome to the Saturday shift in the ICU. Is this your first ICU rotation as head nurse? I heard you are rotating through all of the hospital's wards and clinics as part of the nurse management training program. How do you like it?"

Jan nodded as she flipped through the patient record Gwen handed her. "The program's been pretty interesting, and it's a real opportunity to move up into management. I'm an ICU nurse by training, but this is my first day heading up this particular ICU. Besides the coronary cases, anything I should know right off?"

Gwen glanced from one end of the ICU to the other. They stood at the main patient—monitoring console, a long semi-circular counter that looked more like the command console for a battleship than a hospital work station. Twenty-six video screens stretched along its fourteen-foot length. A Formica work surface and two lab stools sat before the electronic maze, and Jan scooted into place on one of the stools.

The glass-fronted rooms where each of the patients was housed were visible in a semi-circle from where they overlooked the ICU. Through the glass walls of the patient rooms, Jan could see the staff as they worked their patients. Heavy curtains hung next to each bed, tucked back against a tower of electronics stacked at the patient's head. The requisite wires and tubes flowed from the towers to various parts of the patient.

"Despite how it looks, the patient monitoring station is simple to operate," Gwen said. "Take everything you've ever used at other ICUs and pack it into this single work area, and there you are. Scan the monitors for a minute or two and let me know if you have any questions. You'll recognize what you see. Beyond that, as I see things, the only issues you've got besides the impossibly challenging patients, are the staff."

"As usual."

The other woman grinned. "You *have* done this work before."

Gwen was a slender woman with the sallow appearance of a librarian, but when she smiled, her face transformed. She became pretty, with kind eyes and a cheerful expression accentuated by lips that naturally curved upward. That look would go a long way toward comforting any patient.

"Keep an eye on Stan and Gemini, your two nursing aides. They're good, but they're young and have a terrible crush on each other. I found them in the supply room last week, and they weren't discussing any medical protocol I'm familiar with. Your RNs are top rate, although you've barely got enough on shift to cover all the beds. If one gets sick, we may have to close a bed down, unless there's a backup in the nursing pool. That's always an iffy proposition. Stella is the name of your assistant head nurse, and you can count on her. I've known Stella for two years. The three LPNs are pretty good, too. They don't have the skills of their higher-rated RN peers, but they've all been around for a while and we've trained them pretty well."

Gwen indicated a nurse administering meds to the patient in Room Three. "I would keep an eye on Judy."

"What's the issue with Judy?"

"She's become very attached to Mr. Parsons. She's a split-shift nurse, so I get to watch her for five hours before you come on board. She's spent a lot of time in there with him today, and even though she knows he's terminal, it seems to me that she's taking his condition too hard. Something else must be going on with the woman. She's worked for me for two years and never been like this. I've caught her crying several times this evening. We don't need that. The patient doesn't need that."

"She's lost her objectivity?" Jan asked.

"At least."

Jan reached for the Parsons chart, flipped it open. "He's a vehicle accident case. Snapped his neck going through the windshield—second and third vertebrae. The brain stem has been compromised. You don't get much more terminal than that."

"Yeah. It's pretty sad. He's in his early fifties. You'd think people would learn to wear a seatbelt."

Jan snapped the record shut. "The prognosis is bleak but that respirator is doing the hard work for him. He's comatose. I see that the family has refused to pull life support. Any chance of that changing?"

Gwen shook her head and stepped over to the coat rack and retrieved a sweater. She shrugged into it, the weariness of the past shift, twelve long hours, finally catching up with her.

"There's really no hope, but the family's loaded. They had a cast of thousands in here yesterday, half a dozen top neurologists from around the state. They all agreed that Mr. Parsons is one for the books, but the family is old-Olympia and Mr. Parsons is much beloved, so they don't want to give up. There's word they may bring in some Swiss specialist who's developed a new procedure for regenerating nerve cells. He's due later this weekend, so until then we keep our Mr. Parsons clicking and whirring along."

Jan grimaced.

Gwen stifled a yawn. "Sorry about that. Guess I'm becoming a little calloused after too many long shifts without a break. This may be the greatest hospital in the state, but they need more staff so some of us can get a weekend off now and then."

"It's an industry-wide problem. About Judy...?" Jan said.

"Just keep an eye on her. She's handled patients like Parsons before, but she's way too distraught. I think you can rely on her, but keep it in the back of your mind."

"Will do. Have a nice evening."

"Yeah. Maybe I'll actually get a few hours of sleep while the kids are at day camp, before Soccer, and before ballet lessons. I can only hope."

Jan returned to her review of the charts, noting critical medication schedules, patient update schedules, and the other usual things important to the administration of an Intensive Care Unit. It would be a busy shift, but it seemed like she had a good crew. In her experience, that usually made all the difference.

She signaled for the assistant head nurse, a young woman named Stella, to join her at the console. The nurse hurried over and Jan asked her to monitor things while she made her initial rounds. From there, Jan moved quickly from room to room, speaking briefly to the patients if they were awake, and scanning monitors and patient charts. She spoke to each nurse and technician that she found at the bedside, offering a suggestion here, a word of reassurance there.

As she approached the Parsons room, she steeled herself to deal with what she anticipated to be a nurse on the edge. She'd seen the same sort of things a couple of times during her career, and in each case the nurse had been able to recover themselves, regain their professional detachment. She hoped to find out what was bothering Judy, before someone got in trouble.

"Judy," she said. The humming of the ventilator drowned out her voice and when she came up behind the nurse and tapped her shoulder, the woman jumped.

"Gwen said things have been pretty rough for you and Mr. Parsons. Everything all right?"

Judy sniffed and rubbed her nose with the sleeve of her paisley smock. Her eyes were red from crying, and her complexion was blotchy.

"I'm sorry. My life's a little complicated right now and Mr. Parsons kind of set me off, I guess."

Judy seemed to relax when Jan laid a gentle hand on her arm and patted it. "We've all been through that rough combination of personal difficulties and tough patients. Would you rather take some time off? I'm sure I could arrange for a replacement from the nursing pool if you'd like to go home."

"Oh, that'd be..."

"Excuse me. Sorry, but I need to talk to Judy, right now."

Jan turned to find Carole at the door to the patient room. Jan didn't consider herself and the hospital's Deputy Administrator to be good friends, but they had eaten lunch together many times while she'd been on rotation in the administrative wing. Jan had great respect for the woman's dedication to the hospital and her commitment to her job, and was genuinely pleased to her whenever they encountered one another.

Carole's hostile expression, abruptness, and tone of voice, though, suggested that this might not be one of those times.

"I'll be finished with her in a second, Carole. Please wait at the nurses' station and I'll send her right over."

"I need to talk to her, now."

Jan felt her back stiffen as she turned to face Carole more directly. She kept her voice carefully neutral. "I appreciate that, and she'll be with you in a minute if you will remove yourself from the patient's room, and wait by the nursing station, out of the way."

Carole glared at Jan, but then seemed to reconsider and stepped away from the door.

It was a cardinal rule in healthcare that you didn't bother patient care personnel at bedside and Jan was thankful that Carole at least knew enough to take the cue without making any more of a scene.

"Guess I won't be going home, after all," Judy murmured.

"Why's that? You're my staff member, not hers. I can get her to come back later, if you want."

Judy squared her shoulders and wiped her eyes with a tissue from the bedside cabinet. "No, I'll handle our illustrious Assistant Administrator. I've dealt with her before. It shouldn't take long, and then I'll be back to assist with Mr. Parsons."

"I'll stay with him until you get back."

Judy stepped away to join Carole. Jan observed much of their meeting as she monitored the patient's condition. There was anxiety written on Judy's face as the two women talked. After a short time, the two moved out of sight, into the supply room behind the nurses' station, and Jan lost track of them.

Jan kept busy running through the paces with Mr. Parsons' equipment. He had several catheters in place for body secretions, nutrition, fluids and the other things necessary to keep him going, and they all took management. The breathing tube extending down his trachea was in good shape and the ventilator kept up its regular, wheezing hum without much assistance. She checked his pupil response and found none. His eyes were dilated and didn't contract when she shone light on them with a tiny, handheld flashlight. The man was essentially a vegetable. She'd seen so many of these cases over the years and wondered if he had ever envisioned himself being kept alive like this.

She called up the patient record on the patient information management system's bedside monitor and found a copy of the man's living will posted to the file. It specified that he did not want to be kept alive artificially. It didn't surprise her that it hadn't been honored. She knew that a doctor was unlikely to shut off life support if a close family member protested. Later in the record, she found a note from the doctor, documenting a request by the man's wife that he be kept alive at all cost.

Death is so often an issue for the survivors, and so seldom an issue for the patient.

Jan felt another person's presence behind her. She glanced over her shoulder to find Judy had returned. Carole was nowhere in sight.

"Did you notice Mr. Parsons' living will when you reviewed his files?" Jan said.

Judy edged closer. "No. I'd been told he didn't have one, so I didn't think to look. That's odd. Why would the doctor say Parsons didn't have one when he did? I wonder if his wife even knows? I've met her a couple of times. She doesn't seem like the type to go against her husband's wishes. It's been a long battle for her, and I think she's tired. She'd let him go, if she knew there was a living will. I'd bet on it."

Jan hit a button and cleared the screen. If Judy was right, then it suggested that the physician's note was a fabrication. If that was the case, was anything in the record legit? Was Mr. Parsons being kept on ice for other reasons? It wasn't much of a leap in reasoning, considering the other things that might be going on in the hospital. What better way to store valuable organs than in a living body? She made a mental note of the name of the doctor who'd written the file.

She would pass the information on to her brother during her break.

Jan moved away, so Judy could check her patient. "I'll make a point to bring it up when the docs come by, later. Grand Rounds are at ten. I'll catch him then."

Judy nodded and turned away to check her patient's equipment.

"He's set up very well, Judy. You do nice work," Jan said.

Judy didn't reply, just sniffed loudly and went about her tasks.

Three hours later, Jan was finishing a pile of paperwork when Judy and two other nurses said their goodbyes for the day. She waved them out of the ICU and welcomed their replacements, running each through the introductions and backgrounds of the patients they'd be handling. Martha, Judy's replacement, was a woman in her mid-fifties and appeared to be a stable, mature type. It pleased Jan to have her at Parsons' bedside. The rest of them seemed equally competent.

Fifteen minutes had passed without incident when the amber light next to bed twelve's monitor began to blink, and the life sign monitors at the bedside began to scream. It was loud enough that every nurse on the ward stepped out of their patient's glass enclosed rooms. Parsons was in distress.

Jan looked over to the bedside in the same instant that Martha looked up to meet her eyes and gave an animated, come-help-me wave. Jan scanned the console, and then hit the red call button on two monitors. Two RNs dashed from their rooms to meet her on the way to Parsons' bedside.

Parsons' body jerked violently as the light on the patient monitor shifted from amber to red. One of the two nurses, a competent middle-aged woman named Gail, checked respiration. "Respiration's down," she said.

"Check his tube for blockage," Jan called as she grabbed at wires to check for broken connections. She needn't have said it. When she glanced over, Gail was already checking the tube.

The second nurse, Jaree, checked Parsons for papillary response, blood flow and sensitivity in the extremities. Sensing Jan's question, Jaree looked over after a brief exam and said, "He's non-responsive."

Jan cut her gaze to the vital signs monitor and recognized heart patterns consistent with a ventricular fibrillation. This all took only seconds, and in the next instant, she slapped the broad blue button on the wall a few feet above the patient's head. "He's flat-lined. I'm calling the code."

The intercom came to life a split second later, the soft voice calling out in a synthetically stable voice, "Dr. H, report to the ICU 12. Code Blue. Dr. H, report to the ICU 12. Code Blue."

Several more of the ICU nursing team streaked from the room and into the hall, where the unit's crash cart was stored. In another minute, they had the paddles out while Jan cleared Parsons' chest.

In that same instant, the hospital's Crash Team sprinted through the ICU doors. There were six members of the team, two doctors and four nurses, highly trained professionals whose job was to bring the near dead back to life.

One of the doctors immediately took the paddles from Jan's hands, and with gratitude she surrendered them. It was a drill that every ICU nurse was familiar with.

She stepped away as the team closed in around Parsons' bed. The lead physician called for the monitor readings, "I need the latest, folks. What's his readings?" Jaree read him the latest from all the monitors.

"Doesn't look that great, but we've seen worse," the physician replied. "I want epinephrine every three minutes until we're done here. Get the defib going, now!"

From the background, Gail came forward with the syringe and jammed it into the port on the IV line running directly into Parsons' vena cava, the artery leading directly to his heart.

The second physician, holding the defib paddles, yelled, "Clear," and the staff all backed away.

Volts streamed through Parsons' body, and his back arched. The monitors at bedside all showed a continuous flat line. No heartbeat.

"Nothing," said the nurse positioned by the monitors. "The ventilator's keeping him breathing, but that's all we've got."

The doctor yelled "Clear" again, and again the patient's back arched.

No change on the monitors.

One of the doctors said, "Shit. This is a tough one. What's his name?"

"Parsons. Samuel Parsons," Jan said.

"All right, Mr. Parsons, one more time. Do us all a favor and wake up."

Again the electricity, and again nothing.

"Epinephrine," the second doctor said.

A nurse slapped a 50 cc syringe into the doc's hand. The needle was six inches long and looked like a weapon.

"How much time since arrest?" someone asked.

The nurse working Parsons' station checked a paper in her hand and said, "Five minutes."

"I want someone on heart compression, and I want the CPR continuing until I say to quit. Come on, Sam. You can do it. Here comes the big boost."

He plunged the needle into Parsons' chest, directly into the heart muscle.

The monitors still didn't change. The second physician moved in and put his hands over Parsons' sternum, measured two fingers up from its bottom most point and leaned down to compress Parsons' chest. Sweat formed on the doctor's forehead as he pumped on the chest, again and again at carefully timed intervals. This was hard work and after three minutes, the lead physician stepped in and took a turn.

"How long now?" the doctor asked between compressions.

Jan looked at the clock on the wall. "Just over ten minutes, doctor."

"We've got a pulse!" Gail said from head of the bed, where she monitored the patient's bedside monitor.

Everyone cheered.

Jan stepped over to confirm Gail's observation. "Gail's right. We've got a pulse, but we've got no brain activity at all."

The lead physician stepped away from Parsons' bedside and joined Gail and Jan at the monitor.

"Crap. We've got a heartbeat but no brain wave activity. What's the patient LT?" He used the common shorthand for the patient's long-term prognosis.

"He's been comatose for his whole visit. He's not expected to recover." Jan said. "There's a living will on file, but some confusion regarding next of kin's wishes."

The team worked intently for ten more minutes before the head of the team called things off. "It would be wasted effort," the lead doc said as he stepped back from the bedside. He called up the patient record on the bedside monitor and shook his head grimly as he read the comments that Jan had seen when she'd reviewed the patient record, earlier. "This man has been brain-dead for days. I can't imagine why he's been kept on life support all this time. It's a waste of money and bed space. Must have been a family request. Well, that's old news at this point."

As the team packed up their equipment, Jan, back at the nurses' station, watched Mr. Parsons' heart beat with a weak, but stable rhythm. Brain activity remained flat, with not a peep of activity. She'd seen this happen in the past, but it still gave her the creeps to see it again. It was hard to imagine the body continuing life, while the brain had ceased to function.

The team lead, a doctor with a nametag on his scrubs that read Thompson, came over a second later and leaned against the front of the console. He was a young man, near her own age, with boyish good looks but sad eyes.

"Bad day for Parsons. Sorry I couldn't bring him around."

"You did what you could," Jan said. "In some states, the law says that if there's a heartbeat, the patient is technically still alive. It's only a few states like Washington where they recognize that the patient has gone beyond the pale if the brain stops functioning. You want to see the chart?"

The doctor accepted a metal-clad, hard copy version of the same record that was stored in the hospital's automated system. He flipped through the pages. "I see he was Farley's patient. I know Ian. I'll give him a call and break the bad news when we get our gear cleaned up and out of your way."

Jan took the record back and laid it on the counter top. "Thanks. I'm surprised that he crashed like he did. With all the equipment and the way he was set up, I expected him to linger on for some time."

The physician raised his eyebrows and wiped the palm of one hand across his face. "Me, too. The guy was a classic veg, with low-level brain waves, but could have hung on for years before he gave out. It's uncommon for cases like his to crash, although it does happen. I'll submit my report on-line from my office. You can add your notes to it in a half hour or so. Need anything else from me?"

"No. I'll notify the family and call the transplant team in. He's an organ donor. Says it all over his record. At least he's a perfect candidate for that. His death won't go for nothing. Thanks for being around."

Doctor Thompson smiled. "It's the job. Hope the rest of your day goes better."

Perfect transplant candidate?

The thought ran through Jan's brain like a skipping record, as she remembered what she'd been told about patients dying at Wilkes, and the suspicion that it was all tied to a death-for-money conspiracy. Was that what Parsons' case had been? Had he been set up to become the hospital's latest organ donor?

Someone would have had to slip him some meds to stimulate death and ultimately put him into a brain-dead state while his other critical organs still functioned. To be an organ donor, a deceased patient's heart had to keep beating. That was the only way you could hope to save the valuable organs like the heart, lungs, liver, kidneys, pancreas and small intestine. If the brain-dead person's heart continued to beat, and the person was maintained on a ventilator, the organs would continue to receive a blood supply. If the heart stopped, the only things that could be preserved would be the patient's tissues, skin, bone, cornea, and perhaps the heart valves.

As Thompson walked back to join his team, Jan's thoughts flashed back to earlier in the shift, when Carole and Judy had disappeared into the supply room. Did that meeting have something to do with Parsons' death? The timing would have been right if Carole had directed Judy to slip something into Parsons' meds. Could that have been why Judy was so upset?

No, it was too crazy. Jan had been listening to her brother for too long. She was no detective. She needed to focus her attention on her live patients, not some conspiracy that her brother was investigating.

The rest of the shift did go better. Mr. Parsons' body was wheeled away by the pathology crew twenty minutes later. In another two hours, bed twelve was filled once again, this time by a post-operative splenectomy case that was expected to recover fully. Jan's mind shifted from Mr. Parsons' unexpected demise to the care of her new patient.

Her day finally over and her replacement briefed, Jan stripped off her nursing uniform and called Jake from the locker room shortly after 4 pm. He showed a definite interest when she described the Parsons case.

"We've kept an eye on the assistant administrator for some time, although she frankly doesn't seem like the murdering type. We'll keep watch on this Judy person, as well," he said.

When she hung up the phone, she felt a nagging desire to give Bill a call. The last time they'd been together had been nice, and she could use a little "nice" right about now.

The thought brightened her mood and she decided on a more direct approach. She checked her watch. He might still be at the office and it was only a few minutes' walk from the ICU. Seeing Bill might be just what the doctor ordered.

Chapter 21

Bill was in the hall, a short distance from the ICU when the Code Blue was called in the ICU. He had a lot on his mind, and most of it was contained in the rolled up notebook pages he slapped against his thigh as he walked, oblivious to the nurses, doctors and technicians streaking along the hall toward the intensive care unit.

A short while ago, he'd talked to the clerk in E.R. She'd seemed a likeable woman, a little domineering, maybe, but good-natured. When he asked about the young man who'd died from the car crash on I-5 a few days before, she'd been as surprised as he that the boy had died. She'd showed him an abstract from the attending physician's notes, suggesting that the boy had a good chance to survive.

Did she know that he'd been an organ donor?

To that question, she'd gotten genuinely misty eyed, and suggested that at least his death hadn't been totally in vain. Bill felt inclined to accept the woman's surprise and concern as genuine.

His next stop had been the OR to have a conversation with the head nurse. The reception there had been totally different. He'd been treated politely enough, but OR crews were notoriously close knit and he could feel the suspicion the second he, an outsider, walked through the wide, double doors leading to the suite of operatories.

"Of course it was a tragedy," the head nurse had said when he asked about the splenectomy that had gone bad a few weeks before.

"Yes, at least the patient's death had some benefit. Thank goodness for the organ transplant program."

Was she aware that the patient's sudden "crash" had not yet been attributed to a clear cause?

"No," she'd replied. The cause of death that had been reported to her was massive post-surgical iatrogenic infection. "It's an unfortunate reality that those things happen sometimes. What's sad is that my OR crew, with its nearly spotless record, was involved. We've been drilling them on that issue ever since. We owe it to our patients to be as close to perfect as humanly possible."

When he'd shown her statistics that revealed a relatively high number of sudden crashes in the OR, all leading to organ harvests for the hospital's transplant program, the head nurse's tone and expression had grown stressed, almost angry.

"I think you should leave now, Mr. Deming," she said. "If you think something is amiss with those cases, you should report it to the hospital's administration and to the person you work for. My teams are under enough stress as it is, with the long hours, too many cases, and testy surgeons. The next time you want to come in here and ask questions, or make accusations, I'd suggest you schedule an appointment. I'll be sure to have Dr. Harrison, our head surgeon, and our lawyer, here to meet with you."

He couldn't fault the woman's response. She may have not liked his questions or suggestions, but her reaction and words were by the book. She was protecting her teams and her hospital from potential litigation. She had been professional, surly maybe, and certainly her tone had been defensive, but her answers had left little doubt about her loyalties.

Still, that last interview hadn't set well with him at the time, and something still felt a bit wrong when he ran through it in his mind again.

As he was thinking the situation through, the fact that a "code blue" had been called, and that people were responding, finally filtered through his subconscious. Like anyone who'd worked in a hospital for more than a week, he registered "codes" with a detached sort of interest: who was the patient? Did he know the person? Who would be talking to the family? It was hard not to project something of oneself into the situation, but there was little you could do personally, so you kept yourself detached.

So it was with some surprise that he found himself at the intersection of two corridors, near the entry to the ICU. To his left was a bank of windows that looked out on a large staff parking lot. He watched absently as the wind picked up dramatically outside, and a heavy branch crashed down from overhead, landed on the hood of a Chevy Explorer and set off its alarm.

"Mr. Deming?"

Bill glanced around. Ruth, the CEO's administrative assistant, approached from the hallway to his left. His smile was automatic. He liked this woman. He liked her nosey parental concern for Jan, how she treated everyone with a kind sort of respect and courtesy, and how she carried herself in spite of her advancing years. Ruth personified confidence and poise, like you'd expect from some ancient, wise relative.

As she got closer, he was surprised to notice Ruth limping slightly. The edge of a bulky bandage peeked from beneath her skirt hem.

"Are you all right?" he asked.

"Just a skirmish with a picture I was hanging in the living room last night. I fell off the stepladder. Twisted something. It's rough getting old. I remember a time when I would have bounced right back, with hardly a bruise. Now I'm all wrapped up like a surgical patient."

"At least you're all right. This seems off the beaten path for you, down here in the bowels of the patient care wards."

"There aren't many places in Wilkes Memorial that this old bat doesn't get to during a day, I'll have you know. If there's a beaten path, I've been on it before and will cover it again in short order. When the CEO, Mr. Sterling, wants something done, he wants it done now and it's usually me who docs it. I've found the best way to get things done is for me to take care of them myself."

Bill smiled. She very much reminded him of his grandmother. She was strong-willed, too.

"Did you hear the Code Blue?" he asked.

"Yep. I think it was one of Jan's patients. She's doing her ICU rotation this week, although you probably know that already." Ruth surreptitiously checked her watch. "You should go over there and see her. She ought to be getting off shift about now."

"You do realize that your attempts at matching me up with Jan could be misinterpreted as meddling with a very important audit."

Ruth grinned, and rubbed softly at her bandaged arm. "Is it working?"

Bill's sheepish grin and his unspoken response apparently gave her all the validation she needed.

"Someone has to keep you young folks in line and headed in the right direction. Jan's a good girl and I want to see her happy. If I had a daughter, I'd want her to be like Jan. Straight, strong, beautiful and smart, that's Jan. But then maybe you don't see as much in her as I do. Maybe you see more in some floozy like Carole."

It was Bill's turn to get flustered. "That's an odd thing to say about the hospital's second in charge. Besides, Carole and I have known each other since we were in high school. We're just friends."

"From what she told me, you must have been pretty darn close."

"Like I said, Carole and I are good friends."

He felt his good mood dissipate under the woman's not-so-subtle insinuation. How much did she know about Carole and him? Had she told Jan anything?

Ruth harrumphed. "Friends. Right. If that's what you want your story to be, I won't get in the way of it, but a horse with stripes is still a zebra no matter what label you put on it. If you want a good woman in your life, you focus your manly moves on Jan. It won't be some clamoring, clinging vine like Carole who will make a man happy in the long run. My man, Henry, now he was a good man. If he just hadn't died like that..."

Bill interrupted before she could take the discussion any further. He wasn't prepared for a long family history at this point. He'd had enough of this kindly old lady. "I really have to get going. Thanks for the chat, Ruth."

He ducked around the corner and left her staring after him.

Bill approached a maintenance worker replacing bulbs in the hallway as he made his way toward the ICU. The man was a giant, dwarfing the eight-foot ladder he was standing on, huge muscles straining his overalls and work shirt. Near the man was a small sign pointing to the hospital's morgue. It gave Bill an idea.

He approached the man on the ladder. "Excuse me, but can you tell me where I might find the pathologist? His name is…"

"That would be Dr. Pigeon, sir," the maintenance man replied. His words were slow and measured, with just a touch of a New England accent. The man stepped off the ladder and pointed down the hall.

"His office is straight down that away, at the end of the hall, on the left. It's the last room in the wing. The morgue is right next to it, with a big sign on the door. You get to the morgue, and you've gone too far. Next stop after that is the loading dock and you're outside."

"Thanks for the directions."

"I was here when they poured the foundation and I'll be here when they tear it down, I reckon. You ever need directions, you come to me."

Bill followed the repairman's instructions and found himself outside the pathologist's office a few minutes later. He knocked and when he didn't receive an immediate answer, cracked the office door open and peered in. No one was home, but there was a briefcase poised atop the large desk that dominated the room. It looked as though someone had been planning to leave for the day, but had been interrupted or forgotten to take the case with them.

Bill eased the door closed and moved off down the hall to the morgue. A sign on the door said "Restricted Access." He ignored it and pushed his way in through a broken automatic door and found Doctor Pigeon bent over the inert form of a recently deceased patient.

"Come in, young man, and close the door behind you. I don't want my patients catching cold. It could kill him, don't ya know." The man laughed loudly at his own joke. It was a roaring, baritone laugh that jarred the senses.

The pathologist looked grizzled and old, nearly as tall as Bill but with the stooped shoulders of old age. He stood at a stainless steel autopsy table with a bone saw in one hand and a skullcap in the other.

"Do you have a second, Dr. Pigeon?" Bill said.

The pathologist raised the skullcap in Bill's direction. "Does it look like I have a second?"

Pigeon cocked his head toward the ceiling and said, "Recorder off."

A young man stood across the body from Pigeon, most likely the pathologist's assistant. The technician reached over to a switch located on the side of the autopsy table and flipped it. "Recorder's off, sir."

Pigeon set the bowl-shaped piece of bone aside, turned to Bill and stripped off a surgical glove. He reached out a hand.

"Walter Pigeon. Pleased to meet you. You're that hot shot auditor I've heard about, aren't you?"

"Word does get around, doesn't it?"

Pigeon chuckled. "It's a hospital. Every hospital I've ever worked at has had one thing you can count on: a well-developed gossip network. You'll be happy to know that you're the current subject."

Bill took the man's hand and felt like his had been captured in a bone crunching vice. The old man seemed to find humor in Bill's discomfort as they shook hands. In spite of his advanced age, the pathologist had a grip like a wrestler.

"I guess I can afford a few minutes." He waved a hand at the cadaver on the table. "This character isn't going anywhere."

"I read a report about missing organs from a deceased Jewish patient, and wanted to ask a few questions. The people I work for are very interested in the hospital's transplant program, so it's an issue I need to wrap up before I can finish my work at Wilkes."

"I remember the Jewish patient. They take some special handling, but missing organs? I never wrote any report about missing organs," Pigeon said.

Bill reached into the breast pocket of his blazer and pulled out a neatly folded piece of paper. He handed it to the pathologist. Pigeon took it, scanned it briefly, and then cast an accusatory look at this assistant.

"I let Cory write this report, along with a few others that day. We'd been overrun with work, and when that happens I generally do the hard stuff and let him take care of the paperwork. I guess it'd be best if he filled you in on the details. I don't know anything about any missing organs. You can beat him if he made a mistake. I give you permission. Now turn that recorder back on so I can finish my work."

By the look on the old man's face, Bill could tell that Pigeon's good humor had evaporated. Bill nodded to Cory and the technician followed him out of the morgue and into the hallway, where they could talk without interrupting the man.

They stopped just outside the door to the morgue. The maintenance guy that Bill had asked directions of earlier, worked quietly on another fixture nearby, but otherwise the hallway was empty.

Cory was a skinny, sallow-faced young man. He reminded Bill of Barney Fife, a character from old Andy Griffith Show reruns. The man's hands shook constantly, as if he were perpetually nervousness.

"Can you tell me anything about the missing organs you listed in this report?" Bill held up a copy of the document.

Cory took the paper, reviewed it briefly. When he spoke, his voice was raspy, like two sheets of sandpaper rubbing together. Bill guessed that the man had probably smoked all his life, and it had affected his vocal cords, even at his young age.

The technician hitched a thumb back toward the morgue. "No matter what he says, it happened exactly like I put in the report. The kidneys and liver were missing. I never know what happens to a body in the OR, or in a patient care unit. I just report what I see. If I check a corpse and an organ is not where it should be, I make a note in the record. It's routine. It's no big deal."

"This kid was Jewish. It's against their religion to have organs taken from the body. They consider it mutilation. Were you aware of that?"

"No way! And I don't need to know anything about any missing organs that weren't supposed to be gone from the body. I do my reports exactly like the doc tells me to. I've still got the notes that I used to transcribe the report, if you want to see them. I keep 'em in a file cabinet next to my desk. I've got someplace I have to be in a few minutes, so right now's not a real good time, but I could get them to you tomorrow."

Bill checked his watch. "I'll pick them up first thing in the morning."

Cory nodded, but Bill could tell from his expression that the man was concerned about something. Then again, he was the perpetually nervous type that always seemed to be concerned about something.

Either way, Bill decided that it would be best not to pressure Cory too much at this point. From his military intelligence days, he knew that often the best way to get something from an informant was to give that person time to relax, to get used to the idea of talking to someone outside their normal sphere of associates. He'd used the same approach countless times during audits, and it generally got him the information that he needed.

Cory shrugged, his bony shoulders rising like the wing stubs of a vulture hunkered on a telephone wire. "Don't see why not. Come by first thing. There's nothing in the files that could do anyone any harm."

"Thanks," Bill said and hooked a thumb over his shoulder, toward the morgue. "Anything missing from that body on the table in there?"

He'd intended it as a joke, but Corey wasn't fazed.

"Sure," the pathology assistant said. "The kidneys are gone. It's pretty common. There's a big demand for 'em. This hospital's got one heck of a transplant program. It's kind of nice being a part of an organization that helps so many people, when you get right down to it."

"Yeah, real nice."

On the way back to his office, Bill swung by the administrative wing and poked his head into Sarah's office. No one was home. From his perception of the woman, that had to be unusual. It was only five p.m., and that was early for a woman as dedicated as Sarah.

Bill felt the beginnings of concern nagging at the back of his mind. What if she had uncovered incriminating information and whoever was responsible knew about it? She said that she'd told Carole and the CEO about her suspicions. What Sarah had been right about her suspicions, but the hospital's management team was in on the deal and had done something to Sarah, to get her out of the way?

He shook his head to clear the thought. He was getting too wrapped up in the whole conspiracy thing. He needed to retain his objectivity. She was probably already on her way home. Maybe she had a big date tonight. Who knew?

He'd keep a lookout for Sarah over the next few days, and if she didn't turn up, he'd say something to Carole, maybe even report it to the police.

Jan called Bill's office from the hospital lobby. She'd stopped by his office, but he hadn't been in. His phone rang several times before the voicemail kicked in. Frustrated, she hung up without leaving a message and glanced at her watch. It was five-thirty. She'd give him one more try in a few minutes, but first she'd call Judy and see how the RN was holding up. Something about the nurse's state of mind hadn't set well with Jan, and nagging thoughts lingered.

The death in the ICU this afternoon didn't feel right, just like

Judy's attitude. The man was terminal but was hanging in there on the respirator. He shouldn't have died the way he did, not that soon. Judy's attitude, Carole's visit to the ICU, the patient's sudden death – nothing about that shift in the ICU felt right.

She'd give Judy a call. Maybe she knew what had happened, beyond what was on the record. Maybe the woman just needed a shoulder. Jan had lost patients she'd cared about, too. She knew what it was like.

Then she'd call Jake and report what had happened.

Chapter 22

Bill slumped in his desk chair and stared through the dull reflective glass of his office window. The garden outside was empty of birds. The Junco had flown the coop, and the clouds drifting overhead seemed to gang up, blocking it out. There'd be rain in another couple of hours.

He swiveled back to his desk and the stack of papers waiting for him. When he'd left yesterday, they had been neatly piled and ordered to match the outline he'd drafted for his final report. One pile for each major area, six stacks in all. This morning, there were only five. The financials, policies, strategic plans, accreditation results, and Medicare audit files were all there. The patient case reviews for the transplant program were gone.

He had searched each desk drawer and his briefcase in the hope that he'd misplaced the file, but had turned up nothing. Even odder was the fact that the drawers of his desk were totally empty, as though someone had cleaned them. He'd stocked those same drawers with supplies days ago, so there should have been paper, pens, folders, and the usual assorted office items that a typical desk jockey needed to survive. Now it was all gone. Someone had cleaned

151

him out, and taken the file, but why?

The scanner! He'd scanned the patient charts from the file into his laptop computer, along with the rest of the source data for his report, and then downloaded it all onto a zip disk.

He took the laptop from his briefcase, placed it on the desktop and flipped it open. When the screen lit with his company's logo, he hit a three-key shortcut that took him to his draft of the final audit report for Wilkes Memorial. He blew out a long breath when he located the unlabeled zip disk in his briefcase and jammed it into the computer's zip drive. As the file of case reports opened and spread out before him on the computer screen, he nearly cheered. They were all there, including the section he'd created for the particularly sensitive files Sarah had given him. Those were password protected to ensure their security.

As he studied the computer files, he noticed that Luke Harrison's name was listed as the backup surgeon on the vast majority of the cases where questionable transplants were involved. The first couple of times he'd reviewed the records, he'd been focused on identifying the primary surgeon, or the physician in charge, and had missed that. Harrison's name was in every questionable file as the backup surgeon. He'd been in the OR every time a patient listed in the files had died.

Another idea popped into Bill's mind, so he scanned the files again, now looking for the name of the referring physician. Sure enough, there was Harrison's sidekick. With one exception, the referring physician had either been Dr. Harrison, or his buddy, Dr. Ian Farley. It didn't seem to matter if the case originated in the OR, ER, or in an outpatient clinic, one of the two doctors was always listed in the file.

Now he had a definite link between two of the hospital's key staff members and the questionable cases. W.M. had more than fifty physicians listed on staff, and those two names regularly showing up in the questionable files had to be more than mere coincidence. Bill didn't believe in coincidences.

He was so focused on his findings that he practically jumped out of his chair when the door to his office suddenly swung open.

Carole peeked around the door jam. "You busy?"

Bill inhaled a deep breath to force his racing heart to slow.

She didn't wait for a response, but closed the door behind her, came across the room and around his desk, and sat on its corner, smiling down at him. She ran a tapered, manicured finger down the sleeve of his jacket.

"I haven't heard from you for a couple of days. What's the matter? I thought we had a good time the other night." She swung a leg around and rubbed her knee lightly against his.

Bill slid his chair back out of range.

"I believe the last time we saw each other, you were trying to reshape my face with your fist. I'm not anxious to go through that again." He stood, and turned away to face the window. Though he was facing away from her, he could see her clearly in the window's reflection.

"Maybe I want to give you another chance."

He wanted to laugh, but failed to see the humor in any of Carole's behavior. She could change her color at the drop of a hat. One minute she was pummeling the side of his face. The next, she sauntered into his office like a seductress, looking for a willing sacrifice. No matter what they'd had, or how she'd been twenty years ago, she was dangerous now.

He turned back to face her. "I don't think I'm up to it. I think you had it right the other day, when you said our being together like that was a mistake."

She swung off the desk, slid up beside him and caressed the sleeve of his shirt.

Bill felt anger rise inside him, anger at himself for letting things get out of hand, and anger at her for continuing the charade. She didn't want him for any lasting relationship, he was sure, and he didn't want anything further to do with her, except in as much as it affected his need to complete his job at the hospital. The Carole he'd known before no longer existed. The new Carole was way too complex, maybe even disturbed, and he desperately needed to keep his distance from her. That he'd slept with her hadn't helped the situation at all. How could he have been so stupid?

He looked down at Carole, at the smug smile, the confidence in her eyes, running her eyes over him like he was some sort of prey she had cornered.

No. His feelings for her were gone. The things he'd felt the other day were the fleeting imaginings of a Bill from twenty years ago. He'd been wrong to indulge those fantasies.

He put his hands on Carole's shoulders and moved her back a step. "You're a complex woman, Carole. You always have been. After all these years, you can still stir my blood, but this isn't going anywhere."

He saw the anger light up her eyes, the same fire he'd seen in the parking lot at the hotel. He dropped his hands from her shoulders and stepped back.

Carole spun on her heel and stalked to the other side of the room. "You didn't think that way the other night when you were ripping off my clothes."

"I didn't know how I felt a few days ago. And besides, what happened then was mutual and instigated by you. It happened, there's no denying it, but it's past, over."

"It's that Jan McDonald woman, isn't it? I'll fire the little slut for this."

Before he could respond, she raised her chin and pointed a long-nailed finger at him, like a weapon. "I came by to let you know that Wilkes Memorial has terminated your audit. We no longer require the donation offered by your client. We have found an alternate source of funding. We have contacted your firm in California and advised them of that fact. You, Mr. Deming, are fired."

Carole gripped the doorknob, her trim form rigid and outlined in stark relief against the deep mahogany of the office door. "I want you out of here by the end of the day. You can take until then to write your reports, but stay out of my way in the meantime."

"All this because of one night, because you feel scorned?"

"I told you I'd never let what Kurt did to me happen again. You should have listened.

"You messed up in more ways than you can count, Bill. You used me, and you can't imagine what I can do to someone who does that. You're only seeing the first piece of what this is going to cost you."

Bill's voice was low and cold as his own anger flared.

"I used you? It was you who met me at the door and practically *ripped* my clothes off. I am sorry I had a part in what followed, but I'm not totally to blame."

Carole's chin went up and she opened her mouth, but Bill

continued before she could speak.

"You wouldn't know anything about a file that's missing from my desk, would you?"

She smiled, but the expression held little warmth.

"You're in my hospital. You can say what you like, deny what you did to anyone you like, but you will be held accountable for what you've done to me. I'm not the weak little schoolgirl you once knew. I do know that one of our clerks presented you with some information that you shouldn't have received. There were patient records in that file, which must be protected by this organization from prying eyes like yours. I had the files removed from your office and shredded. You can request access to the same files, of course, but short of a search warrant, you will have a difficult time getting any cooperation from Wilkes Memorial, now or in the future."

Bill met her leveled gaze; his words slicing out like the sharp edge of a knife. "Then I'll be in touch with the police regarding my findings, and I'll suggest that they provide a search warrant to continue the investigation."

After all he'd been through, the trashed hotel room, a painful sock in the jaw, the threats; he decided that he was more determined than ever to finish the job he'd started. He was certain his employer would back him – or there would be no huge contribution to the hospital – but the issue was now larger than a charitable donation. This was about human lives, and the trust that patients placed in their health care giver's hands.

"You have to be a cop or a lawyer to get one of those. You're no policeman. You're a bureaucrat, an auditor. You're nobody. Come see me when and if you can find someone who will support your delusional theories."

Carole nearly ran over Jan as she strode out of the room. Jan smiled as she passed, while Carole gave Jan a withering stare, and then stormed off.

"Did I interrupt something important?" Jan hesitated just inside the door.

Bill shook his head and sat down. "I don't know. How much did you hear?"

"Everything after the part when she said you're going to pay for what you did to her. What did you do?"

155

He waved her to a chair across from the desk. "It's not important. Although, apparently I've just been fired."

Jan eased into the high-backed chair, folded her hands in her lap, and waited for Bill to continue.

Bill looked up from examining the tips of his fingernails, after some minutes of silence. He might as well tell her. If his feelings for Jan were developing like he thought, it would have to come out sooner or later. Bad news never got better over time.

"A long time ago, Carole and I had a relationship. We were just kids, back in high school. When I got back into town for the audit, we got together again."

Bill could see the flush begin to fill Jan's cheeks as she put two and two together.

"Together?"

Bill nodded his head. He was bad at hiding the truth; it had been his downfall during his brief stint in Military Intelligence. He felt he was probably wearing enough of an explanation on his face when he met her eyes.

"You slept with her?" Jan's tone sounded half question, not wanting to believe, and half accusatory. The effect was crushing. Bill felt his heart sink. Enemies had yelled at him, pointed rifles at him. He'd been threatened by CEOs of some of the largest corporations in the world, but it had not felt like this. He felt like something valuable was slipping away from him, and there was nothing he could do about it.

"I didn't realize the feelings I would develop toward you. The thing with Carole was before that. I was probably guilty of being insensitive, of not appreciating the impact the encounter would have on Carole, or her state of mind. I could have handled things better."

He averted his eyes from the pain in Jan's expression and looked, instead, to the garden outside. The sun was just peeking through the clouds, although it dimmed as quickly as it came. The lone Junco was back, flitting about the plants, pecking at the ground for seeds.

"You say you have feelings for me, yet you go to bed with her? How could you be so insensitive, to her and to me?"

Bill continued to stare out the window. "At the time, it was a fling with an old girlfriend, which she initiated. I hardly knew you at that point."

"Making love to a woman is just a fling, like it's nothing? Carole's probably a wreck over this. I see why she stormed out of here. Carole fired you?"

"Yes."

"I'm not surprised. It's probably better than you deserve."

Bill winced. Those last words felt like he'd been smacked across the shoulders with a club. He turned slowly to face Jan. Maybe he was an insensitive monster. He opened his mouth to offer a reply, but Jan saved him the trouble by cutting him off.

"I don't want to talk about this any more, and we don't have the time. Jake called a few minutes ago. He's at Sarah's house. There's a body there, and he asked if we'd come down and ID it. You've met Sarah, and I'm not sure that I could pick her out of a crowd."

Bill's gut knotted. Sarah? Dead? He'd just seen her a few days ago. First his hotel room, then Sarah? Someone was scared, and there didn't seem to be any limits to what they'd do to protect themselves.

He retrieved his jacket from the back of a chair, and led the way to the door. "We'd best get over there to meet him. We can take my car."

A half hour later they pulled into Sarah Laughlin's driveway. The house was a small, white Cape Cod style building, with dormers along the roof. It was nestled on a cul-de-sac in North Olympia, the old part of town that dated back to the early nineteen twenty's. Quaint would have adequately described the place, with its blue-on-blue shutters and neat garden bordered by a flagstone walk.

Jan got out without a word, slammed the car door behind her and headed for the front door, then stopped halfway up the walk and turned back to Bill. She held her hands out to her sides as if she was about to say something, then muttered, "I don't want to do this." As Bill was about to say that he'd go in alone if she wanted, she suddenly reversed course again and headed for the front door.

Bill followed silently behind.

Jake met them on the front porch, glanced briefly at the expression on his sister's face, and cocked an inquisitive brow in Bill's direction. When Bill ignored the gesture, Jake shrugged and waved them into the front room.

As they entered the house, Jake said, "We questioned the man who worked in the office next to Sarah at the hospital this afternoon.

He'd called the Olympia PD earlier in the day to report her as missing. Seems like the boy had a crush Ms. Laughlin."

When they were all through the front door, Jake held up a hand to hold them from proceeding further into the house. "This won't be pretty. Whoever killed her made quite a mess of it. The dining room where we found her is covered with blood, as is the kitchen where we think the fight started."

They walked through the house, and Bill noticed the odd collection of furniture that seemed to suggest that Sarah was more than just a little complicated, as an individual. The living room was a hodge-podge of antique furnishings. A sofa that must have dated back to the thirties, but looked like it had recently been recovered sat against one wall, covered by a collage of small, crocheted doilies. Several more contemporary overstuffed chairs of contrasting blues and greens were scattered around the room, spaced among a half dozen occasional tables of dark mahogany and walnut. Of the latter, Bill could not see one that wasn't covered with pictures of Sarah's cats and dog.

"Kind of like stepping back in time by half a century," Bill said.

Jake took them deeper into the house, to the dining room. "We questioned her neighbors," he said. "They said she pretty much kept to herself. Few visitors ever came to the place. No one knew much about her, although she's lived here all her life. She inherited the place from her folks when they died."

They paused at the arch that opened to the dining room. It was worse than Jake had said. Blood was everywhere. It was smeared on the furniture and walls with big blotches across the wall-to-wall carpeting.

Jake paused at the archway leading into the kitchen. "While this is bad enough, what you're about to see is much, much worse. You both up to this?"

Jan and Bill nodded silently, and followed Jake into the kitchen.

"The weapon was a large kitchen knife. She was stabbed repeatedly, and didn't die easy. We've got blood from a second person, probably the attacker, so we know she put up a fight. Don't touch anything. I've got a team on the way to collect samples for DNA testing."

Dead bodies were nothing new to Bill, but what he saw reminded him of his worst days in either Egypt or Haiti, where death of this kind had been a daily occurrence. Jake lifted the edge of a light tarp that covered the body and Bill felt bile rise in his throat. Jan turned suddenly and left the room.

Bill forced down his reaction and examined the face of the dead woman carefully.

"That's not Sarah," he said. "I don't know who it is, but it's not Sarah Laughlin."

Jake let the tarp fall back across the dead woman's face. Jan came back into the room to stand behind Bill and leaned her head against his shoulder. She held a framed photograph in one hand, and lifted it to show Bill and Jake. "The dead woman's in this picture," she said. "She must be Sarah's sister or a friend"

"Hang on a minute." Jake turned to one of the uniformed officers standing nearby. "Get me the wallet you found on the bedroom desk."

The police officer returned with a thin blue pocketbook. Jake took it and flipped through its pages. "I assumed this was her purse, and didn't spend much time with it. It was a rookie mistake." He fished a license from the wallet, and examined it closely. "Here she is. Luvelle Detwhiller. Florida license. There's a phone number and address. We'll check it out."

Bill walked back through the dining room, his eyes lingering on the aged furniture, so varied in style and age, but obviously well cared for. Now much of it was covered with the dead woman's blood.

Jake and Jan followed a few steps behind.

"It wasn't a professional hit," Jake said. "Professionals are neat, almost sterile when they kill. This was the work of an amateur, someone driven by passion or anger. Those are the cases that are brutal, like this one."

"All killing is brutal," Jan said. "No matter how much death I see at the hospital, it is still the most violent thing I can't imagine someone doing to another person."

Jake ran a hand through his thick hair, and then glanced at his watch. "You're right, of course. It's the perpetual police student in me that says things like that. It's after six. Go have a glass of wine for me somewhere. I'll be here a long time before we wrap this up."

Bill and Jan left without another word. Neither spoke until they were in Bill's car and headed away from the house. "You want to get that glass of wine? Maybe we could talk," Bill said.

Jan's jaw set as she stared out the front window of the Supra. "Just take me home. I think I've had enough trauma for one day."

Bill nodded. Between his affair with Carole and the dead woman at Sarah's house, he could understand how she felt. Even so, his insides churned because it was his actions that had killed their budding relationship, nearly as dead as the woman in the kitchen. The understanding settled into his gut with a sickening certainty as he pulled onto the main road and headed south, toward her place.

When they pulled up to her house, Jan initially didn't make any move to get out, as though she lacked the energy needed to open the door and leave the car. She blinked several times, and then tears ran down her cheeks. Her lower lip trembled.

Finally, Bill got out and opened the door for her. With a considerable effort, Jan climbed out of the sports car and then, in another second, was in his arms. She clutched his waist fiercely as her body shook with heavy sobs. Bill stood numbly, his arms around her shoulders, fighting back his own emotions and any words he might have to comfort her. It was one of those times where silence was the only therapy.

After a few minutes, he felt her grip soften and the flow of tears ebb. She released him then and stepped back. Grudgingly, he let her go.

"Are you going to be all right? I could stay for a while, if you like. Under the circumstances, you might not want me around."

She shook her head, cutting him off. Her expression was sad, weary. "Life's too short for this craziness. That woman at Sarah's ..."

She swayed toward him, and her lips were suddenly against his, tender at first and then hot, passionate. The sensation, the heat, was like a tonic that washed through him. It was a long kiss that deepened and sent tendrils of warmth shooting to every limb. When she released him once more, she took his hand and led him toward the house. "Stay," she said. "I need you to stay."

She led him to the front of the house and paused at the top of the stoop. She gave him a searching glance as she rested one hand on the doorknob. "You understand that I don't believe in casual sex. If you stay with me tonight, it has to be more than that."

Bill's answering smile came slowly, uncertainly, but built from deep inside. He must have looked silly, because Jan's sad expression brightened slightly and she actually smiled.

"I'll take that as an affirmative," Jan said.

Later that night, they drove back to Bill's hotel and rescued Alex from the room. Jan and the dog had a brief discussion about who was going to ride in the front seat, but settled it easily enough with Alex and Jan both crammed into the passenger seat. It was a crowded arrangement, with sixty pounds of dog ensconced in Jan's lap, but it brought out a much-needed laugh from both Bill and Jan as they drove back to Jan's house.

It was late night before they all settled in the warmth of Jan's home. When Bill and Jan headed for the bedroom, Alex joined them, and draped himself around their feet at the end of Jan's small double bed. There they remained, Bill and Jan wrapped around each other with feet entangled in bed sheets, blankets and dog.

The next day, Jan wasn't due at the hospital until after noon for her shift in the ICU. Bill felt no pressure to return to his office to wrap up his reports, so they lingered over breakfast. It was over toast and coffee that Bill mentioned the missing files to Jan.

"If Jake's suspicions are correct," he said, "then Carole is likely implicated in all this and may have taken those files. If she's mixed up in that, and then if the murder at Sarah's home is tied into all of this…"

Jan considered his words through a long silence. "You'd better call Jake and tell him about the files Sarah Laughlin gave you, and what Carole said. Carole has to be involved in this. I don't believe something like the killings of patients at Wilkes could go on without someone in management knowing about it. And I'm not saying that because of what happened between the two of you, but it just makes sense."

Bill found it difficult to challenge her logic, except about the killings. "Carole has certainly changed since I knew her, but it's hard to imagine her killing anyone. Having me fired and throwing me off the hospital campus, now that's more her style, but killing someone? I don't know about that. On the other hand, Sarah has been missing from her job for awhile now, and it's my impression that she would not just get up and leave without telling someone."

"Unless she's in hiding. If someone at the hospital found out she'd given you the information, maybe even threatened her, then she'd be scared and maybe run. Who knows were she could be by now?" Jan said.

Bill stared out the kitchen window toward the long rows of animal pens and bird enclosures in the field behind the house. "As much as I saw death and violence when I was in the Army, it's still hard to think of anyone killing another person over something as empty as profit, and it seems that money is all the people at Wilkes are after, those involved in the organ transplant killings. This tops anything that I experienced in the military."

"These are desperate people. They must have found out Sarah gave you information that would condemn them. They must have felt that they needed to shut her up. We don't know exactly how many patients they've already killed to support their program, so it's not hard to imagine them doing something like that," she said.

Jan slid her chair back and grabbed the phone from the kitchen counter. "I've got to make a call."

Bill sipped his coffee and let his gaze wander out the kitchen window again. He could see one of the eagles in the nearest enclosure. It seemed agitated and strutting back and forth on a thick perch, wings spread wide. A second later, a hawk did the same thing in another cage across the narrow walk that divided the rows of screened enclosures. A minute later, a cat crept up the grassy row between the cages, and then was gone. Both birds fluffed their wing feathers, and then settled back onto their perches.

Jan hung up the phone and slid back into the chair across from him at the kitchen table.

"Problem?" he asked.

"Just a hunch that struck me a minute ago. I called the home phone number of one of the girls who worked the ICU shift with me yesterday. We lost a patient unexpectedly, and she was the nurse in charge of the patient. She was upset before the man died, but now that I think of it, seemed uncommonly distraught for someone of her years of experience. I wanted to check on her. Her roommate just told me Judy went in to the hospital early this morning to resign her position. She said that Judy had already arranged for a mover to ship what little she owned to somewhere back east. Now, why would she do that all of a sudden?"

"That is odd. It takes time to arrange a move across the country, with movers, utilities that have to be cut off, bank accounts that need to be closed. She must have known she was leaving well before today," Bill said.

Jan sipped her cup of coffee and watched Bill over the rim of the cup. "Losing a patient is tough on anyone, but ICU nurses see death all the time. Quitting your job over it seems a bit excessive. Maybe there's another reason."

"You think she played a role in the patient's death, maybe as part of this organ theft issue?" Bill said.

"Maybe," Jan said. "It makes about as much sense as anything we've seen so far. First, Sarah disappears. Then someone dies in her home. According to Jake's records at the bureau, there have been fifteen patients who have died when their prognosis was for a full recovery, or at least a long, lingering death. Each has become an organ donor for the hospital immediately following their death. If Judy was paid off for assisting with the death, or even looking the other way, it would be enough to motivate someone to clear out of the area."

This time, Bill picked up the phone, fished in his shirt pocket for a note he'd written yesterday, and dialed the number of the pathologist's office.

"Pigeon here," the hefty voice of the hospital's senior pathologist answered the call.

"Doctor Pigeon, it's Bill Deming. We talked yesterday. Is Cory around?"

"Ah, Mr. Deming." The pathologist's voice was noticeably cool. "No, Cory doesn't work here any longer. I think he wanted a job closer to his home in Seattle."

"He left Wilkes? He got a new job?"

"I, ah, gave him a little assist on his way, you might say. It was better for everyone concerned. There were some irregularities in the records that couldn't be explained, and he was closest to that sort of thing. You remember. I think you brought up some of those issues when you talked to him the other day. I had to do something and I'm afraid he was the sacrifice that had to be made. Can't tolerate that sort of thing, can we? He didn't leave a forwarding number. Now, I really do have to get back to work. A new body came in late yesterday and

I'm already late with my report."

"Thank you, doctor."

"Don't mention it. Say, didn't I hear that you were done with your audit? Thought you'd be on your way back to California by now."

"I'll be here for a few more days. You have a new body in for autopsy? Would it be the man from the ICU? A Mr...."

Bill waved toward Jan.

"Parsons," she whispered.

"A Mr. Parsons?" Bill said.

Pigeon didn't reply immediately, but the pause was significant and spoke like words never could. "I'm not at liberty ..."

"At least can you tell me if the patient was, by any chance, an organ donor?"

Papers were shuffled at the other end of the line as Bill waited.

"Why, yes. Yes, he was. It's right here in the doctor's report."

"Can you tell me who the doctor was who signed that report? I can get that through the Freedom of Information Act, or you can tell me now." Bill was pushing his luck. The FIA didn't apply to private hospitals, but he was betting that Pigeon didn't know that.

"It was Dr. Farley, the Internist. Now I really do have to get back to work."

Bill thanked the pathologist and hung up.

"So, what did he say?" Jan asked.

Bill set his cup down and faced Jan. "He wouldn't say that the new body in the morgue was Parsons, but it seemed obvious by his reaction that it was. He did indicate that it was an organ donor. Farley signed the death certificate and authorized release of the organs. I'd bet big money that we have another patient murder on our hands, and that, as you say, Judy was involved."

"Farley signed the death certificate?" The tone of Jan's voice went up a notch. "That'd be a real trick."

"What do you mean?"

"Parsons was Farley's patient, but Farley wasn't the attending physician when Mr. Parsons died. I was there. Dr. Thompson was on duty. He would have signed the report. Why would Thompson have Farley sign things when he wasn't anywhere near the room when the patient died?"

Bill's smile was grim. "I think it's pretty obvious. Either

Thompson's in on this or Farley got there afterwards and falsified the record. It wouldn't be the first time a patient record was 'doctored' after the fact, here or at any hospital in the country. People make mistakes and try to correct them every day, sometimes legitimately, sometimes not so legally. I'm going to head into the hospital and see if I can talk to Thompson, maybe even get a look at the report Pigeon wrote up on the autopsy. Why don't you call Jake and fill him in."

Jan glanced at the clock over the kitchen sink, and then back to Bill. "It's only a little past nine. Thompson works the off-shift, like I do today. He won't be at the hospital until noon."

"That's three hours," Bill said. "What shall we do with all that time on our hands?"

"I'll bet we can find something to do," she said.

Chapter 23

Dr. Farley's desk phone rang. Only a few staff and his wife knew his direct the number, so when it rang, it seldom meant good news.

He picked up the receiver. "Dr. Farley here."

"We need to talk," said the voice at the other end of the line.

It was Luke Harrison, and Farley knew exactly how this conversation would go. The man had been sniveling for a week, since Farley had the kid in the ER put away and his organs harvested. You'd think the head of surgery for one of the area's most renowned hospitals would have a little more spine. If he kept making an issue out of the case, it wouldn't be too much longer before he became a major liability.

"What is it, Luke?"

"Pigeon just called. He said Deming's been asking questions about the ICU patient. He said you were listed as physician of record on the death certificate. Deming seemed very interested in that, even asked if the dead man was an organ donor. I'm worried, Ian. First you took the ER patient, and now this one in the ICU. Things are getting out of control."

Farley picked his teeth with the edge of a page from a journal he'd been reading and considered Ian's words. Maybe Harrison had a point. Deming was getting close. Perhaps it was time to shut down the program for a while; let things cool off. The director had eliminated the leak of information from the pathologist's office and reportedly had taken care of the woman in patient records. He didn't know how the director had taken care of the woman, but the inference was that it had been a *permanent* solution. The nurse in the ICU had been a problem, but he'd dealt with her personally. That accounted for most of the loose ends, except for this Deming character. He didn't like the feeling he was getting about Mr. Deming. He might just ruin everything.

"I hear what you're saying, Ian. I'll call the Director and pass on what you've told me. She'll know what to do. She's kept this program going for a long time, and kept us rich in the process. I'm sure she won't want to risk everything we've worked for, so I'll suggest that we shut down for a time, until this cools off."

Harrison's sigh of relief came through clearly over the line. "I hope she agrees. I could use a rest from all this. I can barely operate with all this tension in the air."

Farley chuckled. "You just concentrate on all the money you have in your off-shore account. Even for a surgeon, you have to be the highest paid doctor in the country. Talk to you later, Luke. Stay calm. Things will work out."

Farley hung up without waiting for a reply and dialed the number that accessed the Director's private line. She answered on the first ring.

"Yes."

He thought it odd that she'd never said his name or revealed her own, that they'd never met in person, even though they'd worked together for several years. Once, he'd paid a friend at the police department to try to trace her phone, find out who she really was, but it had been routed through five different switches, including one across the border in Canada. Dead end. He had to admit the woman was organized and effective at what she did. If anyone could figure a way out of this dilemma, it would be her.

"This is Farley. We have a problem."

"Such as?" Her voice was calm, level, but with a hint of malice.

"It's Deming, the auditor. He's getting too close to us. Maybe we should shut things down for a little while until Deming's gone and the situation cools down."

Farley explained what Ian had told him.

"We're not shutting anything down, and don't either you or our illustrious chief surgeon worry about Deming. He's been fired and told to clear out. I doubt we'll hear anything further from him. If we do, he knows he'll lose his job with his firm in California. One of Wilkes's boards of directors is close with his employer. It was how he came to us in the first place. Deming's no longer a problem. Did you take care of the ICU nurse?"

"I bought her off, just like you said. I had to scare her a little, but she went willingly enough. She's on a plane at this very moment, going who knows where with her purse full of money. How about the Laughlin woman? Any problems there?"

"That's not your concern. I told you I'd take care of it. You tell the chief of surgery that he can relax, too."

Farley began to ask another question, but the line went dead with a soft click. He carefully returned the phone to its receiver, using the tips of his fingers as though it were hot.

Chapter 24

They drove to the hospital together that afternoon. Bill felt about as upset as any man would. He'd found the woman of his dreams and had been fired from his job all in the same day.

His termination from the hospital audit was based on the word of a scorned woman rather than anything related to his work, so it was hard to feel totally bad. On the other hand, he knew that if his boss in California put two and two together, he would have a pretty good case against Bill. There was really no way around it: Bill had screwed up, badly. Whether or not Carole was an old flame, she was still a member of the leadership team at a hospital he'd been sent to evaluate, and was off limits. That his professional conduct in the matter would be questioned seemed likely. When he got to the hospital, he'd call the California office, lay the cards on the table and see how they fell. He felt pretty sure how it would go, and it wasn't going to be pretty.

For now, he'd just enjoy the moment with Jan.

Alex was stretched across the sports car's small back seat, his body twisted so that his head rested on the console between Bill and Jan. Jan scratched the dog's head as they drove. Alex's eyes rolled with pleasure when Bill looked over at him.

Jan smiled when she caught him glancing at Alex. "What?"

"I'm just thinking that it's been a pretty busy week. I met an old flame that may have cost me this assignment, even my job. I met a timid little records clerk that may have uncovered a plot to murder patients and who has disappeared. Someone else was murdered at the record clerk's home for reasons that seem pretty obvious. And I met a woman who, in just over a week, captures my heart in a way I'd never thought possible."

Jan reached over and squeezed his hand, where he gripped the car's stick shift. "Sounds like things are working out just fine," she said.

"It's hard to think that someone didn't take you off the market before this." Bill said. "How come I'm the lucky guy?"

He could see her broad smile out of the corner of his eye as he worked the Supra through the thick traffic on Capital Way, the capital city's main thoroughfare. Her chin tipped up a little before she replied. "And who says I'm off the market? You sound pretty sure of yourself, buster."

When he started to apologize for his presumption, she squeezed his hand again, shutting off his words.

"Oh, I've had a few dates, even been pursued, but the relationships never lasted. I've always been too busy with my career. That' why Ruth—you remember Ruth?"

Bill groaned. "How could I forget the original Miss Matchmaker?"

"That she is. It's why Ruth is constantly pushing some poor unsuspecting soul my way or giving him my office number. My record at relationships has not been great, and she knows it, so she keeps trying. I've asked her to stop, but she says someone has to look out for my interests. It's actually kind of sweet."

Bill laughed, as he ran the car from second to third gear. "I seem to run into that woman constantly around the hospital. I saw her just yesterday, down near the lab, when I was on my way back from talking to Dr. Pigeon. She gets around."

"Ruth is a pretty vigorous woman. I hope I'm in as good a shape as she is when I'm her age. She has a very nice old house in North Olympia, you know, on a hill overlooking Puget Sound. It's a big place, and since her husband died, she's kept it up all by herself. I don't know how she does it. The expense alone must be monumental, not to mention all the cleaning, repairs and such. The work she puts in to keep the yards mowed, the gardens tended… It's no wonder she's in such good shape. I don't think there's an ounce of fat on the woman."

Jan released her grip on his hand as he pulled into the hospital's parking lot. As they stepped out of the car, Jan's voice sounded almost shy as she asked, "Did you mean what you said earlier, about me capturing your heart?"

Bill nodded, came around the car and took her arm. "And I'm not too proud to say it, even as a confirmed bachelor."

She put her arms around his waist and pulled him toward her in a warm embrace. "Well, I'll have to give that comment some thought and see where I stand on the issue."

There was a stack of messages on Bill's desk when he unlocked his office door fifteen minutes later. That they were there, that the deliverer hadn't hesitated about entering his unoccupied office and compromising the confidentiality of his records, attested to the fact that they had little fear of him any longer. Fortunately, he'd kept all of the important papers in his briefcase, and he'd kept that with him. Anything of critical importance, he'd been careful to scan into his laptop, which he kept locked in the back of the Supra, with Alex on guard.

Bill laughed at the thought of the big Labrador retriever guarding anything. Who would have thought that once, long ago, he'd actually had Alex trained to work as a guard dog? It had been one of his many failed attempts at having a hobby while stationed for three long years in Germany, where dog training was considered a serious undertaking, and all dogs were trained.

Alex had actually done pretty well with the training, until the point where he was supposed to attack a well-padded attacker. Instead of charging the assailant, Alex had simply sat down in the grass and stared at the man, tail thumping as he apparently waited for a pat on the head.

That had been years ago, and all the training had since been lost under the comfortable roles of the dog's thick flesh and fur. At least Alex was big enough to discourage intruders, even if he wasn't very fierce. They might think twice before breaking into his car, as long as they didn't know the dog.

Bill dropped his briefcase next to his desk and picked up the messages. He recognized Ruth's handwriting at once. She had delivered many such messages to him over the past weeks, although if he hadn't been in the room, she'd normally taped them to his door.

The first was from his employer in California, asking that he call at once. Elliot Farewell, his immediate supervisor and principle owner of the company, was not the type to call if it wasn't urgent, and Bill expected that he knew exactly what they'd be talking about. They'd known each other from their military days. They'd been good friends ever since. But Elliot was also a political man, a savvy businessman, and Bill had a bad feeling about where their conversation would go as he picked up the phone and dialed his boss's number.

Elliot's secretary answered the call on the first ring. "Farewell Consulting, may I help you?"

"Alice, it's Bill Deming. I got a message to give Elliot a call."

"I'll put you right through. He's in a meeting, but said to interrupt him if you called. Is everything going well up there?"

"It's interesting, Alice, very interesting."

Bill heard a click as the call was transferred.

"Bill, you there? Is everything all right up there?" Elliot's voice was its usual mix of unbridled enthusiasm and diplomacy, but sounded more tempered than usual, wary.

Bill paused to gather his thoughts before responding. "I thought so until a few days ago. In fact, I figured I'd be done by today, but something came up."

Elliot cut in as Bill took a breath. "So I've heard. You think you've uncovered some sort of conspiracy, and the hospital's management team is really upset. They say you're creating a stink with our client, alleging that you've gotten caught up in some sort of fiction that could ruin the hospital's reputation. They're threatening a lawsuit. Bill, you've encountered conspiracy theorists at every site we've sent you to. It's commonplace enough for all of our consultants. You know better than to get caught up in these things, to listen to those people."

"The police are involved in this one, Elliot."

Bill could hear Elliot's frustrated intake of air and braced himself for what he knew was coming.

"You're not down there to play cops and robbers. You're there to do a job. You represent this firm at that worksite. You will not engage in damaging speculation outside the scope of your audit."

"You know me better than that. I wouldn't allow myself to get sucked into something fictitious. This is different. We go way back, Elliot, to when we were both working in intelligence. You know I'm experienced enough to know the difference between conspiracy games and the real thing. There is criminal activity here, not just business irregularities. They are killing patients in this place. I'm convinced of it, and so are the police. At least one patient was murdered, and perhaps many more. What I've uncovered seems to validate that there is much more to this place than meets the eye. The police were already involved before I got here."

Elliot's voice came back soft and low, which Bill knew did not bode well for the conversation. When Elliot had been a colonel in the Army, and Bill only a major, Elliot had dressed him down once using that voice. He'd deserved it back then, and would never forget the agony the quiet voice had caused.

"This is your first job for us in Washington State, Bill, and we do a lot of business up there. The state's medical industry is growing in leaps and bounds, and there's a lot of opportunity for us, particularly in Olympia. Many of Wilkes' board of directors are important in state politics. We mess with them, and we lose business. It's as simple as that. We can't afford to lose the business. We're paying you a great deal of money for what you do, and there's nothing in your contract that calls for you to conduct a criminal investigation, real or imagined."

"But..."

"No buts, Bill. Back off from this issue, and do it now. Finish your report today and fax it to me. If you feel strongly that something may be going on there, include it in the report and then let go of it. Wrap this up before you do us serious damage and get out of there."

Bill slumped down in his chair, and then swung it around and gazed out at the garden beyond the window as he considered his response to Elliot's demand. The Junco was back, pecking at the ground around the base of a large bush. That's me, he thought, just pecking away at the seeds. Maybe it's time for a change.

"I can't do that, Elliot. I'll write up my report, and I'll fax it to you like you said, but I'm not heading home just yet. Too much is involved. People are losing their lives up here, and I can't just walk away from it. The State Bureau of Investigation has asked me to help with their investigation. It would be wrong for me not to help them out, given what I know."

Elliot's tone relayed his increasing impatience. "I've been informed about your involvement in an unwanted romantic affair with one of the hospital's officers, the assistant administrator. Are you sure her rejection of your advances hasn't clouded your judgment, sent you on a crusade to ruin her hospital? Really, Bill, what's happened to your judgment? You've always been so reliable, so grounded."

Bill's anger flared. This time it was his voice that came out soft, quiet, and tempered with cool steel. "I can be pretty sure where your information came from, and I can tell you what you're hearing is off the mark. And I resent the fact that you would accept any of it as fact without first checking with me. For the record, my relationship with any woman is separate from business matters, particularly when it was I who was pursued and not the other way around. You getting that information was just a weak attempt by someone who wanted to divert attention away from what's really going on here. The point is that patient lives are being lost and the hospital staff is likely to be involved. I will send you my report, Elliot, but I will also ship a copy directly to your client, advising him of my findings."

"You do that and you'll leave me no choice."

"I'll do what I have to do. You know me well enough to know that. Ethics force me to resolve what I've found before I quit this location, and also to inform the client of those findings. I'm sure he wouldn't want to see his money go to an organization engaged in the sort of activities I've seen here."

Bill could hear the long sigh escape from Elliot before the man's next words. "If you feel that strongly, you must do what you believe is right. I respect your position on this, as I always have respected your position on things in the past. You cannot, however, do what you suggest as an employee of Farewell Consulting."

Bill watched as the Junco flew off and disappeared into the bushes at the edge of the garden. "That's too bad. I've always enjoyed working with you and the rest of the gang at the office. I'll fax you a letter of resignation today."

"It'll be accepted. Goodbye, Bill."

As Bill hung up the phone, Ruth poked her head through his doorway. Bill smiled at the woman's open grin. She wore a Pendleton jump suit of a dark blue and green plaid. Blue-white hair was swept back from her lined face in a stiff hairdo, right out of the sixties. Her pale blue eyes lit up as she hesitantly stepped into the office, then dimmed when she noticed Bill's frown.

"Everything all right, dear? I just stopped by to see if you found the messages I left earlier. I have another one, from a Mr. Jake Williams. He said it was very important."

"Thanks, Ruth. Everything's all right," he lied. "But thanks for asking."

Ruth set the note on the corner of Bill's desk and folded her arms over her thin chest. "Carole tells me you're leaving us. Are you finished with your work, then?"

"Yep," he replied. "All done today, right this moment, actually."

"I'll be sorry to see you go. Did you and Jan ever make a connection?"

Bill brightened at her prod. "You know we did, Ruth, and I'd actually like to thank you for introducing us. She's a wonderful woman."

"But you'll be leaving the area."

"No. Actually, I'm thinking about staying around for a while. I think I've missed being in the northwest."

Ruth gave him a lopsided grin. "And then there's Jan. That's a pretty good incentive to stay around, too, isn't it? Well, you keep in touch, whatever you do. And have a care with Jan. I feel a responsibility to the girl."

Ruth turned and disappeared out the door.

When she was gone, Bill picked up the phone and punched in Jake's number.

A second later, Jake came on the line. "Bill. What can I do for you?"

"You called me."

"Right. Sorry. Real busy at this end. Can you fill me in on anything you've found? The state attorney general got word that we're investigating Wilkes, and we're getting pressure to deliver our findings, or cut and run. Lots of politics in this case, it seems."

Bill described what he and Jan had uncovered. "It seems likely that the patient who died in the ICU yesterday was an organ donor and another victim."

"Too bad for the patient. We have got to stop what's going on at that place now. I recorded what you just said, and I'm glad I did. You and Jan have provided some good leads. Based on what you two have uncovered and your audit findings, I could probably get a search warrant now to go through the hospital's records. On the other hand, our showing up with a warrant would alert whoever's involved to the fact that we're on to them. They might go to ground, and blow the investigation. Any chance you could get into the Pathology Department and get a first-hand look at the autopsy reports on that patient? Maybe Jan could take a look at the body before it's moved to the funeral home. As a nurse, she might be able to spot something about the body that suggested unauthorized organs had been removed. If she did, it would definitely be a 'smoking gun', the sort of thing we'd need to take this case to the next level."

"Without a search warrant, that'd be breaking and entering, wouldn't it? I've just been fired from my job, Jake. I've got no real reason to be in the hospital once I clean out my desk. Jan might be able to explain her presence in the path lab or morgue, but for me, it'd be pushing things pretty far."

"I would never ask you to do anything illegal," Jake said. "On the other hand, we have cause to issue a search warrant now and what we're talking about is no more than a chance to make sure that when we do execute the search warrant, we get what we need on the first try. I know there's risk involved in what I'm suggesting, and I can't officially ask you to break the law. However, by entering the morgue and locating what we think is there, you'd help us to focus our search. What you find could be invaluable.

"My experience with killers of any social standing, like these doctors, is that at the first evidence of someone sniffing about their heels, they go to ground. Then it's almost impossible to get the goods on them. They're too high-society and well connected to touch without practically being caught in the act. Why do you think MEDICARE fraud cases take so long to get to court? These people may be criminals, but they're powerful, connected, and they're definitely not dumb. It can take decades to close a complex case if we screw up the first try to get at the culprits. What we need is confirmation that the case in the ICU is organ rip-off and murder. Then we get a warrant to seize the records. To make sure we're headed in the right direction, we need Jan's hands inside the body cavity and you staring at a report that lays out the facts."

Bill swiveled his chair and looked for the Junco in the garden beyond the windows. It was nowhere to be seen.

"So, we go in, take a look at the body and the report and give you a call?" Bill said.

"That'd be the ticket. I'll have a couple of investigators hanging around the hospital in case you get into trouble." Jake said.

"We'd better do this today, while I still have some kind of reason to be around here. Tomorrow, I may not be able to get into the place. What about communication with your people?"

"Jan carries a hand-held CB in her car for emergencies. My crew will monitor Channel 11. You call out on that radio and they'll come running."

"Thanks. I'll give you a call when I have a chance to talk to Jan. I should see her in another hour or so."

Chapter 25

Bill glanced at the remaining phone messages on his desk. They were from a variety of people: his secretary back at the office in California, his parents, and the hotel. He stuffed the one from his parents in his pocket and filed the rest in the wastebasket, then spent the next forty-five minutes putting the finishing touches on his final report and expense sheet. Without a lot of fanfare, he emailed the documents off to his office in California.

His ex-office, he corrected himself.

After that, he typed out a brief electronic mail message, a letter of resignation, and sent that off to his ex-boss, too. There was no satisfaction in watching the email disappear from his computer screen, as it dashed off through the ether to his old employer. He'd liked his job, the company, and the people he worked with. He'd miss all of it.

Finally, he sent a copy of his final report of audit findings to the man who'd commissioned the audit of Wilkes Memorial. He felt a sense of responsibility to the man who'd requested a clear picture of W.M.'s operation, and there was no way he'd let his boss or anyone else edit the report when so much was on the line. In a separate note, he provided the man with Jake Williams' phone number at the

Washington State Bureau of Investigation, in the event more information was desired.

Bill powered down his laptop computer, boxed up the few things he'd accumulated in the temporary office, and then walked down to the loading docks, where he threw it all into a dumpster. He was headed back into the hospital when Dr. Pigeon, the pathologist, came out through the same doors. Their greeting was civil enough but curt, the pathologist making no pretense about wanting anything more to do with Bill.

Bill accepted the slight with a nod and continued through the doors, then paused and turned. He pushed back through the doors and looked around. Pigeon was nowhere to be seen. He glanced toward the road leading away from the docks and saw a small pickup truck heading away. Pigeon had driven off, and that gave Bill and idea.

Bill glanced up and down the length of the loading dock's long concrete ledge, with its evenly spaced rubber bumpers, hydraulic lifts and tall, sliding metal doors. There was a single personnel access door a few feet to the right of the last of those doors. The sign above it read "morgue. He knew from experience that hospitals often left the door to the morgue unsecured if a funeral home was expected to remove a body sometime during the day. He stepped over and tried the doorknob. It opened under his hand.

Bill checked up and down the long loading docks a final time. No one was in sight. He'd have a few minutes, anyway.

He slipped into the morgue and quietly eased the door shut behind him. The room was small, cold. The floor, walls and ceiling were tiled in green marble. The air was cool and smelled aseptic, with just a lingering trace of some preservative. A portable lift and sling stood in one corner, ready for transferring particularly large bodies. Along one wall stood a bank of twelve large sliding drawers set in into the front of a gleaming stainless steel refrigeration unit. That's where the bodies would be.

Across from the reefer was another door, leading back to the hospital's interior. A clipboard was hung on the wall next to the door. Bill flipped on the lights and the room filled with the glare of a half dozen florescent tubes. He slipped the clipboard from its hanger and rummaged through a thick sheaf of papers. Near the bottom of the third page, he found the late Mr. Parsons listed, the man who'd died during Jan's shift in the ICU. Only two other bodies were logged in that day, a baby that didn't survive six weeks of premature birth and an elderly lady listed as ninety-six, who died of natural causes. In spite of the deceased woman's age, he had to wonder exactly what *natural causes* might mean at Wilkes Memorial.

Bill heard the doorknob on the door leading to the hospital's interior rattle, and then quiet. Someone seemed about to enter, but had paused. He heard the low rumble of voices beyond the door, and quickly replaced the clipboard, switched off the lights, and slipped back out the door leading to the loading dock.

Bill lowered himself over the edge of the loading dock to the asphalt below, and headed around the corner of the building, out of site of the morgue and the docks. His heart was racing. That was close, and there was no telling who might have been about to enter the morgue, but the last person who would be expected to be in the morgue was Bill Deming, and he didn't want to be seen.

At least he'd been inside and had a chance to get the lay of the land. Later, he'd head back to the morgue and do some of the digging Jake had suggested. He'd give Jan a call, see if she could take a long dinner break and give him a hand when he went back in. With any luck, they could do what needed to be done, and be in and out in an hour. She could go back to work, finish her shift, he'd head back to the hotel with no one the wiser, and Jake would have his information.

It sounded so simple when he thought about it. Maybe this wouldn't be so bad, after all.

Dr. Walter Pigeon stared through his office window and watched Bill lower himself from the loading dock and head around to the far side of the building. What had he been doing in the morgue? What could he have wanted?

Pigeon knew Bill had just been fired from his job – word of the termination had spread rapidly through the hospital's corridors. He was surprised to see him at the hospital at all. If it had been him, he knew he would have been too embarrassed and angry to stay around the place for more than a few minutes. Deming impressed Pigeon as a nosey little cuss and if he was still here, then it could only mean trouble.

When Deming turned the corner and disappeared, Pigeon walked across his office and retrieved the shopping list his wife had faxed him. It was when the fax came through that Pigeon had heard a noise in the morgue, which shared a wall with his office, and went to check it out. He hadn't gone into the morgue initially, although he'd had his hand on the knob. A member of the housekeeping staff had stopped him to ask a question. When he'd finally opened the door to the morgue, the lights had been out and the place apparently empty. That's when he'd gone back to his office and noticed Deming step through the morgue's door and slip over the side of the loading dock.

None of this smelled good to the pathologist. Not that he had a lot to hide regarding his work in the morgue, unless Deming had discovered …

Just the thought of Deming tripping across his involvement in all that the activities here drained the color from Pigeon's face. The shopping would have to wait. He had a call to make.

Chapter 26

Jake Williams liked being a cop. Even in his academy days, when the other candidates were complaining about the studying, the early morning workouts, the tests, he'd been in heaven. He loved the challenge to his mind, to his body, and his life. For him, police work was an all-consuming job, an occupation that defined who and what he was.

For five years before joining the SBI, he walked a beat in downtown Olympia, getting to know the people and learning the ropes. Then, one day the old downtown Pacific First Federal Savings and Loan had been robbed in the middle of the night. It had seemed like the perfect crime to everyone except a rookie cop with a passion for detail.

Jake had been single back then, lived on the reservation, and didn't share his bachelor friends' lust for late nights and heavy drinking. He'd seen too much of that sort of thing on the reservation, seen too many destroyed families and lost kids to touch a drop of alcohol. What he did with his time instead was study the town he patrolled. He found it fascinating, studying old maps of the area. The more he got into it, the more he became transfixed by how the old part of town had been laid out by the city's elders. Old city maps, construction plans for the town's first buildings, ancient street plats from the 1850s, they all captured his imagination. As a result, Jake developed an intimate knowledge of every underground passageway, and every sewer that might serve as an escape route for someone with something to hide.

When other officers gave up on the Pacific First Federal robbery, Jake took another tack. He knew something the rest of the force didn't. He knew there was an old underground sewer line, dating back almost a hundred years that ran right up underneath the building where Pacific First Federal was located. It connected with a large cistern the city had long ago abandoned.

With that information in hand, Jake approached a Sergeant Jamie Smathers, a well-respected officer on Olympia's police force. When he explained his theory, she was fascinated. She offered to invest some of her own personal time to help him check it out.

The night after their initial discussion, with the bank manager's assistance, he and Sergeant Smathers entered the bank's basement and found an old access hatch that led to the cistern that had been covered by an old carpet and empty storage boxes. Jamie noticed a bloody rag on the basement floor near the hatch, and a trail of dried blood that led down into the cistern and along the course of the abandoned sewer line.

With the entry and escape route established, the next challenge was to figure out how the thieves had gotten into the bank's vault. The vault hadn't been damaged during the robbery, and that suggested the robbers had inside assistance. A check of the bank manager's files showed that a limited number of employees had access to the vault. The time sequenced lock on the vault was state of the art, and could only be overridden by the bank manager, the assistant manager, and the maintenance man who serviced the bank's equipment.

With the information they had regarding how the thieves got into the building, their theory of an inside job, and a warrant in hand, Jake and Jamie confronted the bank's manager, assistant manager and maintenance man and requested a DNA sample from each. The bank manager readily agreed, but the assistant manager and maintenance man immediately called their attorneys.

The maintenance technician sang for the District Attorney. The assistant bank manager and three outside accomplices, including the maintenance man, were convicted and sent to prison, and the stolen money was recovered.

The story made all the papers, and a few weeks later, the Washington State Bureau of Investigation approached Jake and offered him a job. He accepted without hesitation, and was the first Native American to be chosen as a member of the SBI.

A year later, he and Sergeant Jamie Smathers were married.

Even after all he'd seen since his appointment to the Bureau, this Wilkes case nagged at him like no other case ever had. The possibility of health care professionals abusing the trust that patients placed in them particularly angered him. On top of that, he couldn't seem to get a handle on the facts; at least not enough facts to nail down a case.

Jake tossed his notepad onto his desk and swiveled his old wooden desk chair to retrieve a cold cup of coffee from atop his gray metal desk. He glanced through his cubicle's glass front to see Jamie walking across the open bay at the center of the bureau's bullpen, headed his way. She was carrying an armload of paperwork.

He groaned. Jamie had left the OPD and joined the bureau a few years after he had made the move. Between them, they shared a passion for their jobs, for each other, two amazing children, but their approaches to criminal investigations couldn't be more different. The most frustrating aspect of their differences was that she was frequently right, or at least more right than he was. Her contrary opinions could be ill timed, inconvenient and annoying, but he'd learned from five long years of working together to grit his teeth and hear her out when she had an opinion about something.

She had that look about her as she approached his office.

"Hello, dear," she said, leaning into his cubicle. The smell of freshly washed hair and just a hint of perfume wafted into his workspace. He glanced at his watch. She must have just finished her workout in the office's dojo. She always worked out at this time of the morning, and among her other many talents, his wife was a second-degree black belt in a rare form of Okinawan karate. That was another thing she had over her street-brawler husband.

"I have some nice reports for you to look over and sign."

Jamie dumped the pile on his desk and waggled a finger under his nose. "And no whining. I'm shift supervisor today, so you have to do everything I say."

She waggled her eyebrows suggestively.

He laughed and could feel the color rise in his cheeks.

She never failed to perk him up when things got tough at the office, and this time was no different.

She stepped into his workspace and lifted a hip onto the corner of his desk.

"You've got that look. The Wilkes case got you down?"

Jake leaned back in his chair. "Things are tough, right now. Sarah Laughlin's sister has been found, murdered in the Laughlin house. We confirmed the victim's identity yesterday. Sarah, our key witness, is missing in spite of an APB put out across a five state area. Now my sister's boyfriend may have discovered information to make things even more complicated."

"I've got confidence in you. If you can find your way through sewers to solve the perfect bank robbery, you can figure out a little organ theft. Besides, I have a theory. I've looked over your case files, and I think someone pretty high placed in the hospital is in on this, someone who has blanket access to patient records, operating schedules, staff rosters, the whole administrative smear."

"Interesting concept," Jamie said. "I'd had much the same thought.

Jamie stood up and turned to leave, but Jake snaked out a hand and slapped her on the butt.

She spun on him. "Sex abuse. Harassment! Insubordination! I'll tell the Chief."

"Right. You'd tell him that your husband is stalking you at work. You should be so lucky."

"All right, you two. What have I told you about PDA in the office? No public displays of affection or you'll make us all jealous."

The chief approached from the opposite side of the bullpen. Alan Finney was the single most decorated police officer in the state. Recruited directly from the military after retiring as the Army's top cop, the man had a quick mind, a faultless memory, and a quirky sense of humor that kept his investigators on their toes.

Jamie squared off with the man, looking down her nose from her prodigious five foot ten to his diminutive forehead, at barely five feet four inches tall. Jake had to wonder which one would win an actual fight, should it ever break out. With Jamie's black belt, and Alan's background in boxing and Ju Jitsu, an actual confrontation would be something to behold.

"No public display of affection here, boss," Jake said.

Alan looked past Jamie and nodded to Jake. "Good to hear it. Wouldn't want to have to can my best married team for illicit sex in the workplace. The Governor frowns on that sort of thing."

Alan's face shifted from his trademark face-splitting smile to serious. "So how's the investigation at the hospital going?"

Jake explained about the murder, Sarah Laughlin's disappearance, and caught them both up on the information Bill had provided. Cases usually didn't frustrate him, but this one was truly twisted. Doctors, nurses, or other staff in a hospital, killing patients—it violated every Florence Nightingale image a person had grown up to believe in. Sarah Laughlin's mysterious disappearance continued to frustrate him. A conscientious employee who never missed work, who could tell you every name in her files, should not leave work and not return, especially since no one seemed to be looking for her.

Alan frowned. "Those responsible for this have crossed into the pale, from helping terminal patients to outright murder of others with no ability to protect themselves. No crime could be more predatory than this. You've got to get these guys."

"If I made a habit of swearing, I'd do it now," Jamie said.

Jake drummed his fingers on the desktop. "If what I believe is true, they're killing people right and left over there, and have been doing so for years. Someone goes to that hospital expecting help, and the next thing, they're dead and their liver, kidneys, eyes and heart are gone."

Jake took a deep breath. "And now we have this." He waved a single sheet of paper.

"It came in a few minutes ago over the fax from Seattle PD. A roommate returning from a long weekend found the body of one Cory Alexander in a Seattle apartment in the University district. He was stabbed to death. Lots of blood, according to SPD. The MO for the killing was much like the one for Sarah Laughlin's sister. Multiple stab wounds, obviously done by an amateur, someone he must have known to let him or her get that close to him. The killer had to have gotten right up next to him to inflict the wounds described in the report. The angle of attack suggests a small person, the depth of the wounds also suggest someone who's not all that strong."

Jake frowned as he reviewed the next paragraph in the report. "Cory's occupation was listed as assistant pathologist at Wilkes Memorial. How do you figure that? SPD confirmed that he was let go by the hospital the day before his body was found."

Alan swiped a hand across his forehead. "I think we all know what that means."

Jamie nodded. "The killer may have struck the first time out of passion or defensiveness, but if it is the same person, this second killing means premeditation. One murder could mean an act of passion. The second usually means that the suspect has turned into a cold killer now. It's just business to her, a way of tying up loose ends. She won't hesitate to kill again if the need arises."

"She? You think it's a woman?" Jake asked.

"Yep," Jamie said. "Everything we've seen suggests a smallish, weak-limbed person. Combine that with the flailing manner of the stabs, which means a lot of emotion. It could be a man. Someone as short as Alan could have done it."

"Thanks for the vote of confidence," Alan replied.

She turned back to Jake. "Do you think it's someone from the hospital?"

Jake stood, took his nine-millimeter pistol from the desk drawer, and clipped its holster to his belt. "I do. We're too close, and the perp is covering his tracks by knocking off the weak links in the organization. Bill and Jan are going to try to get into the morgue today to check out a body for me. Whoever's doing this may have harvested another patient's organs from the ICU where my sister was working yesterday. It had all the markings of one of this group's victims. Deming thinks it's connected, and I've got a hunch he's right. I sent two men over to hang around the hospital with instructions that Jan and Deming will give us a yell on Jan's radio if they need help. I'm heading over to join the back-up crew."

"I'll go with you," Jamie said. "They have great coffee at the hospital snack bar. I could use some."

Alan cast a frown at the two investigators. "You guys be careful."

Jamie reached out and pinched her boss's cheek. "You old softie."

Alan shrugged away her hand. "You mind your manners, Investigator Williams. Get her out of here, Jake."

As Jake and Jamie walked out of the office, Alan called after them, "And close this case before we lose any more citizens."

Chapter 27

Jan stepped through the ICU door and hesitantly reached for Bill's hand, squeezed it. Her expression was furtive, and the shyness of her approach made Bill's heart leap.

"I feel like a fugitive, slinking around like this," she said.

"You look wonderful."

Jan pushed his hand away, but smiled broadly, nonetheless. "Keep your mind on the job, Mr. Deming. We've got murderers to catch."

Bill glanced up and down the hallway outside the ICU main entrance. It was late and the housekeeping staff had finished and gone home for the night. Only one person was visible along the long stretch of hallway, a painter touching up baseboards. The man waved at them when Bill glanced his way, then gathered up bucket and brushes and wandered off.

"We've scared the poor man off."

"Good for us," Bill said, and started for the morgue.

"I can't," Jan said. "I've got a patient who needs supervision until after his evening meds. The nurse overseeing the man is new and inexperienced. I can't leave. I need another hour or so."

She glanced at her watch. "Why don't I meet you on the loading dock in an hour? We can check things out then"

Bill shook his head. "People around here know I've been fired. If I'm seen hanging around, someone might get suspicious."

"Another hour shouldn't mean that much."

Bill nodded. "OK. I'll meet you then."

Ninety minutes later, Bill stood alone on the loading dock. Jan was a half hour overdue, and he was starting to get worried. If he waited too long, someone was bound to come along and find him. He couldn't risk that, not at this point.

He glanced along the length of the long dock. She must have gotten caught up with a patient. In her business, things like that happened all the time.

It was full dark now and the security lights had come on a few minutes earlier, washing the forty-foot concrete platform with a too bright light. The lamps hummed like a whispered secret. A single blue pickup was parked near the dock, backed up near the morgue door, the hospital logo on the passenger side door. It was a quiet, lonely place and seemed abandoned by all but Bill, who glanced at his watch once more.

Where is she? With so many people coming up missing at the hospital lately, she had to know he'd worry. He thought of going inside to call her to see what was going on, but that might raise suspicions with the staff in ICU. At this point, there was no way to identify everyone who was in on the murder for profit scheme. Maybe he should call Jake. Jake had said there'd be cops stationed around the hospital in case they got into trouble or found something worth examining immediately. Jan carried the only radio capable of contacting them.

He checked his watch again. Time to get moving. He'd just have to catch up with Jan later. When he got done in the morgue, he would go find her, take the results of his search to her so she could interpret.

Bill padded silently to the morgue door and breathed a sigh of relief when it opened under his touch. The tape he'd used to cover the lock earlier was still in place.

With a last glance along the length of the loading dock, he stepped through the door and into the pitch darkness of the morgue. His footsteps echoed hollowly off the tiled floor as he made his way to the opposite side of the room. He located the light switch next to the interior door and flipped it on. The room's tile walls gleamed under the overhead florescent tubes. The air smelled too purified, too sterile to hide the death stored in the refrigerator cabinets that lined the walls. He grabbed a clipboard from where it hung next to the light switch, scanned it and found the name he was looking for. Drawer seven.

Bill set the clipboard aside and located drawer seven, one of a dozen three foot by two-foot squares of stainless steel that fronted the hospital's huge refrigeration unit. He threw the latch and slid out the long, frigid tray with the body on it. It was Mr. Parsons, the patient who'd died earlier that day.

The cadaver was covered with a taupe sheet. Bill pulled it back to reveal a long, jagged opening that ran from the body's throat to groin. It had been stitched up and there was no blood. It was a gruesome sight. No matter how many times he'd seen this during his time in Army Medical Intelligence, it still made him nauseous.

He replaced the sheet and rolled the refrigerator's grisly contents back out of sight. Jan would take care of examining the body, if she arrived in time.

Bill moved over to the small, stainless steel desk next to the door leading to the interior of the hospital and rummaged through its drawers. He found nothing, and then realized that autopsy reports wouldn't be left in the morgue in any case. "Of course, they'd be in Pigeon's office," he muttered.

Bill slipped through the door to the hallway and down the hall to the hospital laboratory. The Lab would still be open, staffed by the night crew, and he knew Pigeon's office adjoined the lab. Jan had described its location when he'd informed her of his visit with Pigeon and the late pathology technician.

When he got to the lab, the place was deserted. A sign propped up on the front counter read, "Gone for dinner. Back in 30 minutes. Call pager 2743 for emergency assistance."

Pigeon's name was listed on an office door a few feet behind the lab's front counter. Bill stepped around the counter, through a swinging partition and over to the office door. It was open, so he stepped inside and flipped on the lights.

He glanced around the cluttered room. "Now, where would I put an autopsy file I'd just finished dictating?"

The office was large, with heavy walnut paneling that gave the room a dark, studious feel. A Tiffany lamp sat on an expensive-looking desk of immense proportions. Matched the man, Bill thought as he considered the pathologist's large girth and over-sized physique.

Book-lined walls were on two sides of the room, and a huge computer hutch, complete with the latest model computing hardware, sat behind the desk. Bill considered turning on Pigeon's computer to see if he could access the patient report from there, but dismissed the notion a moment later. Computer access throughout the hospital was monitored. If he logged on to Pigeon's files, the transaction would be recorded and he'd be discovered.

Bill prowled the office's perimeter. Pigeon had expensive tastes. A collection of fine Hummel porcelain decorated one shelf of a bookcase. An illuminated, antique world globe sat on a coffee table between two leather occasional chairs opposite the desk. Another Tiffany lamp, a floor model, stood beside an occasional chair and lit the room with a rose-colored glow.

He found Pigeon's outbox on a credenza at the side of the desk. "Bingo. Right where it should be."

The file on top was labeled "Parsons Autopsy."

Bill picked it up and flipped through the pages. He found a note showing that the kidneys had been taken for transplant. Now, if the transplant office's records reflected both kidneys as being available, the hospital's pathologist was in the clear... unless Jan's search of the body showed other organs had been removed. If others had been taken, Jake would have his case.

Bill glanced at the computer hutch and noticed a multi-function copier, printer and fax machine. He took the page of the report that summarized the pathologist's findings and inserted it into the machine, grimaced as it noisily whirred and chunked out the copy. He replaced the original paper in the autopsy file and returned it all to Pigeon's outbox. He was turning to leave when the office door opened and Carole stepped into the room, followed by the man who had been painting in the hallway.

"What do we have here?" Her face held an expression of innocent concern. "A little extra-curricular breaking and entering? Why I declare, I've trapped myself an intruder."

Bill shrugged and tried to appear unconcerned. "I'd left some papers with Dr. Pigeon earlier. I came back to get them and found the door open. You did say you wanted me out of the hospital today."

Carole smiled and stepped closer, and Bill stepped instinctively. From where he stood, he could smell the sweet scent of her perfume, the fresh aroma of soap that lingered in her hair.

"Maybe you shouldn't leave, after all," she said, as she reached out a long-nailed finger and ran it up the sleeve of his shirt. "Maybe I was presumptuous, a little too spiteful for what I perceived as your betrayal. Maybe we could make up, let bygones be bygones. I talked to Jan, you know."

"She told me."

Carole's voice was a purr, the seductive tones of a cat with a mouse in its sights.

"She told me nothing happened between you the night you took her out. Maybe I was wrong about you. Or maybe she lied."

He stepped back, but Carole kept with him, and pushed up against him. Her breasts brushed the front of his shirt. Sexuality radiated from her like a wave of heat, wrapped around his senses and made it hard to keep his mind on what he was doing.

He stepped back again and found himself against the front of Pigeon's desk, trapped as she moved in on him. He placed both hands on her shoulders and gently held her away from him.

"Carole, I am leaving the hospital in a few minutes, and I doubt I'll be back. There is something between me and Jan, and there is absolutely nothing left between you and me."

"Wrong answer." Carole knocked his hands away and leaned into him. She nuzzled his neck with her mouth, ran her hands down low and moved against his legs.

With a sickening sense of disgust growing in him, Bill pushed her away again, but then felt strong hands grab him from behind and jerk him over hard, backwards, onto the desktop. Carole climbed up onto the desktop to straddle his chest as the painter, who had quietly moved around Bill during the conversation, held Bill down, with his arms trapped at his sides.

He felt the sharp jab of a needle entering the side of his neck, directly into the jugular. He was too startled by the suddenness of the attack to react at first, but quickly gathered himself and shoved upward, hard from the lower back, with all his strength, and twisted to one side.

Carole gave a little cry and slid off him, off the desk, and fell to the floor. The painter, a big man, but with leverage working against him as he reached across the desk from behind to hold Bill down, gave a grunt and fell forward onto the desktop as Bill rolled to the left, slid off the desk and struggled to his feet.

Bill reached up to his neck, where the syringe still dangled, and wrenched it out. Big mistake. It stung like fire as the needle emerged from his artery, followed by a trickle of blood.

He stared at the syringe in his hand. It was empty. He looked over to Carole, who was climbing to her feet and straightening her skirt around her legs, and tried to form a question, but he couldn't, and then heard her laugh as if from a great distance.

He saw her smile at him again, and the expression formed by her thin-lipped grin and sharp eyes was one of consummate anger and victory.

"Now, if you had said you had no feelings for Jan, that might have saved you. As it is, with the trouble you've caused me and my hospital, I'm afraid you've just become a victim of your own plans."

Bill tried to speak, but his mouth wouldn't function. He tried to raise his hands to reach out for support against the desk, but found they wouldn't respond.

His knees began to buckle, but Carole came over and held him up.

"Your client pulled his offer for our cardiac wing, based on the report you sent him earlier today. I just got the call a few minutes ago. We needed that money and that report was bad enough on its own, but then there's the matter of your betrayal of my love, twenty years ago and now, again. What you did to me was unforgivable, both times. I can't tolerate that sort of thing."

Bill felt panic rising inside him, but his limbs wouldn't respond. What had she injected into him?

Carole traced a long fingernail down the side of his face. "Don't worry. I'm not going to kill you. You're not worth that much trouble. I'm just going to punish you a little. You'll be dumped outside of town at some trashy dive, coated with alcohol and filled with enough drugs that you'll be convicted of use and possession, once the police find you. I'll make sure they find you. When you eventually get out of jail, your life will have been destroyed, just like Kurt and you destroyed mine."

She slapped him lightly on the cheek, not enough to hurt, but enough for the sound to echo through the office. The lights of the room began to dim as Bill finally managed to mutter a weak, toneless question, "Why?"

Carole snorted. "I thought I'd explained that clearly enough. I've worked too hard to put this place on the map, to build my life the way I want it, to get the things I want and need. This game you're playing could end all that. I won't let you do it. You can abuse me emotionally and physically, but I won't let you take away the rest. I'm going to remove you as a threat to all the things I've built here. If you'd only played nice ..."

She patted the side of his face once more as he felt his last strength ebb away. "You're so weak, I could do anything I want to you, and you could do nothing in return. You're weak and I'm the strong one. Isn't that nice? Feel lucky I let you live."

As Carole's last words faded, Bill's knees buckled. Through a haze, he saw Carole open the office door and felt the painter lift him and drag him out of the office. His head bumped painfully against a door jam as he was taken out the loading dock doors and dumped into the back of the small pickup. As the truck's engine sputtered to life, his final consciousness faded to black.

Chapter 28

Darkness had closed in on the hospital and the vapor lights suspended over the asphalt driveway of the loading dock at the rear of the main building projected an illumination that was too white, almost garish. The tall, white liquid oxygen tanks at the edge of the drive, a few yards away, hissed and sputtered, and cast off intermittent clouds of freezing steam that briefly floated through the area and then dissipated like wraiths on the hunt.

Jan paced the cold length of the loading dock, multiple shadows following her as she moved from lit area to shadows, to lit area. Where was Bill? A last minute admission to the ICU had taken longer than anticipated, and the shift change had seemed to go on forever, but she'd been sure that Bill would wait for her.

A loud crack sounded from beyond the darkness. She spun around, and the big flashlight she carried jerked its beam of light in the direction of the noise. The beam illuminated the huge liquid oxygen tanks. A large chunk of ice had fallen off the heavy tank's regulators, a common enough occurrence when liquid oxygen tanks were involved, but nerve-wracking tonight.

Jan sucked in a deep breath of air to calm her nerves. How had she let herself get into this position, lurking in the dark to meet a man, to uncover a murder ring? She was a nurse, not a detective. First, she agrees to become a part-time cop to help her brother, who, after more than thirty-five years, she knew was crazy. Then, she meets and sleeps with a man she hardly knows, who two-timed her with his old girlfriend, of all things. Then, it all comes together, and she's waiting here for a man she isn't all that certain she should trust, to help him help her brother track down a bunch of homicidal maniacs.

Why do I do these things to myself?

The answer to the first part of the question was clear enough: Because she loved her brother, trusted him, and placed a great deal of value on human life. She'd really had no choice but to help him.

The second question was a bit more complicated: Did she love and trust Bill?

Trust? Probably. Trust assumes great importance in a relationship if you want to keep that relationship alive. Bill seemed to know what he was doing, and was committed to helping the patients at Wilkes. The love issue would just have to wait, to see how things worked out.

She rolled her shoulders in a weak attempt to ease the tension that knotted her muscles. It didn't help.

There was the soft click of a door as the entrance to the morgue opened a crack. She approached the door and peered inside, but the room was too dark to see a thing. "Bill? Is that you, Bill?"

She eased the door wider and slanted the flashlight's beam into the room.

"Can we at least have a little light in here, please?" she called out. "There's no one out here but me. All the smart people are home eating dinner by now, Bill. Maybe we should join them."

She stepped through the door and raised the flashlight. As the light's powerful beam illuminated the far side of the room, she felt a strong hand grab her shoulder from behind and the sting of a needle entering her skin at the base of her neck.

Jan twisted toward her attacker and swung the heavy flashlight, felt a thud and crunch as it connected with her assailant. She heard a soft curse as her legs gave way and her vision blurred. Whatever she'd been given, it was strong and working fast.

Jan saw the room's overhead fluorescents switch on, the flood of light warring with her fading consciousness. She vaguely recognized the face of the person who held her, lowering her to the floor, but the drugs overwhelmed her system before she could fix the face with a name.

And then there was only emptiness, darkness.

Chapter 29

Bill awakened with the taste of mud in his mouth. His head throbbed with a dull ache. Whatever Carole had given him, it wasn't going to include a gentle recovery.

There was a shudder and then a hard bump that lifted him into the air briefly, and then sent him crashing down on a cold, hard metal surface. He raised his head from where he lay and looked around him, and an icy wind ripped at his hair and ears. He was in the open back of a small pickup truck, speeding down an unknown highway. The tall, dark silhouettes of fir trees whipped by on either side of the road and there was a slight salty taste to the air. The truck was headed west, out of Olympia and toward the Puget Sound or the ocean.

The truck hit a pothole and this time he was nearly bounced out of the truck. He cracked his head on the floor and cursed as his vision swam.

Something chaffed and dug at the skin at his wrists, locked behind him, and through the thin socks at his ankles. He was tied, hand and foot. In the moonlight, he could see thick strands of twine wrapped around his ankles.

Bill craned his next and twisted his position to see forward through the truck cab's back window. A heavyset man with practically no hair was at the wheel. He remembered that dark profile. It was the painter he and Jan had seen at the hospital when they met outside the intensive care unit. The man met Bill's eyes in the rear view mirror and gave him a little wave.

Bill let out a low curse. How many times had he seen that man before all of this happened? He'd been a fool to let it go. Years ago, he'd been a trained intelligence officer. He knew better. He'd grown complacent in his work-a-day life. He should have picked up on the fact that the man was following them.

If that was the case, what about Jan? Had she been abducted, too? Bill felt his heart sink at the thought. She was on her own, and there was nothing he could do about it, trussed up like a pig, on the way to its execution.

At least he hadn't forgotten all of his old training. Bill rolled onto his side and exhaled deeply. His lungs deflated, he drew his knees up and forced his hands down and around his feet. The move stretched the twine tightly around his wrist and he felt the first few drops of warm, sticky blood seep from around his bonds. In another second, he'd passed his feet through his arms and had his hands out in front of him where he could see them.

He used the opportunity to glance at his watch's luminous dial. It was after nine o'clock. How long had he been unconscious? Two hours, at most, he decided. Carole must have botched the injection, or didn't figure the time it would take for her buddy, the painter, to get where they were going.

That gave Bill an advantage. He dug through long dormant memories of Escape and Evasion training from his years in the service. The first rule was to be patient, find an opening, and use that opportunity to get away. Don't be rash and fling yourself at the situation. Be smarter than your captor, and once you're free, keep moving. Most escapees got caught because they ran out of steam or courage, and stopped moving.

First, he had to find a way out of the truck.

He watched the driver through the cab's rear window. The man was intent on the road ahead and paying little attention to his cargo.

He worked his hands free with his teeth, gnawing on the twine until it finally loosened. Once his hands were free, he felt at his pockets. His wallet was still in his rear pants pocket. That meant he had a calling card he could use to reach Jake or Jan or the local police, if he got away and could find a phone.

Now, how to get out of a moving truck? There was no way to accurately gage the speed, but at the rate the trees were rushing by, he'd guess they were doing at least fifty miles an hour. Jumping at that speed was out of the question. His best chance would be to jump when the truck slowed for a turn, while it was still moving but going slower. It would be a hard fall, no matter how he did it. He'd done moving jumps while still in the military, during parachute drops and air assault maneuvers. He was definitely out of shape for that sort of thing, but he'd have to take his chances if he wanted to be free.

As the truck sped down the road, he used the time to get his bearings. From the terrain, it was likely that they were headed west, toward the coast along the southern end of the Olympic Peninsula. It had been one of his favorite trips as a kid, and he recognized many of the landmarks. Somewhere ahead, the driver would have to slow to pull onto a side road to dump his cargo. How far he'd go after the turn-off was anybody's guess, but the woods were thick in this area. It would be Bill's best chance to make the jump and get away into the dense growth beside the road. On the other hand, if he didn't get away, the dense woods were the perfect place to hide a body, where it wouldn't be found for months or years.

He would wait until the driver slowed to make that turn. That would be his chance.

A few minutes later, he heard the switch in the rear taillight click as the driver activated his right blinker. Bill gathered his feet beneath him, staying low so the driver wouldn't see, and forced his back against the side of the truck bed.

The truck bounced across another pothole and the metal of the truck's side jarred him painfully across the back, jostling him and threatening to throw him back across the bed. Painful as hell.

He braced for the turn as the truck began to slow, and felt the truck bed tilt as the driver swung the truck in a tight arc to the right. Huge fir trees whipped past only ten or fifteen yards from the edge of the road. It wasn't much room to land, but it looked like this would be his best opportunity.

Jump and tuck. Jump and tuck.

He repeated the words over and over in his head, just like in airborne training in the Army. Back then, he'd had a few bad landings and he hadn't been jumping from a moving truck onto gravel. This was likely to rate right up there with the worst of those landings.

As the truck hit the apex of its turn, Bill saw his chance. He stood briefly, teetered as the truck shifted position, and jumped for the shoulder of the road.

He cleared the gravel at the edge of the road by inches, and tumbled into the mud and weeds beyond, landing on his left shoulder. Then he was rolling, the momentum of his fall sending him like a top, out of control. Desperately, he grabbed his knees with his hands, then reached out and slapped at the ground to ease the impact as he continued to roll. One shoe flipped off into the distance, a long piece of twine trailing it as it sailed away. Rocks gouged through his thin jacket and tore at his pants.

After a half dozen revolutions, he came up hard against the base of a tree, a tall, ancient fir. When he took a deep breath, pain lanced through his side. He touched the point of the pain and found a gash in his side, the blood seeping through his shirt. *Must have gouged myself in the fall, maybe broken a rib.*

At least he was out of the truck. He was free.

Bill blinked his eyes to regain his orientation. *Escape and evade. Remember the rules. Keep moving.*

When he tried to regain his feet, the world spun and he had to lean back against the tree until his vision settled and the dizziness passed.

Stomach still churning and his broken rib screaming each time he moved, Bill did a more thorough, but quick inventory of the rest of his body. A dozen spots would eventually develop into dark, painful bruises and he'd sprained his wrist, but all things considered, he was miraculously intact.

He glanced up toward the shoulder of the road. He couldn't see the truck, but the sound of skidding tires was loud as the driver reversed direction and pulled the truck back toward his direction. He must have felt the truck lurch when Bill jumped from the truck. He was some distance off, but the revved engine meant the man was coming on fast. Bill had to move, and it had to be now.

Carole couldn't afford to let him get away, and he was sure she'd paid this man handsomely to ensure that it didn't happen. She needed to ruin Bill's credibility in order to protect the hospital, and she wanted him punished for what she perceived he'd done to her.

No doubt the driver had his orders to dispose of Bill without any witnesses. If the driver of the truck was willing to be part of a kidnapping, he was liable to go to any extreme.

Bill saw the glow of the pickup's red taillights as they smeared the darkness, getting brighter as the truck backed toward him at high speed. If he could get the man away from the truck… But he'd have to be patient and lucky to pull it off. Those were two characteristics he'd never been known for.

Bill ducked behind the tree, and the truck stopped just above his position. He could hear the crunch of the man's boots on the gravel as he emerged from the vehicle. The man edged his way along the shoulder, scanning the woods for any sign of his escaped prisoner. From Bill's position, he could see the man's silhouette against the darkness of the forest and the moonlit sky. The man turned away and walked down the road in the opposite direction from the truck and Bill's position. He carried a large bat or board in one hand, and a flashlight in the other.

The man clicked the flashlight on. Sooner or later, he would figure out that he'd passed the point where Bill was hiding, turn around and retrace his steps, back to the area where Bill hid. Bill had to get to the truck before that happened, get it going and get out of there before he had a chance to react. The only advantage he had at this point was that the driver had no idea where he was, but Bill could see him and the truck.

Bill slipped off his remaining shoe to avoid crunching the gravel, and climbed to his feet. He stayed low and crept up toward the shoulder of the road as the man walked slowly along the edge of the road, his back to Bill's position. The rocks of the roadside dug painfully through Bill's thin socks.

Bill paused at the crest of the shoulder. He could just make out the top of the man's head in the distance as his abductor continued down the shoulder of the road, the flashlight's beam roaming through the trees and underbrush as he searched. He was looking in the other direction. There simply wouldn't be a better time than this to make his move.

Bill slipped off his watch and heaved it toward where the man was looking, beyond the trees and into the brush. It landed with a light crack and soft rustling of dried grass.

"Got you," the man yelled and charged off down the slope and into the trees.

Bill raced to the driver-side door of the truck. It was ajar, so he eased it open and slipped into the driver's seat. The cab dome light flashed on and off like a strobe, and his pursuer spun around as the light flashed.

"Hey! You stop right there!" the man yelled, and charged for the truck.

The keys were still in the ignition, and he kicked the truck's engine to life. He wrestled with the brake release, and then jammed the automatic shift into drive. The man was fast, coming on hard, and reached the passenger-side door as Bill got the truck into gear.

The engine grabbed and the vehicle swerved as the man grasped the passenger-side door handle, but he couldn't hang on as the truck gained speed. Bill heard the satisfying sound of gravel flying as the truck's rear wheels dug in and flung debris in his kidnapper's face. In the rear view mirror, Bill saw the dark form of the man sprawled on the ground where the truck had been only seconds before.

A mile later, Bill swung the truck around, crossed the median and headed south and east, past the point where he'd left his captor and toward Olympia. As he drove, his heart rate slowly returned to normal. He flipped on the truck's dome light and took a quick inventory of what lay in the truck's small cab. He could have shouted for joy when he saw the open cell phone on the seat beside him.

He picked it up and dialed 911. It was the only number he could remember. After explaining his situation to the operator, he was put through to SBI headquarters. The dispatcher patched him through to Jake's car radio.

"It's Bill. I've had some trouble."

"Where are you? You're supposed to be at the hospital. When I didn't hear from you or Jan, we came over to check out the situation. I couldn't find either of you."

"I'll explain later, but Carole Fletcher, the Assistant Administrator for the hospital, found me in the pathologist's office. She drugged me and had me taken out of town to be dumped, killed or whatever. I just now managed to get away."

"I don't understand. You and Jan are supposed to be together, getting a look at the morgue. Where's Jan?" Jake asked.

Bill explained that Jan hadn't shown up at the meeting point and his assumption that she'd gotten tied up in the ICU.

"You may be right," Jake said when Bill finished. "I'll have my men at the hospital go in and check on her, see if she's still in the ICU. She's probably all right; still working on a patient that went south or something like that. She never was one who could leave a patient's side if care was needed. As for Carole, you have to admit that she had a good plan. Even if they didn't kill you, the drugs would have been found in your system and you'd be ruined as a witness. Your credibility would be shot."

"Right. I'm headed back to Olympia. I'm in one of the hospital's trucks. I should be back in the area in an hour or so, depending on traffic."

"I'm looking forward to hearing the rest of that story," Jake said. "I'll arrange to have Carole picked up. Where did you leave her friend?"

"He's somewhere along Highway 101 north, last I saw him. He shouldn't be too hard to find. Look for the man with the gravel down his shirt."

"I'll have the state bulls pick him up and bring him in. Maybe our interrogation crew can get something out of him. By the way, what time was it when you last saw my sister?"

Bill felt a tight knot form in the pit of his stomach. It had been hours since he and Jan were supposed to meet. "It's been too long, Jake, and I'm worried about her. Let's find her quickly."

Chapter 30

Bill called Jake on the cell phone as he neared the outskirts of Olympia. They agreed to meet at Jan's house. Jake had already searched the hospital and found no sign of his sister.

Bill dropped the truck at the hospital and swapped it for his Supra. A plainclothes investigator met him and took possession of the pickup. When he'd finally opened the door to his sports car, Alex had lunged for the bushes and relief, after hours of confinement. Bill felt bad about leaving Alex for so long and vowed never to leave him locked in the car like that again. At least he'd managed to leave the windows cracked and park the car in the shade.

"Sorry I left you here for so long, buddy. Too bad you weren't with me," Bill he'd told Alex, when the dog had finally returned from the bushes and climbed back into the car. "I could have used some of that guard dog training I paid for when we were stationed in Germany."

Two hours later, Bill pulled up to Jan's house. Jake and a very attractive woman stepped off the front porch to greet him. She was petite, but with an athletic appeal to her stride. She wore her red-brown hair cut short, in an old-fashioned tomboy cut. She had an outdoorsy look that Bill liked. Jake introduced Bill to his wife, Jamie, also an investigator with the State Bureau of Investigation. As he made the introduction, Jake's normally casual smile seemed forced.

"Jan's not here, and hasn't been here all day," Jake said. "We checked inside. There are dirty dishes in the sink. I know my sister well enough to know they wouldn't be there if she'd been here today for more than a few minutes."

Jake took a step toward Bill and the intensity of the man's glare forced Bill back a step. "Are you sure you don't know any more about my sister's disappearance? Have you told me everything you know?"

Jamie put a restraining hand on her husband's sleeve. "Sorry, Bill, but it's not like her to disappear. Mister Big Detective here is naturally protective of his baby sister."

Bill could understand the man's worry, but he squared himself and returned Jake's glare. "I'm the one who was drugged and kidnapped. The man who kidnapped me, the one who drove the truck, was the man painting in the hospital this evening when I met Jan outside the ICU. Whoever is arranging all of this must have had him waiting for us. They probably had someone else snatch Jan. Carole has to be part of this. I'm convinced of it. If we find her, we find Jan. I'd bet on it."

Jake's shoulders drooped and he ran a hand through his long hair. "You're saying that she, they, or whoever it was, knew there was a connection between the two of you, and knew that you were investigating the murders at the hospital?"

Jake turned on his heel and led the way back up the front stairs and into the house. Bill and Jamie followed, with Alex close behind. Bill dropped into the overstuffed recliner near the door, while Alex curled up at his feet and was instantly asleep.

Two other men, both in sports shirts, slacks, and bulky sweaters materialized from the sides of the house and stepped up onto the front porch. Each wore an earphone, and from the look of the bulges at their hips, was heavily armed. Bill nodded in the direction of the men.

Jamie dropped onto the couch next to her husband. "You're still pretty new around us; new to us. For all we knew, you might have been involved in Jan's disappearance." She let the word hang in the air. "We're just trying to cover all the bases."

Jake's face was like stone, unreadable as he shifted positions and eased himself deeper into the couch's cushions. To Bill, the big man looked like a predatory cat, coiling to strike at something, at him, and it was unsettling.

Jamie continued while Jake glowered. "A State Patrol car wasn't too far from the scene when you called in. Your man wasn't hard to spot. You apparently ran over his foot on the way out and broke his ankle. He tried to run when the bulls arrived, but only made it a few steps before they apprehended him. He's at the hospital being treated for the ankle. He's swearing that you attacked him and stole his truck. Later, he'll be transferred to the Bureau's headquarters for questioning."

Bill sat up straight. "You believe him?"

"Give us a little credit. Everything the State Patrol officers could gather from the scene where you claimed you jumped supports your story, right down to the skid marks in the gravel." Jake's voice came like a low growl.

"Thanks for the confidence." Bill didn't bother to hide the sarcasm in his voice, and stood up suddenly. "This sitting around is senseless. We have to do something."

Jamie raised a hand to cut off his next words. "We need to do this by the book, take it one step at a time. You have to be patient. We questioned some of the crew that worked with Jan in the ICU today. The way I figure it, she disappeared shortly after Carole had you taken. We had the same thought about Carole's involvement in the murders and perhaps Jan's disappearance, but we haven't been able to locate her to get any answers."

"I should have put two and two together when I saw Carole's house that first time," Bill said. "She lives way over her head for someone in her position. She has to be involved in this to live like she does. It should have tipped me off."

Jake sat forward on the couch. "What's that mean?"

"You'd have to see the place to understand. It's a palace. Original art on the walls; expensive antiques everywhere."

"Maybe we should have a look at Ms. Fletcher's home," Jamie said. "Could be we'll find something there that will help. It wouldn't take much to get a search warrant at this point, with what she did to Bill."

Jake called out to one of the officer's on the front porch. "Farrell, get a call into HQ. Tell them I need a search warrant for Carole Fletcher's house, now! All the information they'll need to have it prepared is in the case file on my desk."

Farrell reached for the door, then turned back and gave Jake an uncomfortable smile. "The boss is at the Performing Arts Center with his wife tonight. We'll have to call him out to get his approval. He's going to be steamed."

Jake's laugh was harsh and without humor. "They're showing the *Mikado*. Jamie dragged me to it a week ago. Believe me, he'll probably give us all medals for busting him out of there."

Jamie glared at her husband and thumped him on the shoulder with a small fist. Jake's reaction suggested that the punch carried more force than was apparent.

"I have a suggestion." Bill said.

Jake cut him off. "You don't suggest anything. This is a police matter, and we're going to wait here until we get that search warrant. Then you can go with us when we check out the house. From what Jan told me the other day, you can probably be a big help to us at that end, with your *intimate* knowledge of the place."

Jake's attitude suggested that he knew about Bill and Carole's relationship, and the tone of his voice made Bill feel more like a suspect than an ally. He stood, forcing down anger and humiliation. He turned his back on Jake, stepped across Alex's inert form and went to a small window to gaze at the trees silhouetted in the darkness beyond the house. Alex cocked one eye open as Bill stepped over him, and then closed it again a few seconds later.

"If you didn't already know, when I first arrived in town, Carole and I ran into each other." Bill didn't look at Jake and Jamie. "We were old, very good friends from high school, over twenty years ago. She invited me over to her place. That was before I discovered my feelings for your sister." Bill kept his tone flat, emotionless. He didn't like where this was headed, but felt the need to clarify things.

"You had a relationship with her." It was a statement, not a question, and Jake's words were spit out like charges for a heinous crime.

"What happened between Carole and me is none of your business." Bill kept his tone flat, his gaze out the window, toward the tops of the evergreens that swayed back and forth in the stiff breeze.

Jake lunged from his chair, crossed the room, grabbed Bill by the shoulders, and spun him around. "It is my business, and don't you doubt it. Carole is a suspect and Jan is my sister. If you had a relationship with Carole, you could be in this up to your ears. Maybe you know where Jan is right now. Maybe you've known all along."

Bill's control broke, and he whirled, ducked under Jake's left arm, and stepped around him in one swift motion. He grabbed Jake's wrist as he moved, twisted it low and around, up between the man's shoulder blades, and then slammed Jake up against the wall. In another instant, he had a knee in the small of Jake's back and felt the man grunt as his face struck the wood paneling.

Bill's ribs and wrist were throbbing with pain, but he ignored them as he put even more pressure on Jake's back. "I'm in love with your sister, you idiot. I'm not her kidnapper. And if you don't get that, take a look at the needle marks on my body where I was recently drugged, kidnapped, and driven half way across the county to be killed. You getting any of this through that thick skull of yours?"

The policeman standing outside pulled his gun and headed through the screen door. Jamie smiled and waved him off. "Don't worry about it, Sam. It's just a lover's quarrel."

The man re-holstered his gun and stepped back outside, the look on his face suggesting that he accepted Jamie's assessment but wasn't totally convinced.

Jamie walked over to where Alex lay, stooped down and stroked the rough hair of the dog's back. She glanced casually toward the two men as Jake struggled vainly against Bill's grip. "If you boys are about done," she said.

"That depends," Bill said. "On your husband's next move. Any more accusations like that and …"

"It's his job to be suspicious, Bill, and Jan is his sister. When you worked with military intelligence, weren't you just a little bit paranoid from time to time?"

Bill dropped his knee from Jake's back and eased the man's wrist down to his side, then stepped away.

Jake rubbed at his sore left shoulder as he turned around to face the room. His hand strayed to the back of his right hip, where a nine-millimeter Beretta was holstered.

"Don't even think of it," Jamie warned her husband. "You started this, Jake. If you calm down a bit, you'll realize he's right. You've no real cause to suspect Bill of anything."

Jake glared at Bill, but dropped his hand to his side. "Maybe you're right. It's just that when he confirmed that he'd had a relationship with the same woman who might be behind Jan's disappearance, the murders at the hospital…"

"We don't actually know that Jan's kidnapped. She's just missing at this point. There's been no ransom note," Jamie said. "We're cops, here, you know. We're supposed to have evidence before we label someone as a suspect."

Bill joined the conversation at that point. "Jake has a point, though. Jan's been missing for too long already. We have to act quickly to find her."

Jamie stood up from petting Alex and patted Jake on his sore shoulder hard enough to make him flinch.

"Yeah, I feel the same. It's killing me that we don't know what's happened," Jake said. "Sorry I got on you like that."

Bill gave Jake a wary smile. "Just don't try to handle me like that again. I'm not your garden variety accountant or consultant."

Jake rubbed the shoulder again. "I guess. Jan said you were in the army, right? She said you were medical, but I'd guess something more like Special Forces."

Bill headed for the door, paused before he stepped outside. "Something like that, but I never got the beret." His words were clipped, short. He was in no mood to make friends with the man who accused him of complicity with Jan's kidnappers, if she had indeed been kidnapped. That was the problem with all this. He simply didn't know what was going on, and he needed to do something to figure things out. "If I'm not under arrest, I'm heading back to the hospital. Maybe I can figure something out, get a lead on where Jan might be."

"Boss?" It was Farrell, standing at the door in Bill's path, with no intention of moving out of the way.

"Let him go. He's not a suspect, not yet, anyway."

Farrell stepped back to let Bill pass. "The office said they'd have the warrant in a few minutes. The Chief wants you to meet him at Ms. Fletcher's house."

"I'll meet you there after I stop at the hospital, if you like," Bill said.

Jake started to protest, but Jamie cut him off and they followed Bill out the door. They were in their respective cars and pulling out of the driveway a few minutes later, having agreed to meet later at Carole's house. Alex once again snoozed on the passenger seat as Bill pulled out of the drive behind the two unmarked State cars, and headed back to Wilkes Memorial.

Where could Jan be? Did Carole have her? The frustration of not knowing gnawed at his gut.

He dropped the car into third and picked up speed.

Chapter 31

It was close to midnight when Bill pulled the Supra into the hospital parking lot. The clouds had closed in overhead and a fine mist was filtered down through the still night air. As he brought the car to a stop in a parking place near the hospital entrance, Alex opened groggy eyes and thumped his tail once on the passenger seat.

Bill noticed the reserved sign on the spot that he usually used was gone. "I suppose they've already given it to someone else. No matter, let's get you settled in for a while. I need to do a little digging. No one kidnaps this boy and gets away with it. I'm going to get to the bottom of who's involved in all this."

Alex kicked a hind leg and closed his eyes, but Bill reached over and pushed at the dog until he got both eyes open again. Then he reached across and opened the passenger-side door.

"Out the door, you lazy thing. You need a walk before I head inside. This may take a while."

Alex stretched, and then eased his bulky body out of the car. Bill joined him among the shrubs a moment later, following the dog into the darkness beyond reach of the of the admin wing's entry door lighting. He cursed softly as Alex led him deeper into the tall rhododendrons and cedar hedges, and he tripped on an exposed root.

Just as the big Lab seemed to find the perfect bush, two people emerged through the hospital's entrance. The first was tall, perhaps a few inches over Bill's height and wide across the shoulders. The other was smaller, slender, less distinct, and walked with a limp. Both wore dark overcoats that hung to mid-calf. Hats shielded their faces from the rain and easy recognition.

"You listen to me," the taller one said. "I'm out of this, effective right now." The voice was familiar, even muffled as it was by the distance. "I wasn't in on this to take a murder rap."

As Alex finished his business, Bill squatted down beside him and placed a quieting hand on the dog's head. That person had definitely said the word 'murder.'

The other voice was softer but so muffled that Bill could barely make out the words, let alone recognize the voice. "You're in this too far to get out. What do you think a judge would say about what you've done? People died with our help. You were just a little subtler than the average murderer. Believe me when I say if we all go down, you're going down with us, no matter what."

The tall man reached out with a dark arm, clutched at the other person's shoulder, and shook it violently. The smaller person staggered and nearly fell. "I never lifted a hand directly to kill anyone, or to let any patient die. I think the police would understand if I went to them. I could work a deal and turn state's evidence. Then where would you and your big plans be?"

Alex wiggled under Bill's hand, wanting to head back to the warmth of the car. Bill calmed him with a slow, deep chest scratch.

The smaller person's voice rose to where the words came clearer. It was a woman's voice and familiar, but it wasn't Carole's. Bill searched his memory as he tried to identify the speaker.

"Don't you ever touch me like that again. If you ever think of getting tough with me, or going to the police, I'll make sure it's the last thing you do. I've got enough evidence planted that you won't see the light of day for the rest of your life, no matter what deal you work out or what you do to me personally. I'll tell you when you're out of this."

She nearly spat the words as she continued, her voice becoming louder, more shrill. "You go home to that beautiful, trophy wife of yours, to your beautiful home, in that expensive car, and sleep off this panic. When you wake up in the morning, I want you to remember exactly who got you where you are today. If I hadn't found you and doctored your files for the Credentials Committee, you'd still be practicing without a license in the backwoods of New England. You'd be lucky if you were getting work treating sheep after what you did to that woman in New Hampshire. I have all the evidence squirreled away, and I can either insure your future success or I can bring you down. Don't you forget it. You do your job, and be happy to have what you've got."

The man tall stepped back, shaken by the woman's speech, but not totally defeated. "Don't you threaten me, you cheap hack. I was never convicted of that crime. I could go to the police right now and tell them enough to implicate you with the death of the Laughlin woman. Remember that I'm the one who bandaged your wound after that incident. If you push me just a little bit more, I'll go to them, I tell you. I will go to the police."

"You do that, and you're as dead as she is."

The woman turned and stalked off toward the parking lot and out of sight.

Bill watched as the tall man lingered in the light at the entryway, then bundled his coat more tightly around him and headed for his car.

Bill's heart raced. They must be two of the ringleaders, people deep into the patient murders! One was a surgeon. Who could it be? He'd met Harrison, but few others on the surgical staff. The identity of the woman was anyone's guess. He should go to Jake with this information, now, but what information did he really have? He'd overheard a conversation, but didn't actually know who was doing the talking. He needed more information.

Bill waited until they were out of sight before he led Alex from the shadows. He hurried the dog to the Supra and kicked the car's engine to life. Maybe he shouldn't go into the hospital. Maybe he should follow one of those two people. He could find out exactly who they are, maybe even confront them with what he knew.

He glanced into his rear view mirror in time to see a car back out of a parking space in the area reserved for physicians and made up his mind.

Bill pulled out of his parking space with the lights off and waited for the car to pull out in front of him. He recognized the low-slung silhouette of a Jaguar sedan as it headed for the parking lot exit. He eased the Supra forward and followed.

The Jaguar wound its way through the streets of Olympia, past the capital building, and then out to Interstate 5. It headed north on the freeway, where Bill finally turned on his headlights. Fortunately no city police had seen him tailing the Jaguar without lights.

It was forty-five minutes before the Jaguar turned off Interstate 5 at the Federal Way exit, an affluent suburb of both Tacoma and Seattle. It had been twenty years since Bill had been in the area. He was surprised to see the number of shopping malls that had sprung up. Restaurants and drug stores seemed to occupy every possible inch of ground. Even at this late hour, the traffic was heavy, and he had to work hard to not lose the Jag.

Beyond the malls and restaurants, on the outskirts of the bedroom community, the Jaguar turned off the main road and headed up a series of low hills flanked by sprawling mansions. A couple of quick turns later, the sedan pulled into the driveway of a tall, columned house built to resemble a plantation estate. One door of a four-car garage opened slowly as the Jag approached, and then disappeared inside.

Bill reached into the glove box, retrieved his cell phone and dialed Jake's number. The phone rang four times before Jake picked up.

"Bill, where the heck are you?"

Bill explained where he was and what he'd overheard. "Have you found Jan?"

The frustration and worry was clear in Jake's voice. "Not yet, but we will."

Bill forced himself to take a deep breath to steady himself. *Where was she? Had they taken her, too?*

"Don't worry. I'm not even close to giving up on finding her," Jake said. "The frustrating part is that while we have enough on the two physicians you named in your report to open an investigation, and probably even get a conviction for several of the patient murders, we don't have a clue as to who killed the pathologist's assistant or Laughlin's sister. We need more about those deaths, and we need to find Sarah Laughlin, the admin clerk. She's pivotal to the case and I've had people calling everyone we can associate with the girl. She apparently kept pretty much to herself, so there aren't a lot of leads.

What you overheard tonight might help with that."

"I'm at one of their houses, now. I suspect its one of the physicians. I'm going to talk to him and find out who he was talking to at the hospital. It could have been Carole, but I couldn't actually tell. I've got to know for sure. If they have Jan ..."

Jake cut Bill off. "You're not a cop, Bill. Wait for us to get there. I can have someone there in an hour."

"An hour's too long. You know what they tried to do to me. They know that we're close. What if this man decides to pull out, make a run for it? He could be gone in that hour. Then what would we do?"

"You have a point. I'll see if I can get someone over there more quickly. Maybe there's a State Patrolman in the area," Jake said. "Remember that you're not a cop, Bill. Don't do anything stupid."

"I'll call you as soon as I've talked to whoever's inside." Bill severed the connection before Jake could say more.

Bill started the Supra and backed down to the mansion where the Jaguar had pulled in. He eased his sports car into the driveway and stepped out. "Guard the car, Alex," he said as he got out and set the locks.

Alex continued his contented snooze on the passenger seat, although one eye briefly flicked open, watching Bill as he stepped away from the car. "Some guard dog you are," Bill said. "And to think that I actually paid for that guard dog training."

Bill knocked at the mansion's front door. The sound of his fist hitting the heavy wood door seemed overly loud. Through the full-length cut glass window next to the door, he could see lights on inside, so he knew someone was still up. A few moments later, the door opened and Dr. Harrison, Wilkes Memorial's chief surgeon, greeted him. The man made a point of glancing at his watch.

"Mr. Deming. It's rather late for a house call, isn't it?"

The man's normally impeccable hair was unruly, as though he'd been running hands though it repeatedly. He shirt was rumpled, his tie askew. Harrison's face was pale, his eyes hollow and distant.

"Sorry to bother you so late, doctor, but I need a word with you. It won't take more than a minute or two." Bill pushed the door open before Harrison could reply and stepped inside.

Harrison stepped out of the way. "It doesn't appear like you're going to take no for an answer. Come on back to the den. I'm just finishing a brandy. Maybe you'd like one?"

Bill followed Harrison through a high, vaulted entry that led to double doors of heavy walnut. Harrison pushed the doors wide and admitted Bill into a richly appointed office. Inlaid wood paneling coated the walls, and it wasn't the cheap variety sold in sheets at the lumber store. This was hand crafted, tongue and groove, exotic grained hardwood that lined the walls and covered the ceiling. Bookshelves filled with leather bound volumes took up two entire walls. An antique French desk sat in one corner of the room and the soothing sounds of Brahms played in the background.

Harrison handed Bill a snifter of fragrant amber liquor and waved him to a chair next to the warmth of a gas-lit fireplace. The doctor took a chair opposite Bill's and sipped at his drink. "Well, this is quite civilized, Mr. Deming, despite the hour. Now, what can I do for you?"

Bill tasted the brandy and frowned. He'd had better, but never with a man whom he suspected of cold-blooded murder. In the Army, he'd had to fire on the enemy on several occasions, and had taken a life in the line of duty. Then, the boundaries were clear, and the methods obvious. Both sides had been fighting for what they thought was right, and the deaths on either side were in self-defense of higher ideals. The deaths caused by this man, for nothing more than financial gain, were something he could never understand.

He set the brandy aside.

"I was outside the hospital this evening and overheard your conversation with a woman in the hospital's doorway. The police know I'm here and are on their way, but I need to know who that other person was."

Harrison swirled his brandy in its snifter and then took a long, casual sip. When he lowered his glass, he smiled grimly at Bill over its edge. "Lurking in the shadows? Eavesdropping? That seems a little low for a high-paid consultant like yourself."

"Not as low as taking advantage of patients who have placed their trust, their lives, in your hands."

Harrison raised his snifter in salute. "Touché. You're working with the police, then? They know what's been going on at the hospital?"

Bill nodded. "They do."

Bill focused his attention on Harrison's eyes. He knew from past negotiations in business and the military, that this was the key moment. Both parties, he and Harrison, knew where the cards lay and what was in each other's hands. The only remaining question was how those hands would be played.

"The person you were talking to has killed twice already and intends to kill again," Bill said. "Jan McDonald is missing and we think that she has her. We're worried that she thinks Jan is onto her and may try to eliminate her like she did the Laughlin girl, or the pathology assistant. On the other hand, what's to keep her from killing you to ensure that her plans are secure and that she's safe from the police? In my limited experience, criminals don't usually have a lot of loyalty. If she gets rid of Jan, you could well be next."

Harrison turned his tired, empty gaze toward the flames in the room's small fireplace, watched as they licked at ceramic logs with tongues of blue, green and orange.

"Sad," he said. "I know Jan. She was the one doing an admin internship at the hospital. We had several nice conversations in the cafeteria. She's in the ICU now, isn't she?"

"That's where I last saw her. Your partner, the person who tried and failed to kill Sarah Laughlin, may have her."

Harrison's head snapped around. "The Laughlin girl isn't dead?"

Bill never let his eyes leave Harrison's gaze. "She killed Sarah's sister, presumably by mistake. We have Sarah and she's ready to testify." The last part was a lie, but there was no way Harrison could know that.

"With what we have, and Sarah Laughlin's testimony to back it up, you will all go to jail, at the least. You know that the woman who died at Sarah's house wasn't Sarah, but was her sister? Either way, someone was murdered, and you and your friends will be linked to the crime. Your only hope for survival is to cooperate with the police, and you can start by telling me who the woman was that you met at the hospital tonight, and where she might have Jan McDonald."

Harrison leaned his head against the back of the chair and sighed deeply.

"Sarah Laughlin is alive? I'm kind of relieved about that. It makes things a bit easier. And frankly, I've had quite enough of this. The killing's gone too far. The patients were bad enough, even though at first we only selected those who were likely to die, anyway. The thought of Sarah being murdered was too much. Call your friends. I'll cooperate."

Harrison pounded a fist against the arm of his chair. "I didn't sign up for this, not for any of this. The patients we harvested in the beginning were terminal, but then we moved on to questionable patients that were simply convenient, ones we could at least argue would have died anyway. But then there was the patient in the E.R., who should have lived. I knew that. Everyone knew that. And the one in the ICU a few days ago—I think Jan was on duty then. It should not have happened."

Bill stood from his chair and stepped over by the fireplace, then spun on his heel to face Harrison. "You won't get any sympathy from me for your plans gone astray. You played games with patient's lives, deciding who will live and who'll die like some sort of demigod. 'Above all else, do no harm.' Isn't that the oath that you took when you got your medical degree?"

Harrison shook his head and his eyes welled up with un-shed tears.

"What about Jan McDonald?" Bill said. "What about her? Do you want to add her to your list of murdered innocents?"

Harrison groaned. "No. Not Jan. Not anyone, not anymore."

The doctor lurched from his chair and over to his desk, legs obviously unsteady. From a desk drawer, he retrieved a pad and pencil and scribbled a name and address. "This is who you need to find. That's who I talked to when you saw me tonight. She's the one who killed the pathology assistant and Laughlin's sister. When you're done with her, call Dr. Ian Farley, the hospital's Chief of Medicine. He probably won't cooperate with you but the conversation should prove informative. He's in this up to his little bald head. Now, leave me. Come back with the police and a warrant and I'll cooperate, but until then, get out of my house."

"Right. Thanks," Bill said.

"Don't thank me yet," Harrison said as he handed the slip of paper to Bill. "The woman whose name is on this paper told me earlier today that she planned to get rid of Jan. If Ms. McDonald is missing, I'd say there's a good chance that she has her."

Bill took the paper and read the address and the name, the shock of its contents settling over him with a cold chill. He grabbed for his cell phone in his coat pocket, realized it was in the car with Alex, and picked up the phone on Harrison's desk. He had Jake's number memorized and punched it in.

When Jake answered, he explained what he'd learned and gave Jake the name and address where Jan might be held. "Stay with him until the police arrive. I'll call them now," Jake said.

"No way. I'm not waiting here when I know where Jan may be. Harrison's not going anywhere. I'm headed for the address I just gave you. If Jan's there, I want to find her before anything happens."

"Stay where you are, Bill. That's an order," Jake yelled.

"I stopped taking orders years ago." Bill hung up the phone and turned for the door.

"The police will be here in a few minutes. After all you've done, what you've told me tonight could actually help save someone's life."

"Yes." Harrison slid into the chair behind his desk and dropped his head into his hands. "That's something, I guess."

"Harrison? You going to be all right?"

The surgeon chuckled into his hands, but there was no humor in the sound, only defeat. "Of course. I'll be just fine. I'll be right here when the police come along. But Deming …"

Bill turned back to face Harrison. "What?"

"After Jan, she said you'd be next."

Bill felt a cold chill race up his spine as he left the house and climbed behind the wheel of the Supra. Minutes later, he was back on I-5, headed south to the address Harrison had given him.

Chapter 32

Jan's senses reeled. She was falling, falling. Things were spinning around her, out of control. She braced herself for impact, and awakened instead on a cold concrete floor, hands and feet securely bound with something rough.

What happened? Where am I?

The back of her throat was lined with a thick, viscous fluid and it was hard to breath. She gagged, and it took several fits of uncontrollable coughing for her throat to clear.

"Give it a second and you'll feel better," a voice said from the darkness that surrounded her. "The falling sensation, the clogging of the throat—it's an after-effect of the drug I gave you."

The voice sounded familiar, but her head was still fuzzy. She twisted her head to identify its source, but could see little in the dim light. She was in a basement; that much she could tell. The place had a damp, cool feel that only concrete walls provided. Dusty boxes were scattered haphazardly around the room, and when she managed to roll off her side and onto her back, she could see the hazy forms of cobwebs hanging from floor joists above her head. What little light there was came from two narrow windows, high on the far wall. A large chest freezer with a badly scarred exterior hummed and clunked in one corner, next to an aged washer and dryer.

The image of the face she'd seen when she was attacked flashed through her memory as the drug's effects wore off. Her mind cleared, and now she placed that familiar voice.

That same person was on the stairs now. She could tell someone was there by the dark silhouette, framed by ambient light filtering down from an open door at the top of a steep stairwell. Jan could just make out the hem of a gingham dress and the edge of a bandage peeking out below one knee.

"Ruth. Why have you done this to me?" Jan asked.

"You and your man-friend got too close. You would have spoiled everything. I couldn't let that happen, not after all the good we've done for the hospital, after all the money we'd made."

"What are you talking about?" Jan's voice was scratchy, her throat parched.

Ruth stepped down the final stairs and into the dim light. "You know exactly what I'm talking about. You and Deming figured out what we were doing at the hospital. My people overheard your conversations. You were going to the police. I couldn't let that happen. What would all those people do, the ones who need transplants but can't get one because of that silly bureaucracy, that endlessly long waiting list?"

"I don't understand," Jan said. She had to stall for time. Ruth was very capable of killing her, and her only hope was that Jake and Bill would figure things out, or that she could talk Ruth out of doing anything rash. They had been friends when she did her training in the hospital's administration wing.

The windows outside were dark, so it must be night. What time it was exactly, she couldn't tell. There was no way to know how long she had been unconscious. Bill would have Jake out looking for her by now, since she'd missed their meeting at the morgue.

She had to stall, keep Ruth talking until someone came to find her. But had they figured out the Ruth was involved?

"Don't be coy, Janette. You knew we were doing special services for some of our customers at Wilkes. You knew we harvested organs from terminal patients. What I can't figure out is why you or anyone else would object. Why should people who can afford an organ transplant be denied what they need because some terminally ill patient refuses to die, or because doctors can keep a patient alive

220

beyond when they should have died? It's not natural, keeping patients alive like that, when they can do so much good for others. I'm just sorry that I, we, had to …"

Jan detected a hitch in the voice, a sniff and small shudder that indicated the woman might be crying. She decided to bank on the woman's emotions, use that to buy herself some time.

"But you killed innocent people, Ruth. Some of them would have survived if you hadn't killed them. And what about the records clerk's sister? Did you kill her to help someone?"

"You can't know what a person like me could, or could not do." The woman's voice was tight with anger. "No one can know that. Those patients that we helped die would have passed on sooner or later. We were very careful about that, always. If other people had been willing to do what we're doing at Wilkes, my Robert would still be alive today. As for that woman at the house, she shouldn't have fought me. It could have been much easier on her if she hadn't done that."

Robert? Ruth's husband's name had been Robert. And the way she talked, Ruth must have been much more than a participant in the transplant operation.

The reality of the situation struck her all at once, and Jan was suddenly very scared, more so than before. Ruth was the leader of the transplant operation at Wilkes. It was the perfect setup. Ruth worked for the CEO, and answered only to him. She knew everything that went on in the hospital, had access to all of the files. She could have arranged virtually anything that she wanted, with the resources of the CEO behind her.

Incredible! Through her fear, Jan found herself laughing as tears began to stream down her face.

Good old Ruth, there when the hospital went up, and everyone assumed she'd be around when it came down. The woman was a paragon of virtue – at least in the perception of those who worked around her.

Ruth reached out a hand and switched on the room's overhead light, and the glare blinded Jan momentarily. As her vision cleared, she looked up into the kindly face of a woman she had thought to be her friend.

"How could you do it, Ruth? How could you kill all those

patients?"

Ruth squatted down at the end of the stairs. "You mean, how could Good old Ruth do those things? Well, I'll tell you, dear, it's hard the first time. Believe me, I know. I must have cried all night when I arranged for the first patient to go away. It got easier after that. It was business.

"Sadly, I now have to make you go away like I did the others. This time I'll be sure to make it so they don't find your body, not like that other girl. I'll make up some story about you going off to study. People will believe that. You're always studying something. It's why you never met anyone before that Deming character."

Ruth reached down and touched Jan's cheek with a rough, dry hand. "But don't fret. Maybe I'll make you an organ donor. I'll see if I can't find a way for you to be discovered so your organs can be harvested, so you can help someone else continue to live through your death. Maybe I can arrange an automobile accident. Yes, that might do the trick."

Ruth paused to consider her plan. Then her eyes swept back to meet Jan's. "Yes, an automobile accident would do nicely. Then that persistent Mr. Deming might see that you were gone, give up on his silly investigation, and we can all get back to our business."

Ruth eyes were glassy, distant when she brought them back to bear on Jan. "Don't worry. I liked you, so I'll make yours a clean end. Painless. Things have been most messy of late, and I just don't care for all that mess."

"You're going to kill me? But we've been friends."

Ruth waved away the question with a pale, vein-streaked hand. Her blue-white hair caught the glow of the basement's single bulb and glistened with sparkles of many layers of hairspray.

"It's actually rather easy if I keep my mind on my goals, and I have certainly been doing that long enough not to let a little thing like disposing of you get in the way. Someone will get a transplant because of you. I need the money your organs will bring, and if things go right, the hospital could get a nice donation in the process. We'll all benefit. My husband Robert died because he couldn't get a kidney transplant. We had the money, but no one could let him get what he needed in time. Too many others were ahead of him on that cursed priority list.

"I decided to do something about that so others wouldn't suffer the same kind of fate. It gave me a new reason to live, when I realized that I could make a difference. I found a surgeon who was more than willing to participate. He'd been disciplined in New England for questionable practices and was going to lose his license. I took a trip back there and intervened on his behalf, in the name of my CEO, of course. I have a sister who lives in Vermont. It was a nice excuse to visit her.

"When I tracked down that doctor, he saw the sense of what I proposed, so I arranged some paperwork in our illustrious CEO's office so that he could be recruited for Wilkes's staff. I fudged his credentials package so that no one would find out about his unfortunate past.

"That Mr. Sterling is a trusting, wonderful man, but he is rather inept as a hospital CEO. I'm the one who actually runs things at Wilkes, so it wasn't hard to get the doctor's credentials approved and the man hired as our chief surgeon. We did our first case a few months after he was admitted to the medical staff and it was a wonderful success. You might be interested to know that the organ recipient was a Native American, just like you. His father was a tribal elder and made a sizeable donation to the hospital after the surgery. It worked so very well, and gave us the idea for starting the program that we have today. We've allowed some of the community's most influential people to help their relatives or themselves receive treatment they might not have gotten if they'd been forced to wait in line for a liver, kidney, or even a heart. We get quite a lot of money for hearts, you know."

Ruth smiled at Jan as though she felt Jan would see the sense in her words.

"That's sick. You killed innocent people to get those organs, and you took money to do it. For yourself," Jan said.

Where are Bill and Jake? Will they ever come?

Ruth laughed, low and soft. The sound was like sandpaper on rough metal. "Of course I did, dear. After my Robert died, there was no way I could have kept this house up on a secretary's salary."

Ruth sat down on the last step of the stairs and ran a handkerchief across her forehead. Her breathing was hard, labored, as she continued.

"The old fool never invested a dime. I didn't know anything at all about finance back then. So, when the money came flowing in, I took enough to keep me going, although most of it went to the rest of the team, to my trusted advisors and helpers. There must be six or seven people on my staff by now. They call me the 'Director'. Isn't that nice? Of course, except for Dr. Harrison, most of them don't know who I am. We're very careful about that and they're all paid handsomely, so no one ever asks questions."

"Ruth, you can't be serious. You're going to get caught. You must know that. Bill and I got close enough to figure things out. Sarah Laughlin discovered what was going on, and she was just a records clerk. How long can you expect to keep going? If you kill me, it will only make people hunt harder for the truth."

"Of course you're right. I just hope Mr. Deming will stop his inquiry when your body is discovered. The records clerk was enough, but if I have to, I can take care of him, too. It's for a good cause, you know."

Ruth gave a small grunt as she stood up from the step, her knees shaking as she braced herself against the stairway banister.

"Sarah's death should not have happened. She should have minded her own business. I offered to pay her a lot of money for her silence. I even tried to explain how what we were doing was helping the hospital and our patients. She just kept running away from me, claiming she didn't know what I was talking about. She even claimed to not know who I was. She was lying, of course. Everyone knows me at Wilkes, and I couldn't let her ruin all we've accomplished. I couldn't let that happen. She yelled at me. It made me so angry. The knife was there on the kitchen counter, so I..."

"You killed her?"

Ruth looked down at her hands and rubbed them, as though trying to remove a stain from her palms.

"I didn't intend to kill her. I'd never met the girl before, except to talk to her on the phone. When I explained that I worked at the hospital, she acted like I'd never called her at the office. She wouldn't let me into the house at first, until I asked for a drink of water. Her play-acting just made me so mad, and there was that knife on the counter."

"That wasn't Sarah, Ruth. It was her sister."

Ruth's eyes snapped up, wide and startled. "That can't be."

"It's true. You killed the wrong woman, another innocent. I don't know where Sarah is, but you didn't kill her. What about Cory, the man from pathology? Did you kill him, too?"

Ruth's breathing was coming hard now, and sounded labored. "It was easier with Cory, after the Laughlin girl. He'd met me before and trusted me. He let me right into his apartment, and this time I brought my own knife. Everybody trusts me." She shrugged as though the death meant nothing more than swatting a fly.

Crazy. This is a crazy woman, and not a thing I can do about it. Where are Bill and Jake?

"Both of them were rather messy. I'll be more careful with you. I'll drug you like I did at the hospital and you won't feel a thing. You'll just drift off to sleep."

Ruth turned and headed up the stairs, her steps tired and laborious. She paused and turned back to Jan with a friendly smile. That smile sent an icy chill up Jan's spine. "Don't worry about yelling, dear. The walls of this old house are so thick that no one can hear. Robert used to run his saws and machinery down here and I couldn't hear it ten feet from the house when I was gardening outside. I'll come down and check on you later. It won't be long now, dear. I won't keep you waiting."

Ruth climbed the stairs slowly and disappeared through a door at the top. She turned off the basement light as she went and left Jan alone in the darkness.

Chapter 33

Bill pulled his car to the curb a block from the address Dr. Harrison had given him.

The quiet, old money suburb on Olympia's north end hardly looked like a place where a killer would live. Row upon row of manicured lawns, aged red brick houses and ancient, giant rhododendrons spoke of affluence, grandeur, but not murder.

His was the only car on the street. The single streetlight a half block away cast a puddle of light around its base that was washed out and faded by the gloom. Low clouds swirled in a sky of black and gray, and rolled west to east with the freshening wind. It smelled like rain wasn't far off.

Bill hoped that Jake and the police weren't far behind him, but wasn't sure whether to wait for them or not. On one hand, their suspicions could be wrong and Jan wasn't at the house at all. Then again, if the murderer had her and was planning to kill her, he couldn't afford to wait.

Bill gave the yellow Lab snoozing in the passenger seat a sidelong glance as he considered the situation. "I must be out of my mind, Alex. I'm a consultant, an auditor, not a cop. But if anything happened to her …" He glanced at the clock on the car's dash. "I'll give Jake two minutes, and then I go looking for Jan."

At the sound of Jan's name, Alex lifted his head and thumped his tail against the passenger side door.

Bill ruffled the fur on Alex's neck. "Guess we're both in love with her," he said, and glanced at his watch.

Where is Jake?

A minute later, he checked the clock on the dash a final time. "Time's up, Alex. I'm off. You guard the car. I'll leave the window open in case something happens and you need to go outside."

He remembered back to when he'd been kidnapped and the yellow Lab had been shut in the small sports car for most of a day. "Too bad your guard dog training didn't take. I could use a hand with this."

Alex dropped his head back to the seat and closed his eyes with a sigh.

Bill turned off the car's dome light, eased open the driver-side door and stepped out into the night. He made a beeline for the house, sticking to the shadows and skirting glow cast by streetlight.

He paused in the shadow of a tall oak to examine the house from a distance. No lights were on. He could see a set of French doors on the north side of the house, partially hidden by tall shrubs. They might be his best bet for getting inside. He stepped quickly from the shadows and headed for them, across the freshly mowed lawn.

He cut through a small garden, and then pushed his way through thick shrubs at the side of the house, hoping to make his way to the doors without drawing attention. The fragrance of crushed Daphnia surrounded him as he peered in through a low window.

Nothing. All he could see was an empty dining room full of heavy antique furniture. He edged along the wall, toward the open French doors, and noticed a small cellar window at his feet. A faint glow of light came from it, dim, as though not from a fixture in the room, but from another floor of the building, perhaps a stairwell. He bent down and crouched on all fours to get a look inside.

He but he could see the familiar, dark silhouettes of a washer and dryer, stacks of boxes, and the vague outline of something long and angular lying on the floor that looked like... It looked like a person!

He pushed his face closer against the window for a better look, and as he did so, the dark form lying in on the cellar floor stirred and turned its head toward him.

Even in the gloom he recognized the dark shadow of her hair, the profile of her face. Jan!

As his eyes adjusted to the light, he could make her out more clearly. She appeared to be bound, hand and foot, and lay against the far wall of the cellar. He felt his heart pounding. She was alive.

Bill sat back on his heels and took stock of his options. The first thing he had to do was get into the house. He could break in through the cellar window, but it was small and he wasn't sure he could get his shoulders through.

He could sneak around to the French doors, like he originally planned, maybe jimmy them open. But then, if Jan was in the basement, her captor was sure to be close by. If he was seen or heard working the doors open, there was no telling what might happen to Jan before he could find his way to the basement.

One thing was for sure: he couldn't wait for Jake and the troops. Jan was there, in the basement, and he needed to get her out.

Regardless of the risk, the French doors seemed like the best option. His mind made up, he gathered his feet beneath him to rise as something hard, and shockingly painful crashed down across his shoulders. The loud whack of the wood meeting bone echoed across the lawn.

Bill's knees buckled. Searing pain shot down his spine and flooded through his body. His stomach roiled, and threatened to empty itself.

He raised his hands and tried to turn toward the source of the pain, and was struck a second time. The force of it knocked him to the ground, facedown in the dirt and garden mulch. The prickly leaves of heather scratched at the palm of one hand as he struggled vainly to break his fall. Small motes of bright light swam before his eyes and he vomited, uncontrollably. Nauseous, barely clinging to consciousness, he once again tried to gather his legs under him, but they wouldn't work right.

"Really, Mr. Deming, you might as well give it up," said a feminine voice from behind him. "Besides, what would your parents say if they caught you peeking into a lonely old woman's house at this time of night? It's not very gentlemanly, is it? I'm sure the police will understand when they find your body in the morning. I was just protecting myself from an intruder. Too bad it was you, although it is rather convenient. After tonight, I'll have both threats to my little transplant program out of the way. Now you just hold still, and this will all be over in another minute."

It took him a few seconds to place the voice, and when he finally placed it, he nearly laughed. Ruth! It was Ruth, that meddling, matchmaking grandmother of all who worked at the hospital. It made perfect sense. Who would suspect kindly old Ruth of murder, of masterminding an organ-for-money conspiracy ring?

When she hit him a third time, he hardly felt the blow. His body was numb, paralyzed by overwhelming pain. Even when he'd been shot in Haiti while on a mission with Military Intelligence, even then the pain hadn't been this bad. With an odd sort of detachment, he evaluated his situation and concluded that he was lucky she'd hit him across his back and shoulders, and that the back of his head wasn't caved in. He wondered if there was much blood. When he'd been shot, there'd actually been very little. He'd been surprised at that, he remembered

He also calculated that he couldn't take much more of the abuse Ruth was dishing out. Whatever she was hitting him with was doing the job.

Bill heard himself chuckle, as though he were standing outside his body and observing from another vantage point. He wondered just how many times the frail, elderly hospital office worker would have to clobber him before he would finally lose consciousness and die. It would be a blessing, almost, to be free of this pain.

There was a dull thud behind him, but there was no pain associated with the sound, and it oddly confused him.

"Oh, dear," Ruth said. "There I've gone and flung that silly bat off behind me, just about as I was about to put you out of my misery. I do hope I won't have to hit you too many more times before you lie still. I'm not as young as I used to be and Robert's old Louisville Slugger is heavy. Don't you go anywhere until I find that dratted bat."

Groggy and struggling to muster his thoughts, Bill managed to roll onto his back before she could return. *I have to do something. One more hit like that and I'm out for good. Then what about Jan?*

She was back in a few seconds, her small form a dark silhouette against the glow of the streetlight beyond. He lifted his hands and extended them toward her as she raised the bat over her head. He felt the weakness in his limbs and knew it was about over, that he would never be able to save himself, let alone the woman he loved.

Forgive me, Jan.

"It's really too bad that I have to do this, but you've become such a nuisance," she said through gritted teeth. "Now lie still so I can finish this."

Sirens sounded in the distance, but hardly registered in his mind as Ruth swung the bat down toward his head for the final time. He closed his eyes against what he knew was coming next, and then ... nothing.

He looked up in time to see an indistinct form erupt from the bushes. The woman faltered, grunted, and staggered back as though struck, the bat still raised over her head. There was a deep throaty growl that sounded out of character for a woman so small, and another grunt, louder this time, as the dark blur streaked across Bill's vision and rammed into the woman.

Ruth staggered back and disappeared around the corner of the house. There was another growl and he saw the end of the bat beyond the corner of the house, its end still held high, and then disappear as it came crashing down.

As his vision began to fail, Bill heard a loud snarl erupt through the darkness, followed by the sound of something hard cracking against wood or metal.

It was then that blessed darkness finally embraced him, the pain eased, and the little brightness left around him faded to dark.

Chapter 34

Bill regained consciousness by degrees. He felt smooth, freshly washed sheets against his skin, sensed the illumination of soft lights and in the background, heard a regular beeping sound from something near his head. His throat was scratchy, dry, and the air smelled of antiseptic.

A dull throb pounded and ground at the muscles across his shoulders and down his right side. He raised a tentative hand to his forehead and encountered a wad of thick cloth bandages. He probed the bandage and felt a sharp pain as his fingers found the wound at the back of his head.

A sudden rush of panic flushed through him as he opened his eyes and recognized his surroundings. The beeping, the smell, the bed. He was in the hospital! He was trapped in one of their hospital beds! How long had they had him? What were they planning?

He shot a glance around the room, noted the too familiar surroundings, the neutral wall colorings, sterile white covers of his bed, framed by high metal railings and an assortment of monitors, wires and instruments for instruments at the side of his bed.

I've got to get out of here, he thought. He struggled to sit up, but warm fingers wrapped themselves around his arm, restraining him, and he found he lacked the strength to fight back. With a groan and sick feeling in his stomach, he settled back into the too soft pillows and hard mattress of the hospital bed. *They have me. I'm too weak to fight back, to escape.*

"Relax. You're safe, Bill. You're in Tacoma, at Sacred Heart Hospital."

Bill recognized Jake's voice, and its tone immediately set him at ease. He turned his eyes toward the speaker. Jake actually smiled when their eyes met, which seemed a little odd to Bill. In the week or so that he'd known the man, he'd never seen his expression anything but stern.

Jake nodded to a chair at the side of the room, and Bill twisted in the bed to follow the gesture. Jan dozed in a chair against the far wall, near a window. She stirred but his vision blurred and the room began to swim, and he fell back against the pillows.

Jan opened her eyes and saw Bill was awake. She got to her feet, took a pitcher of water from the bedside table and poured some into a flimsy plastic glass. She handed him the water. As he sipped and his vision settled, Bill saw the glint of a tear forming in the corner of her eye.

"The doctor warned me you might come around about now," she said. "The paramedics drugged you up pretty well when they brought you in. You were a mess. You almost got yourself killed."

The water felt cool and soothing against his throat. When he tried to speak again, his voice had lost some of its raspiness. "How long was I out?"

Jan reached out with a hand and smoothed the bandage that draped across his forehead. "You've been sleeping for the better part of a day. It's afternoon now, and they admitted you early yesterday morning around two a.m. When they found you, you were unconscious. You've stayed that way since."

The tear spilled over the corner of her eye and ran down her cheek.

"You okay?" Silly question. Of course she wasn't okay. She was crying.

Jan bit her lip, turned away and gazed out the window. He reached up and fingered the thick, braided rope of ebony hair that fell down her back to her hips.

To think, he might never have touched her like this again.

The ache that had been looming in the back of his brain, displaced by drugs running through his system, flared, and he flinched as though hit from behind.

Memories of what happened came back in a rush. Something hard had smashed across his head and shoulders, again and again, until he'd lost consciousness. He remembered the smell of damp sod, dead leaves and compost, as his attacker drove him into the ground with blow after blow. He remembered Ruth's voice.

Ruth! Kindly old Ruth, who had tried to kill him.

He raised a hand as if to ward off the final blow, and it tangled with the wires and tubes running to him from the vital signs monitor cables and set off several alarms. He ignored the loud chiming, the rush of medical staff into his room.

He remembered rolling onto his back. He'd thought he was about to die, his thoughts oddly detached and objective about the possibility at the time, as though he was viewing someone else's fate. And then, nothing.

"What happened to Ruth? The last thing I remember..."

"Do you remember anything about what happened to her after she hit you?"

"No. Did you catch her?" The pain in Bill's head subsided a bit.

"Ruth's dead," Jake said. "We found her around the corner of the house, with blood on the side of the building where she'd hit her head.

"The coroner found smudges on the front of Ruth's clothes and bruises on her corpse that match the paw marks of a dog the size and weight of your golden Lab, Alex. We hauled him in to do measurements."

"You busted my dog?"

Jake didn't respond to Bill's question, and continued his story. "We also found tracks that match Alex's paw prints near where we found you. They were deep prints, dug in like he'd lunged at something. We're pretty convinced that when Ruth tried to hit you that final time, Alex attacked her."

Jake rubbed a hand through his hair. "I've met your dog, and I'm afraid that sort of thing seems out of character, but that's what the evidence says. In fact, when we arrived at the scene, one of the patrolmen noticed Alex in the passenger seat of your car. We checked the car later and found fresh blades of grass on the floor and seat. They matched the grass at the spot where Ruth was killed.

"I know it seems unreasonable, given Alex's temperament. When Ruth attacked you, you must have cried out. Alex heard you, responded, and took matters into his own hands, uh, paws. Ruth must have regained her feet after he knocked her down the first time, retrieved the bat and was going to take a swing at your dog. We figure Alex lunged at her again, and knocked Ruth against the side of the house. The coroner says she died from a brain hemorrhage that resulted when her head struck the side of the building."

"So the guard dog training finally paid off," Bill said through the haze that still covered his vision. "Guess I owe old Alex a Milk Bone or two."

"I think filet mignon might be in order for the dog," Jake said.

"Already taken care of," Jan said. "Alex has been living the life of Riley at my house ever since we found you. Jake wanted to lock him up, but I know a hero when I see one."

Bill glanced from Jake's face to Jan's, and saw from Jake's embarrassed look and Jan's one of defiance, that she was only half joking.

"I only suggested that we board him at the city pound," Jake said.

There was a light knock on the door, and two policemen came into the room. Jake went to meet them.

"How'd they find me?" Bill asked Jan.

"When you told Jake where you were headed on the cell phone, he didn't waste any time getting there. He found you near the bushes at the edge of the house." Jan paused and took a deep breath before continuing. "Trying to save me like that … coming after me and not waiting for Jake and his men… that was a very stupid thing to do."

"What was I going to do? If anything had happened…" Bill let the words trail off.

Jan wiped away the tears with her sleeve. He did his best to ignore the pain as she bent down to him and wrapped her arms around him. Warm kisses and tears fell on the bare skin of his neck.

They stayed that way for several long minutes before either spoke again. It was Bill who asked the next tough question. "What about Carole?"

Jake went to the opposite side of the bed from Jan. "They picked her up this morning, so I was just informed. She's already worked a deal with the District Attorney, and admitted that she drugged you and had you hauled off. She claims she had nothing to do with the patient deaths, but has promised to help with the investigation of the transplant conspiracy. She's agreed to plead guilty on assault and second-degree kidnapping charges. She's got some hotshot lawyer from Seattle on her case. I bet she's out on bail inside of a few hours. She'll have her day in court, and if she helps with the case against the hospital's staff, she'll probably get off pretty light. What exactly did you do to her, anyway?"

Bill started to reply, but Jan interrupted. "I think I'd rather not know the answer to that one. It's a mystery I don't care to solve."

"If you will excuse me, I need to see my patient."

They all shifted their eyes toward the door, where a white-jacketed physician stood with a broad smile on his face.

"I'll see you later," Jan said. Jake followed her out the door.

When the physician had poked and prodded to his satisfaction, he stepped back from the bed and snapped closed the patient chart he carried. "The good news is that you'll survive. The bad news is that you've got lots of bruises, a few cracked bones, and a mild concussion. You're going to be sore for a good while. Another piece of good news: by this time tomorrow, you're outta here."

"Thanks."

The doctor gave Bill another wide grin. Bill suspected the man had practiced it repeatedly in front of a mirror. It didn't look natural. "No thanks required. Avoid bats and two by fours in the future, and you should be just fine." The doctor chuckled at his own joke, spun on his heel and left.

The doctor was followed a short time later by a nurse, who asked after his comfort in soft, cooing tones. Bill hated those cooing tones, and when Bill mentioned the throbbing in his head and across his shoulders and back, she was appalled. She left the room in a huff, muttering about patient care schedules and incompetent staffing. When she returned, it was with a syringe of clear fluid, which she injected into the IV line running into Bill's arm. A few minutes later, Bill was overcome by a wave of comforting warmth, and he slipped into dreamless, healing slumber.

The room was quiet and in shadows when Bill's eyes finally fluttered open. He had no idea how long he'd been out, and wasn't sure what woke him. The darkness beyond the window suggested that day had transitioned to night, so it could have been half a day or more. He tried to move his arms and legs to get into a more comfortable position, but found they wouldn't respond. His arms, legs, even his neck, simply wouldn't move.

"You're going to find moving to be very difficult at this point."

Dr. Ian Farley stepped from the shadows on the far side of the door. Faint moonlight drifted in through the room's small window and lit his face in contrasting shades of dark. He held an empty syringe in one hand and tapped it lightly against his palm.

"I understand you were a hospital administrator during your career in the military. If so, then maybe you'll be familiar with what I've just pumped through your IV. We call it 'Special K'. We use it to induce a sort of cataleptic state. It's a dissociate hypnotic, similar to phencyclidine, or PCP; one of my personal favorites. It works by disrupting the central nervous system. Oh, sorry. Too technical? Let me make it simple for you: it paralyzes the body. I imagine you're feeling that already. Injected into a vein, like you have been, it works very rapidly. The uncomfortable point for you, most likely, is that while the body is immobile, the mind functions very clearly."

Bill tried to move again, and when he couldn't, panic built inside his gut. He was paralyzed! He knew nothing about the drug Farley mentioned except what he felt right now, at this instant, and he was helpless.

Farley walked over to the bedside and gazed down at Bill with a look of exaggerated concern. "With Ruth gone and Sarah Laughlin out of the picture, you're really the only one with the evidence to implicate me in what's been going on at Wilkes. Without you, all they've got is circumstantial. You've already talked to the police, but what can they do if their key witness is suddenly removed from the picture? They'll be kind of like you are right now, paralyzed."

Farley tossed the empty syringe onto the chair by the window, the one where Jan had sat earlier in the day. It hit the chair, bounced off the plastic seat, and clattered to the floor. He reached into the side pocket of his physician's smock and brought out another syringe.

"That first one just paralyzed you. This one will put you to sleep for good. I expect it will hurt like the dickens, but with the Ace in your system, you won't be able to do much about that, now will you? Too bad you can't tell me what dying feels like. I always wondered about that."

Farley took Bill's IV bag in one hand and made a show of poking the syringe's needle into the translucent plastic bag. He paused as he started to depress the plunger and returned his cold, small eyes to meet Bill's helpless gaze.

"It really is too bad you got into all this. We were doing quite well, helping the hospital with our little program. Of course, we all made our fortunes, as well, but we made a fortune for the institution. Me, Dr. Harrison, Ruth, the OR staff and several others. We brought in a lot of donations that simply wouldn't have happened otherwise.

"Until a few days ago, I didn't even know it was little old Ruth who was directing the program. Harrison was the only one who actually knew Ruth was in charge. Isn't that odd? It's like they didn't trust me.

"You heard about Harrison, no doubt?"

Bill's eyes must have shown his confusion, because Farley went on. "Poor Dr. Harrison took his life the other day. I'm led to believe it was just after you paid him a visit. The police arrived and found him with a bullet in the side of his head. Convenient for me, of course. When I stopped outside your door earlier in the day, while you were talking to the policeman, I overheard him say that Ruth is dead, too. Bad for her – good for me. With her and Harrison out of the way, and now you… Well, I should be pretty much in the clear, shouldn't I? I guess I've prolonged this enough. Time to say good night, Mr. Deming."

Farley dropped his gaze to the syringe and began to depress the plunger.

As Bill helplessly watched the first drop of fluid enter his IV tube from the syringe, the hospital room door crashed open, with Jake right behind it. The big cop dove across the room and slammed against Farley. Both men sprawled across Bill's still form. The hospital bed's wheels squealed as it and its three passengers slid across the room and slammed into the far wall. Bedside monitors screamed a long, piercing whine of protest as electrodes were ripped from Bill's chest and arms. Only the IV tube tied to the IV bag, with the half empty syringe hanging from its side, remained connected to

Bill's body.

Bill, his eyes glued to the syringe, could only stare as drop after drop of deadly fluid began its way down the IV tube toward the vein in his arm. Farley didn't say how much of the stuff it would take to actually kill him. If only he could move …

Farley was the first on his feet after the bed hit the wall, struggling from under Jake's weight. He swung a wild punch at Jake as the cop regained his balance and rose. It connected with a loud crack.

As loud as it was, Jake was hardly fazed by the blow. He grabbed Farley by one shoulder and pounded a single blow to the Internist's stomach. The doctor doubled over, groaned, and crumbled to the floor. In another second, Jake had handcuffs on the man's wrists, both arms bent behind the doctor in a very uncomfortable position.

Bill caught most of this from his periphery, never taking his eyes off the IV line.

Break that line! Do something before that drug hits my vein!

The words were only echoes in Bill's mind, his mouth unable to form the words through his paralysis.

Jake searched through Farley's pockets, and then found the empty syringe on the chair. He didn't see the one hanging from the IV tube, where it had swung behind the head of Bill's bed. Jake dashed out the door of the room, calling frantically for a nurse.

"I must have left my keys … What is Jake all upset about?" Jan said as she stepped into the room.

She glanced at the bed, angled up against the wall, at Farley unconscious on the floor, and ran to Bill's side. "Are you all right? Nurse! Nurse!"

She glanced over at Bill's arm, at the IV line tangled with his bead frame, and then at the IV line. She saw the syringe hanging from the bag, took one glance at the label on it and yanked it out. As she read the label more closely, the color drained from her face and she ripped the IV line from Bill's arm. She screamed for a nurse again, and slipped a thin belt from around her waist. She wrapped it around Bill's upper arm in a tourniquet and tightened it, twisting again and again as she fought to stop the flow of blood from the IV site to Bill's heart.

The IV torn from his arm, the belt cranked endlessly tight around his bicep, all hurt like crazy, but Bill thought it was the most

238

wonderful thing that could have happened. Even as his vision faded and a dark cloud closed over his eyes, he admired Jan's determination, her concern as she worked furiously to save his life. *Why hadn't he found this girl decades ago?* he thought as his vision began to dim and darkness surrounded him.

"Bill! Bill! Don't leave me, Bill!"

He could hear the words as if they came from a great distance. He couldn't move to comfort her, couldn't move his lips to console her. He felt so warm, so comfortable. Farley had said this would hurt, but ...

Bill's last thoughts were filled with irony. *I finally get the girl, and now this.*

Chapter 35

Dawn's first light filtered through the slatted shades of Jan's bedroom as Bill slowly came awake. Light fingertips traced ticklish patterns across his bare chest as he opened his eyes and turned his head for a better view of the woman who lay beside him.

"The last time someone had me immobile like this, it wasn't nearly as much fun," he said as he reached out to take Jan into a full-length embrace.

Jan wrapped her arms tightly around him and snuggled against his neck. "You're not exactly immobile, and last time, it was drugs that had you under a spell. Nothing's holding you back now."

An hour later, over breakfast, Jan read the paper as Bill flipped eggs on an old cast iron skillet. "You are in for a treat," he said. "No one can approach me when it comes to the culinary art of egg preparation."

Bill glanced at the front page that Jan held before her, and saw his picture there. The headline next to it announced the breakup of the Wilkes crime gang, as the media had taken to calling the group involved in the transplant murders.

"You always this talkative in the mornings?" Bill asked when Jan returned his comment with little more than a soft grunt.

She set the paper aside. "It's been over a week since you were released from the hospital, and I've taken care of you all that time. I have pampered you and coddled you…"

"Not to mention other things. I don't think the doctor included those in the patient care plan."

Jan came over from the table and wrapped her arms around his waist from behind.

"I'm a registered nurse. I know what's best for you."

Bill flipped the eggs onto two plates, and they returned to the table where Bill dug into his meal. He tossed a half piece of bacon to Alex, who lay near the base of the stove on an old braided rug. The dog lapped it up with his broad tongue, swallowed it whole and wagged his tail expectantly. When no additional windfalls came his way, Alex curled up in a ball and drifted off to sleep.

Bill and Jan both raised their heads from their food as they heard a car pull up outside. The front door slammed a second later and Jake stepped into the kitchen. He was dressed in pressed jeans, cowboy boots, a blue western shirt that accentuated his dark good looks, and a tweed sport coat. It was his official uniform since he'd been promoted to Assistant Superintendent of Inspectors, a reward for leading the team that broke up the Wilkes organ theft and murder ring.

Jake helped himself to the contents of Jan's coffee mug and took a seat at the kitchen table. "Make yourself right at home, Mr. Head Inspector," Jan said.

Jake smiled and set the empty cup aside and turned his eyes to Bill. "So, how's the patient? Up to a few questions?"

Bill ran a tentative hand down his side and flexed his back. "Better, although I think I'll need a lot more nursing care before I'm ready to venture out on my own."

He was pleased when he saw the color creep across Jan's cheeks.

Jake grinned. "I'll just bet you will. It's time to wrap this case up. We settled the court case with Carole Fletcher's lawyers this morning. She'll get some psychiatric help, then do time in the minimum-security prison for kidnapping and drugging you, and then a lot more time on parole. She's admitted to conspiracy to kidnap and assault, and has agreed to help us wrap up the hospital murders in exchange for the light sentence. Her knowledge of the hospital's administrative processes will help us tie the case up.

"I doubt the charges against Farley will come to trial, either. With Harrison dead, Farley couldn't spill the beans fast enough when he got word that the DA might be going for the death penalty. What he didn't know, and the prosecutor didn't tell him, was that another staff member from the hospital had already pretty much laid things out for the prosecutor."

Jake pulled a pocket-sized notebook from his jacket pocket and flipped through the pages. "The staff member who sang that song was one Doctor Walter Pigeon. Pathologist. You know him?"

Bill mopped up the rest of his hash browns and reached for Jan's leftovers. "Yep. The man was forging autopsy results for the Wilkes group. Was he involved in the death of his assistant?"

Jake shook his head. "I don't think so. That was all Ruth. Guess we'll never hear the full story about that. Too bad she died before she could tell us all the things she was involved with. Darned inconvenient."

Jan and Bill shared shocked glances until they both saw the grin on Jake's face. "Yeah, darned inconvenient," Jan said.

"Did you ever find Sarah Laughlin?" Bill said.

Jake held up Jan's empty cup until she took it and filled it from the pot on the stove. "We found her in Tampa. She'd gotten nervous, and flown out to her sister's place on the same day that her sister had flown out here for a surprise visit. Some surprise.

"Sarah got the messages that we left on her voicemail, but was too scared to return them. She thought they might have been from someone at the hospital who discovered that she'd provided you with the patient files. We finally had the Florida State Patrol help us track her down. We talked to her late last night. She's fine – scared – but fine. She'll be out tomorrow morning to claim her sister's body and will then be helping us wrap up the case. Between her and Carole, I suspect we'll have the investigation complete in record time."

Alex lifted his head as Jan tossed him a crust from across the room.

"You always feed him like this?" Jake asked as he watched Bill shovel through the rest of his food.

"Bill or the dog?" Jan said.

"Either."

"I like my men well fed."

Jake walked over to where Alex snoozed, squatted next to the dog and scratched Alex behind one ear. The yellow Lab rolled onto his back so Jake could rub his stomach.

Jan sipped at her coffee, her eyes bright over the edge of her cup. "Some dog you've got there, Mr. Deming."

"He's shameless," Bill said.

"I'd go easy on Alex. If not for him, you might not be here now."

Bill laughed. "I'd told him to stay in the car. Guess he's not as trained as I thought."

"Lucky for you," Jake said.

"My hero," Bill said. "Who would have thought that lazy lump of Lab would save my life?"

Jan watched Alex as she sipped at her cup of coffee. "It's the quiet ones who'll surprise you."

Jake set his coffee down, reached inside his sport coat and produced a neatly folded sheet of paper.

"One more thing. The bureau chief called your employer in California and explained things. Your old job is waiting for you, if you want it."

Jan reached across the table and took Bill's hand, squeezing it. "That's great."

"I suppose." Bill could only stare at his hands. It was impossible to imagine heading back to California, living somewhere Jan wasn't.

"On the other hand…" Jake slid the paper across the table toward Bill. "The Bureau is setting up a Medical Crimes Unit. I've been authorized to offer you a position as a special investigator. The pays not half what you make as a consultant, but you could do some good in the job, with your background."

Jake cast a pointed glance toward his sister. "Not to mention certain perks that come with the locale."

"Aren't I a little old to become a cop? You have age limits, right?"

"You're retired military. The rules for the state police force wave the age restriction for retired military. If you'll examine the paperwork, you'll see it's signed by the governor himself."

Bill found his heart lifting at the prospect. He could stay here, with Jan. The way things were going between them, there was no telling where the relationship could go. On the other hand, he'd be taking a job that was very close to what he'd done in the military, when he'd worked for the military medical intelligence agency. He'd loved that job.

"Where do I sign?"

Jan cocked an eyebrow. "That's a little quick. Don't you want to think about it for a while? You'd be giving up a lot: your job, the California sun, living near your parents ..."

Bill scooped up the paper. "I'd be giving up a lot more if I left here and went back. Then again, maybe you'd like to try and persuade me one way or the other."

Jake cleared his throat and rose from his chair. "This is where I leave."

"Hold on a second." Bill grabbed a pen from the kitchen counter and scrawled his name at the bottom of the paper, then handed it to Jake.

Jake picked up the document and tucked it back into his coat pocket. "Welcome to the force. It was those other perks that did it, wasn't it?"

Jan and Bill both replied by reaching across the table and taking each other's hands.

Jake shook his head and started for the door. "See you at the office on Monday."

Bill turned back to Jan as Jake slammed the door behind him. "That leaves the rest of today and this weekend, and I don't have a thing planned."

The happy twinkle he saw in Jan's eye told him she knew exactly what he would be doing for the next couple of days, and he approved.

Over by the stove, Alex snored softly.

The End

Printed in the United States
55135LVS00004BA/154-216